Prologue

ASHES, ASHES

#1 BESTSELLING NOVEL,
#1 BESTSELLING AUTHOR!

"THRILLING . . . SWIFT . . . A PAGE-TURNER." —*People*

"IT STARTS OUT, BANG! . . . AS A REPORTER, I HAVE COVERED ENOUGH CRIME STORIES, MURDERS, INVESTIGATIONS, AND TRIALS TO HAVE A FAIR EYE FOR FALSITY, AND I THINK THAT PATTERSON HAS GOT THE MATERIAL DEAD ON."
 —*Baltimore Sun*

"INTRICATE." —*Los Angeles Times*

"BEST CROSS YET . . . Here are a few bits of advice . . . 1. Don't plan on reading 'just a chapter or two' before going to bed; 2. Don't read these books at night if you are home alone; 3. Don't assume you know who all the bad guys are. . . . There are no faster reads than Patterson's Alex Cross books . . . I CAN'T WAIT FOR THE NEXT ONE."
 —*Denver Rocky Mountain News*

"PATTERSON MASTERMINDS ANOTHER THRILLER. . . . Once again, we're left to wonder, how does this man do it? How does Patterson continue to write gripping tales that keep us turning pages into the wee hours of the night until the book is finished, and we're disappointed there isn't more to read?" —*Oakland Press*

"DELIVERS ENOUGH PLOT TWISTS IN HIS NOVELS TO KEEP READERS GUESSING UNTIL THE VERY LAST PAGE."
 —*Delta Sky* magazine

"*ROSES ARE RED* IS AT THE TOP OF HIS GAME. It's another terrific thriller based around his Washington, D.C. detective. This one has twists and an ending that will floor you."
 —*Larry King, USA Today*

more . . .

"ABSORBING . . . BRISK, FUN." —*Publishers Weekly*

"If you like thrillers, *ROSES ARE RED* should definitely be on your reading list. IT'S NONSTOP EXCITEMENT."
—*Daily America Weekender* (Somerset, PA)

"BREAKNECK PLOTTING . . . PATTERSON'S SUSPENSE MACHINE IS ONCE AGAIN IN HIGH GEAR." —*Library Journal*

"GUARANTEED TO HOLD PATTERSON'S MANY FANS SPELLBOUND . . . A JAW-DROPPING CONCLUSION. . . . Should impress readers who enjoyed his earlier Cross books, such as *Along Came a Spider* and *Kiss the Girls*. This one is not to be missed." —*Booklist*

"PULSE-POUNDING." —*Poisoned Pen*

"ONCE AGAIN PATTERSON PUSHES THE ENVELOPE, satisfying fans and the unacquainted alike with an over-the-top plot, his recurrent, engaging, human hero, and best of all in this outing, a villain named Mastermind who scatters his own brand of frenzy anywhere he chooses." —**booxreview.com**

"PATTERSON IS IN TOP FORM IN *ROSES ARE RED* . . . keeps up a frenzied pace . . . definitely in the can't-put-down-until-the-final-page category. The surprises keep popping until the final scene in this clever and engrossing story. COULD ANY THRILLER FAN ASK FOR MORE?" —*Orlando Sentinel*

PRAISE FOR JAMES PATTERSON'S OTHER ALEX CROSS THRILLERS

ALONG CAME A SPIDER

"A FIRST-RATE THRILLER—FASTEN YOUR SEAT BELTS AND KEEP THE LIGHTS ON!" —**Sidney Sheldon**

"THIS READER LOST A GOOD NIGHT'S SLEEP." —**Ann Rule**

"JAMES PATTERSON DOES EVERYTHING BUT STICK OUR FINGER IN A LIGHT SOCKET TO GIVE US A BUZZ." —*New York Times*

"WHEN IT COMES TO CONSTRUCTING A HARROWING PLOT, AUTHOR JAMES PATTERSON CAN TURN A SCREW ALL RIGHT. . . . James Patterson is to suspense what Danielle Steel is to romance." —*New York Daily News*

"HAS TO BE ONE OF THE BEST THRILLERS OF THE YEAR." —**Clive Cussler**

"TERROR AND SUSPENSE THAT GRAB THE READER AND WON'T LET GO. Just try running away from this one." —**Ed McBain**

KISS THE GIRLS

"TOUGH TO PUT DOWN. . . . TICKS LIKE A TIME BOMB, ALWAYS FULL OF THREAT AND TENSION." —*Los Angeles Times*

"AS GOOD AS A THRILLER CAN GET. . . . WITH *KISS THE GIRLS*, PATTERSON JOINS THE ELITE COMPANY OF THOMAS HARRIS AND JOHN SANFORD." —*San Francisco Examiner*

"THIS ONE'S HOT!" —**Liz Smith,** *New York Newsday*

"WRITING IN SHORT, SNAPPY 2 1/2 PAGE CHAPTERS THAT TICK LIKE A TIME BOMB, always full of threat and terror, he hastens us through this parade of horribles to the big bang of an ending." —*Los Angeles Times*

"HORRIFIC . . . SKILLFULLY PUT TOGETHER!" —*Cosmopolitan*

JACK & JILL

"FLAWLESS. . . . PATTERSON, AMONG THE BEST NOVELISTS OF CRIME STORIES EVER, HAS REACHED HIS PINNACLE WITH THIS ONE." —**Larry King,** *USA Today*

more . . .

"A MUST-READ AUTHOR . . . reaches out and grabs you from the opening page and doesn't let go until the last drop of blood."
—*Providence Journal*

"A fine writer with a good ear for dialogue and pacing. HIS BOOKS ARE ALWAYS PAGE-TURNERS." —*Washington Times*

POP GOES THE WEASEL

"Cross is one of the great creations of thriller fiction."
—*Dallas Morning News*

"CROSS IS ONE OF THE BEST PROTAGONISTS OF THE MODERN THRILLER GENRE, AND ONE OF THE MOST LIKABLE. Patterson has a unique gift for making the reader feel Cross's joys and pains."
—*San Francisco Examiner*

"PATTERSON DOES IT AGAIN. THE MAN IS THE MASTER OF THIS GENRE. We fans all have one wish for him: Write even faster."
—Larry King, *USA Today*

"FAST AND FURIOUS. . . . IN THE PATTERSON PANTHEON OF VILLAINS, SHAFER IS QUITE POSSIBLY THE WORST. Best of all, from the perspective of Alex Cross fans, Patterson leaves plenty of room for a sequel." —*Chicago Tribune*

"HE GIVES CROSS A WORTHY OPPONENT—PROBABLY THE SMARTEST KILLER SPAWNED BY PATTERSON'S WICKED IMAGINATION . . . a worthy addition to the Cross saga."
—*San Francisco Examiner*

"PATTERSON MAINTAINS A FAST PACE THROUGH A COMPLEX PLOT." —*San Antonio Express-News*

Also by James Patterson

The Thomas Berryman Number

Season of the Machete

See How They Run

The Midnight Club

Along Came a Spider

Kiss the Girls

Hide & Seek

Jack & Jill

Miracle on the 17th Green (with Peter de Jonge)

Cat & Mouse

When the Wind Blows

Pop Goes the Weasel

Black Friday

Cradle and All

JAMES PATTERSON

ROSES ARE RED

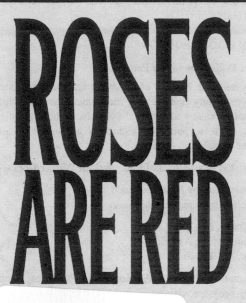

WARNER
VISION
BOOKS

A Time Warner Company

WARNER BOOKS EDITION

Copyright © 2000 by James Patterson

All rights reserved. No part of this book may be reproduced in any form or by any electronic or mechanical means, including information storage and retrieval systems, without permission in writing from the publisher, except by a reviewer who may quote brief passages in a review.

Warner Vision is a registered trademark of Warner Books, Inc.

Cover illustration by Theo Rudnak
Handlettering by James Montalbano

Warner Books, Inc.
1271 Avenue of the Americas
New York, NY 10020

For information on Time Warner Trade Publishing's online publishing program, visit www.ipublish.com.

Visit our Web site at
www.twbookmark.com.

 A Time Warner Company

Printed in the United States of America

Originally published in hardcover by Little, Brown and Company
First International Paperback Printing: July 2001
First U.S. Paperback Printing: October 2001

10 9 8 7 6 5 4 3 2 1

Chapter 1

BRIANNE PARKER didn't look like a bank robber or a murderer — her pleasantly plump baby face fooled everyone. But she knew that she was ready to kill if she had to this morning. She would find out for sure at ten minutes past eight.

The twenty-four-year-old woman wore khakis, a powder blue University of Maryland windbreaker, and scuffed white Nike sneakers. None of the early-morning commuters noticed her as she walked from her dented white Acura to a thick stand of evergreen trees, where she hid.

She was outside the Citibank in Silver Spring, Maryland, just before eight. The branch was scheduled to open in ninety seconds. She knew from her talks with the Mastermind that it was a freestanding bank with two drivethrough lanes. It was surrounded by what he called big-box stores: Target, PETsMART, Home Depot, Circuit City.

At eight o'clock on the dot, Brianne approached the bank from her hiding place in the evergreens under a colorful billboard obnoxiously offering McDonald's breakfast to the public. From that angle she couldn't be seen by the female teller who was just opening the glass front door and had momentarily stepped outside.

A few strides from the teller, she slipped on a rubbery President Clinton mask, one of the most popular masks in America and probably the one hardest to trace. She knew the bank teller's name, and she spoke it clearly as she pulled out her gun and pressed it against the small of the woman's back.

"*Inside,* Ms. Jeanne Galetta. Then turn around and lock the front door again. We're going to see your boss, Mrs. Buccieri."

Her short speech at the entrance to the bank was scripted, word for word, even the pauses. The Mastermind said it was crucial that a bank robbery proceed in a specific order, almost by rote.

"I don't want to kill you, Jeanne. But I will if you don't do everything I say, when I say it. It's *your* turn to talk now, darling. Do you understand what I've just told you so far?"

Jeanne Galetta nodded her head of short brown hair so vigorously that her wire-rimmed glasses nearly fell off. "Yes, I do. Please don't hurt me," she gasped. She was in her late twenties, attractive in a suburban sort of way, but her blue polyester pantsuit and sensible stack-heeled shoes made her look older.

"The manager's office. *Now,* Ms. Jeanne. If I'm not out of here in eight minutes, *you will die.* I'm serious. If I'm not out of here in eight minutes, you and Mrs. Buccieri die. Don't think I won't do it because I'm a woman. I will shoot you both like dogs."

Chapter 2

SHE LIKED THIS AURA OF POWER and she really liked the new respect she was suddenly getting at the bank. As she followed the trembling teller past the two Diebold ATMs and then through the meeter-greeter area of the lobby, Brianne thought about the precious seconds she had already taken. The Mastermind had been explicit about the tight schedule for the robbery. He had repeated over and over that everything depended on perfect execution.

Minutes matter, Brianne.

Seconds matter, Brianne.

It even matters that it's Citibank we've chosen to hit today, Brianne.

The robbery had to be exact, precise, perfect. She *got* it, she *got* it. The Mastermind had planned it on what he called "a numerical scale of 9.9999 out of 10."

With the heel of her left hand, Brianne shoved the teller into the manager's office. She heard the low hum of a computer coming from inside. Then she saw Betsy Buccieri sitting behind her big executive-style desk.

"You open up your safe every morning at five past eight, so open it for me," she screamed at the manager, who was wide-eyed with surprise and fear. *"Open it. Now!"*

"I can't open the vault," Mrs. Buccieri protested. "The vault is automatically opened by a computer signal from the main office in Manhattan. It never happens at the same time."

The bank robber pointed to her own left ear. She signaled with her finger for Mrs. Betsy Buccieri to listen. To listen to what, though? *"Five, four, three, two —"* Brianne said. Then she reached for the phone on the manager's desk. It rang. Perfect timing.

"It's for you," Brianne said, her voice slightly muffled by the rubbery President Clinton mask. "You listen carefully."

She handed the phone to Mrs. Buccieri, but she knew the exact words the bank manager would hear, and who the speaker was.

The scariest voice of all for the bank manager to hear was not that of the Mastermind making very real but idle-*sounding* threats, but someone even better. Scarier.

"Betsy, it's Steve. There's a man here in our house. He has a gun pointed at me. He says that unless the woman in your office leaves the bank with the money by eight-ten exactly, Tommy, Anna, and I will be killed.

"It's eight-oh-four."

The phone line suddenly went dead. Her husband's voice was gone.

"Steve? Steve!" Tears flowed into Betsy Buccieri's

eyes and rolled down her cheeks. She stared at the masked woman and couldn't believe this was happening. "Don't hurt them. Please. I'll open the vault for you. I'll do it now. Don't hurt anyone."

Brianne repeated the message the bank manager had already heard. "Eight-ten exactly. Not one second later. And no stupid bank tricks. No silent alarms. No dye packs."

"Follow me. No alarms," Betsy Buccieri promised. She almost couldn't think. *Steve, Tommy, Anna.* The names rang loudly in her head.

They arrived at the door of the bank's Mosler vault. It was 8:05.

"Open the door, Betsy. We are on the clock. We're losing time. Your family is losing time. Steve, Anna, little Tommy, they could all die."

It took a little less than two minutes for Betsy Buccieri to get into the vault, which was a polished steel thing of beauty with pistons like a locomotive. Stacks of money were plainly visible on nearly all the shelves — more money than Brianne had ever seen in her life. She snapped open two canvas duffel bags and began filling them with the cash. Mrs. Buccieri and Jeanne Galetta watched her take the money in silence. She liked seeing the fear and respect for her on their faces.

As she'd been instructed to, Brianne counted off the minutes as she filled the duffel bags. *"Eight-oh-seven . . . eight-oh-eight . . ."* Finally, she was finished with her part in the vault.

"I'm locking you both inside the vault. Don't say one word or I'll shoot you, then lock your dead bodies up."

She hoisted the black duffel bags.

"Don't hurt my husband or my baby," Betsy Buccieri begged. "We did what you —"

Brianne slammed the heavy metal door on Betsy Buccieri's desperate plea. She yanked her President Clinton mask from her sweaty face.

She was running *late*. She walked across the lobby, unlocked the front door with plastic-gloved hands, and went outside. She felt like running as fast as she could to her car, but she walked calmly, as if she didn't have a care in the world on this fine spring morning. She was tempted to pull out her six-shooter and put a hole into the big Egg McShit staring down on her. Yeah, she had an attitude, all right.

When she got to the Acura, she checked her watch: 52 seconds past 8:10. And counting. She was late — but that was the way it was supposed to be. She smiled.

She didn't call Errol at the Buccieri house where Steve, Tommy, and the nanny, Anna, were being held. She didn't tell him she had the money and she was safely in the Acura.

She had been told not to by the Mastermind.

The hostages were supposed to die.

Part One

THE ROBBERY-
MURDERS

Chapter 3

THERE'S AN OLD SAYING that I've learned to believe in my time as a detective: *Don't think there are no crocodiles because the water is calm.*

The water was certainly lovely and calm that day. My young and irrepressible daughter, Jannie, had Rosie the Cat up on her hind legs and she was holding Rosie's front paws in her hands. She and *"la chat rouge"* were dancing, as they often did.

"Roses are red, violets are blue," Jannie sang in a sweet, lilting voice. It was a moment and an image I wouldn't forget. Friends, relatives, and neighbors had begun to arrive for the christening party at our house on Fifth Street. I was in a hugely celebratory mood.

Nana Mama had prepared an amazing meal for the special occasion. There was cilantro-marinated shrimp, roasted mussels, fresh ham, Vidalia onions, and summer squash. The aroma of chicken with garlic, pork ribs, and four kinds of homemade bread filled the air. I'd even made my specialty that night, my contribution, a creamy cheesecake with fresh raspberries on top.

One of Nana's refrigerator notes was posted on the door of the GE. It read: " 'There is an incredible amount of magic and feistiness in black men that nobody has been able to wipe out. But *everybody has tried*.' — Toni Morrison." I smiled at the magic and feistiness of my eightysomething-year-old grandmother.

This was so good. Jannie, Damon, little Alex, and I were greeting everybody on the front porch as they arrived. Alex was in my arms, and he was a very social little baby. He had happy smiles for everyone, even for my partner, John Sampson, who can scare little kids at first because he's mammoth — and *scary*.

"The boy obviously likes to party," Sampson observed, and grinned broadly.

Alex grinned right back at Two-John, who is six-nine and about two hundred fifty pounds.

Sampson reached out and took the baby from me. Alex nearly disappeared in his hands, which are the size of catcher's mitts. Then Sampson laughed and began to talk to the baby in total gibberish.

Christine appeared from the kitchen. She joined the three of us. So far, she and Alex Jr. were living apart from us. We hoped they would come join Nana, Damon, Jannie, and me in this house. Just one big family. I wanted Christine as my wife, not just as a girlfriend. I wanted to wake little Alex in the mornings, then put him to sleep at night.

"I'm going to walk around the party with little Alex. Shamelessly use him to pick up pretty women," Sampson said. He walked off with Alex cradled in his arms.

"You think he'll ever get married?" Christine asked.

"Little Alex? The Boy? Sure he will."

"No, your partner in crime, John Sampson. Will *he* ever get married, settle down?" It didn't sound like it bothered her that *we* weren't.

"I think he will — someday. John had a bad family model. His father walked out when John was a year old — eventually died of an overdose. John's mother was a drug addict. She lived in Southeast until a couple of years ago. Sampson was practically raised by my Aunt Tia, with help from Nana."

We watched Sampson cruise the party with little Alex in his arms. He hit on a pretty lady named De Shawn Hawkins, who worked with Christine. "He really *is* using the baby to hit on women," Christine said in amazement. "De Shawn, be careful," she called to her friend.

I laughed. "Says what he's going to do, does what he says."

The party had started around two in the afternoon. It was still going strong at nine-thirty. I had just sung a duet with Sampson, Joe Tex's "Skinny Legs and All." It was a howling success. We got a lot of laughs and playful jeers. Sampson was starting to sing "You're the First, the Last, My Everything."

That was when Kyle Craig from the FBI arrived. I should have told everybody to go home — the party was all but over.

Chapter 4

KYLE WAS CARRYING a colorfully wrapped and ribboned present for the baby. And he had balloons! The gifts didn't fool me. Kyle is a good friend, possibly a great cop, but he isn't social and avoids parties as if they were viral diseases.

"Not tonight, Alex," Christine said, and she suddenly looked concerned, maybe even angry. "Don't get involved in some scary, terrible case. Please, Alex, don't do it. Not on the night of the christening."

I knew what she meant, and I took her advice, or warning, to heart. My mood had already darkened.

Goddamn Kyle Craig.

"No, no, and no," I said as I walked up to Kyle. I used my index fingers to make a cross. "Go away."

"I'm real happy to see you, too," Kyle said, and beamed. Then he gave me a hug. "Multiple homicide," he whispered.

"Sorry, call back tomorrow or the next day. This is my night off."

"I know it is, but this is particularly bad, Alex. This one has really struck a nerve."

While he was still holding on to me, Kyle told me he was in Washington only for the night and he badly needed my help. He was feeling a lot of pressure. I told him no again, but he wasn't listening, and we both knew it was part of my job to assist the FBI on important cases here. Also, I owed Kyle a favor or two. A few years back he'd let me into a kidnapping-and-murder case in North Carolina when my niece disappeared from Duke University.

Kyle knew Sampson and a few of my other detective friends. They came over and chatted with him as if this were a social visit. People tend to like Kyle. I do, too — but not now, not tonight. He said he had to peek in on little Alex before we talked business.

Chapter 5

I WENT ALONG WITH KYLE. The two of us stood over the Boy, who was now asleep amid colorful stuffed bears and balls in a port-a-crib in Nana's room. He held on to his favorite bear, which was named Pinky.

"The poor little boy. What a bad, bad break," Kyle whispered as he looked down at Alex. "He looks like you instead of Christine. How are you two doing, anyway?"

"We're settling back into things okay," I said, which wasn't the truth, unfortunately. Christine had been gone from Washington for a year, and since she'd been back, we hadn't done as well as I would have hoped. I missed the intimacy more than I could say. It was killing me. But I wasn't able to tell anyone about it, not even Sampson or Nana.

"Please, Kyle. Just leave me alone for tonight."

"I wish this could wait, Alex. I'm afraid it can't. I'm on my way back to Quantico now. Where can we talk?"

I shook my head and felt anger building up inside. I led him to the sunporch, where I keep an old upright piano that still plays about as well as I do. I sat down on the creaky piano bench and tapped out a few notes of Gershwin's "Let's Call the Whole Thing Off."

Kyle recognized the tune and he grinned. "I am sorry about this."

"Not sorry enough, obviously. Go ahead."

"You heard about the Citibank-branch robbery out in Silver Spring? The murders at the bank manager's house?" he asked. "Manager's husband, their nanny, three-year-old son?"

"How could I *not* hear about it?" I said, and looked away from Kyle. The brutal, senseless murders had saddened me and knotted my stomach when I read about them. The story was all over the papers and TV. Even cops in D.C. were outraged.

"I didn't really understand what I heard so far. What the hell happened at the manager's house? The perps had the money, right? Why did they have to kill the hostages if they had the money? That's what you're here to tell me, right?"

Kyle nodded. "They were *late* getting out of the bank. The explicit order was that the crew member inside had to be out with the money by eight-ten exactly. Alex, the crew member at the bank was *less than a minute late*. Less than a minute! So they murdered the thirty-three-year-old father, the three-year-old boy, and the couple's nanny. The nanny was twenty-five, and she was pregnant. They *executed* the father, the three-year-old, the nanny. You *see* the murder scene, Alex?"

I rolled my shoulders, twisted my neck. I could feel the tension invading my body. I *saw* it, all right. How could they have murdered those people for no reason?

I really wasn't in the mood for police business, though, not even a bad case like this one. "Which brings you out to my house tonight? On my son's christening day?"

"Oh, hell." Kyle suddenly smiled and lightened his tone. "I had to come over to see the promised child, anyway. Unfortunately, this case is really intense. There's a possibility the crew is from D.C. Even if they're not from Washington, there's still a possibility somebody here might know them, Alex. I need you to look for the killers — *before they do it again.* We have the feeling this isn't a one-shot. Alex, your baby is a beauty, though."

"Yeah, you're a beauty, too," I said to Kyle. "You are truly beyond compare."

"Three-year-old boy, the father, a nanny," Kyle said one more time before he left the party. He was about to go through the door in the sunporch when he turned to me and said, "You're the right person for this. They murdered a family, Alex."

As soon as Kyle was gone, I went looking for Christine. My heart sank. She had taken Alex and left without saying good-bye, without a single word.

Chapter 6

RELUCTANTLY, the Mastermind parked on the street, then walked toward an abandoned project within a stone's throw of the Anacostia River. A full moon cast a cold, hard, bone white light on half a dozen crumbling three-story row houses with open, screenless windows. He wondered if he had the stomach for this. "Into the valley of death," he whispered.

To his further dismay, he found the Parkers' hideout was in the row house farthest from the street. They were ensconced on the third floor. Their lovely little lodging was furnished with a grimy, stained mattress and a rusted lawn chair. Greasy wrappings from KFC and Mickey D's were scattered on the floor.

As he entered their room, he held up a couple of oven-warm pizza boxes as well as a brown paper bag. "Chianti and pizza! This is a celebration, isn't it?"

Brianne and Errol were evidently hungry and dug into the pizza pies immediately. They barely greeted him, which he took as disrespect. The Mastermind busied himself pouring Chianti into plastic cups he had brought for the occasion. He passed around the cups and then made a toast.

"To perfect crimes," he said.

"Yeah, right. Perfect crimes." Errol Parker frowned as he took two big sips of Chianti. "If that's what you call what happened in Silver Spring. Three murders that could have been avoided."

"That's what I call it," said the Mastermind. "Absolutely perfect. You'll see."

They ate and drank in silence. The Parkers seemed moody, even defiant. Brianne kept sneaking looks at him. Suddenly, Errol Parker began to rub his throat. He coughed repeatedly. Then he gasped loudly, *"Aaagh! Aaagh!"* His throat and his chest were burning. He couldn't breathe. He tried to stand, but he immediately toppled over.

"What is it? What's wrong, Errol? *Errol?*" Brianne asked, alarmed and afraid.

Then she grabbed at her throat, too. It was on fire. So was her chest. She shot up from the mattress. She dropped the cup of wine and held her throat with both hands.

"What the hell is happening? What's happening to us?" she screamed at the Mastermind. "What did you do?"

"Isn't it obvious?" he answered in the coldest, most remote voice she had ever heard.

The tenement room seemed to be whirling out of control. Errol went into spasms, then fell to the floor in a seizure. Brianne bit a gash in her tongue. Both of them were still clutching at their throats. They were choking, gagging, unable to breathe. Their faces had taken on a dusky hue.

The Mastermind stood across the room and watched. The paralysis from the poison they had imbibed was progressive and extremely painful. It started with the facial muscles, then moved to the glottis in the back of the throat. The Parkers obviously couldn't swallow. Finally, it affected the respiratory organs. A high enough dose of Anectine led to cardiac arrest.

It took less than fifteen minutes for the two of them to die, as mercilessly as those murdered in Silver Spring, Maryland. They lay motionless, spread-eagled on the floor. He was quite sure that they were dead, but he checked the vital signs, anyway. Their features were unbearably contorted and their bodies twisted. They looked as if they had fallen from a great height.

"To perfect crimes," the Mastermind intoned over the grotesquely sprawled bodies.

Chapter 7

I TRIED TO CALL CHRISTINE early the next morning, but she was screening her calls and wouldn't pick up. She'd never done that to me, and it stung. I couldn't get it out of my head as I showered and dressed. Finally, I went to work. I was hurt, but I was also a little angry.

Sampson and I were out on the streets before nine. The more I read and thought about the Citibank robbery in Silver Spring, the more troubled and confused I was about the exact sequence of events. It didn't make sense. Three innocent people had been murdered — *for what reason?* The bank robbers already had their money. What kind of cruel and twisted sickos were they? Why kill father and child and the family's nanny?

It turned out to be a long and consistently frustrating day. Sampson and I were still on the job at nine that night. I tried calling Christine at home again. She still wasn't picking up, or maybe she wasn't there.

I have a couple of tattered black notebooks filled with

names of street contacts. Sampson and I had already talked to more than two dozen of the prime ones. That still left plenty for tomorrow, and the next day, and the day after that. I was pretty well hooked into the case already. Why kill three people at the bank manager's house? Why destroy an innocent family?

"We're dancing around something," Sampson said as we drove through Southeast in my old car. We had just finished talking to a small-time hustler named Nomar Martinez. He knew about the bank robbery in Maryland, but not who did it. The late, great Marvin Gaye was singing on the car radio. I thought of Christine. She didn't want me out here on these streets anymore. She was serious about it. I wasn't sure if I could quit being a detective. I liked my job.

"I had that same feeling with Nomar. Maybe we should have brought his ass in. He was edgy, afraid of something," I said.

"Who's not afraid of something in Southeast?" Sampson asked. "The question remains. Who's gonna talk to us?"

"How about that ugly mutt there?" I said, and pointed toward the street corner we were approaching. "He knows everything happening around here."

"He spotted us," Sampson said. "Shit, there he goes!"

Chapter 8

I SPUN THE STEERING WHEEL hard to my left. The Porsche skidded toward a stop, then hopped the curb with a jolting *thud*. Sampson and I jumped out and started to run after Cedric Montgomery.

"Stop! Police!" I yelled at him.

We shot down a narrow, twisted alley behind the small-time enforcer and all-around tough guy. Montgomery was a source of information, but he wasn't a snitch. He just knew things. He was in his early twenties; Sampson and I were both a whisker past forty. *We worked out and we were still fast* — at least in our minds.

Montgomery could really move, though. He was a blur up ahead of us.

"He's just a sprinter, sugar," Sampson huffed. He was at my side, matching me stride for stride. "We're good for the long haul."

"Police!" I yelled again. "Why are you running, Montgomery?"

Sweat was already forming on my neck and back. The perspiration was dripping down from my hair. My eyes were burning. *But I could still run. Couldn't I?*

"We can take him," I said. I accelerated, turned up my jets. It was a dare — a challenge to Sampson, a game we'd been playing for years. *Who can? We can.*

We were actually gaining some on Montgomery. He looked back — and couldn't believe we were right behind him. Two freight trains on his tail, and there was no way for him to get off the track.

"Put it in full gear, sugar!" Sampson said. "Prepare for impact."

I gave it everything. Sampson and I were still matching steps. We were having our own private footrace, and Montgomery was the finish line.

We both hit him at the same time. He went down like a shocked wide receiver crushed between two very fast linebackers. I was afraid he would never get up again. But Montgomery rolled a few times, moaned, and then looked at us in total amazement.

"Goddamn!" he whispered. That was all he said. Sampson and I took the compliment, then we cuffed him.

Two hours later Montgomery was talking to us at the station house on Third Street. He admitted that he had heard something about the robbery and murders over in Silver Spring. He was willing to trade information if we would look past half a dozen dime bags he had in his possession when we gang-tackled him on the street.

"I know who you lookin' for," Montgomery said, and he seemed sure of himself. "But you ain't gonna like hearin' who it is."

He was right — I didn't like what he told me. Not at all.

Chapter 9

I WASN'T SURE whether I could trust Cedric Montgomery's information, but he'd given me a good hard lead that I had to follow. He was right about one thing: His tip was disturbing to me. One of the people he'd implicated in the robbery was the stepbrother of my late wife, Maria. He'd heard that Errol Parker might have done the bank in Silver Spring.

Sampson and I spent the next day trying to locate Errol, but he wasn't at home or at any of his usual haunts around Southeast. His wife, Brianne, wasn't around, either. No one had seen the Parkers for at least a week.

Around five-thirty I stopped by the Sojourner Truth School to see if Christine was still there. I'd been thinking about her all day. She hadn't answered my calls or returned any messages.

I had met Christine Johnson two years before, and we'd almost gotten married. Then a sad and tragic thing had happened, and I still blamed myself: She was kidnapped by a monster who had committed several murders in Southeast. She had been held as a hostage for nearly a year. *Christine was kidnapped because she was seeing me.* She was missing for a year and believed to be dead. When Christine was found, there was another surprise. She had a baby, our son, Alex. But the abduction had changed her, wounded her in ways she didn't understand, and she couldn't cope with that. I'd tried to help in any way I could. It had been months since we'd been intimate. She kept pushing me farther and farther away. Now Kyle Craig had made it even worse.

Nana usually watched over the baby while Christine was working at the Sojourner Truth School. Then Christine and little Alex went to her apartment in Mitchellville. It was the way she needed it to be.

I entered the school through a metal side door near the gym and heard the familiar sound of basketballs pounding against hardwood and the laughter and joyful screams of kids. I found Christine huddled over the computer in her office. She is the principal at the Sojourner Truth School. Jannie and Damon are students there.

"Alex?" Christine said when she saw me at the door. I read the sign on the wall: *Praise loudly, blame softly.* Was Christine able to do that for me? "I'm almost finished for the day. Just give me another minute or two." At least she didn't seem angry about the other night with Kyle Craig; she didn't tell me to leave.

"I came to walk you home from school. I'll even carry your books," I said, and smiled. "That's all right?"

"I guess so," she said, but she didn't smile back and she still seemed so far away.

Chapter 10

WHEN CHRISTINE WAS READY TO GO, we locked up the school together, then strolled down School Street toward Fifth. True to my word, I carried Christine's briefcase filled with what felt like a dozen books. I tried a little joke. "You didn't say anything about carrying your bowling ball, too."

"I told you the books were heavy. I'm a heavy thinker, you know. Actually, I'm kind of glad you came by tonight," she said.

"Couldn't keep myself away." I told the truth and shamed the devil. I wanted to take Christine's arm, or at least her hand, but I held back. It seemed strange and wrong to be so close and yet so distant from her. I ached to hold her in my arms.

"I want to talk to you about something, Alex," she finally said. She stared into my eyes. I could tell from the look on her face that this probably wasn't good news I was about to hear.

"I was hoping that it wouldn't bother me — your getting on a new murder case. But it does bother me, Alex. It makes me crazy. I worry about you. I worry about the baby. And I worry about my own safety. I can't help it after what happened in Bermuda. I haven't been sleeping since I returned to Washington."

It tore me apart to hear Christine talk like this. I felt terrible about what had happened to her. She had changed so much, though. There didn't seem to be anything I could do to make it better, to help her. I'd been trying for months, but nothing worked. I worried that I wouldn't just lose Christine, but little Alex as well.

"I remember some of the dreams I've had lately. They're so violent, Alex. And they're so real. The other night you were chasing the Weasel again, and he killed you. He stood there calmly and shot you again and again. Then he came and killed the baby and me. I woke up screaming."

I finally took her hand. "Geoffrey Shafer is dead, Christine," I said.

"You don't know that. Not for sure," Christine argued, and pulled her hand away from me. She was angry again.

We walked along the edge of the Anacostia River in silence. After a while she told me about some of her other dreams. I sensed she didn't want me to interpret them. Just to listen. The dreams were all violent — people Christine knew and loved were mutilated and murdered.

Christine finally stopped walking at the corner of Fifth near my house. "Alex, I have to tell you something else. I've been going to a psychiatrist, Dr. Belair, in Mitchellville. He's helping me."

Christine continued to stare into my eyes. "I don't

want to see you anymore, Alex. I've thought about this for weeks. I've talked about it with Dr. Belair. You can't change my mind, and I'd appreciate it if you didn't try."

She took her briefcase from me, then she walked away. She didn't let me say a word, but I would have found it hard to speak, anyway. I had seen the truth in her eyes. She didn't love me anymore. What made it so much worse was that I still loved her, and of course, I loved our baby boy.

Chapter 11

I REALLY DIDN'T HAVE A CHOICE, so I threw myself into the bank robbery and multiple murders investigation. The newspapers and TV were still filled with sensational stories about the murdered father, child, and nanny. The picture of three-year-old Tommy Buccieri seemed to be everywhere. *Did the killer want us to feel outrage?* I wondered.

Sampson and I spent most of one day trying to find Errol and Brianne Parker. The more I followed up on the Parkers with the FBI, the clearer it got that they had probably been robbing small banks in Maryland and Virginia for at least a year. The job at Silver Spring was different. If they had done it, something had happened to change their style; they had become brutal, heartless killers. Why?

Sampson and I stopped for lunch at a Boston Market around one in the afternoon. It wasn't our first, or even second choice, but it was handy and the Big Man was hungry, wouldn't be denied. I could have continued on without eating.

"You think the Parkers are off doing another job?" he asked me as we dug into orders of meat loaf, corn, and mashed potatoes.

"If they're the ones who did the bank in Maryland, they're probably hiding out. They know the heat is on. Errol sneaks off to South Carolina sometimes. He's a fisherman. Kyle already has FBI agents on the ground there."

"You ever spend time with Errol?" Sampson wanted to know.

"Family get-togethers mostly, but he only came to a few that I can remember. I went fishing with him once. He was like a little kid as long as we were catching large-mouth bass and two- or three-pound catfish. Maria always liked Errol."

Sampson kept eating his meat loaf and double order of mashed potatoes. "You think about Maria much?"

I scrunched down into my seat. I wasn't sure I wanted to talk about this now. "Different things remind me of her. Especially Sundays. We'd sleep until noon sometimes, treat ourselves to a nice brunch. Or visit the duck pond near the river. St. Tony's. Long walks in Garfield Park. It's a sad, confusing thing, John — that she died so young. It especially hurts that I could never solve her murder."

Sampson kept on hounding me with questions. He gets that way sometimes.

"You and Christine are doing all right?"

"No," I finally admitted. But I couldn't quite get out the whole truth. "She can't get over what happened with

Geoffrey Shafer. I'm not even sure that the Weasel is dead. We finished here?"

Sampson grinned. "Food, or my cross-examination?"

"Let's go. Let's find Errol and Brianne Parker. Solve the bank robbery. Take the rest of the day off."

Chapter 12

AROUND SEVEN O'CLOCK Sampson and I decided to take a dinner break. We figured we'd be working late, probably past midnight. It was that kind of case. I went home for supper with the kids and Nana Mama.

I ate, and complimented Nana on her cooking, but I didn't taste much of anything. I was keeping the Christine thing bottled up inside me. Not too bright on my part.

Sampson and I agreed to meet around ten to check out a few night crawlers who would be easier to find after darkness fell. At quarter past ten, we were trolling Southeast again in my car.

Sampson spotted a small-time drug hustler and snitch we knew. Darryl Snow was hanging out with his boys in front of a bar and grill that kept changing its name and now was called Used-To-Be's.

Sampson and I hopped out of the Porsche and came up fast on Snow. He had nowhere to run. As always, Darryl was a drug-hustler fashion plate: crimson nylon shorts over blue nylon pants, Polo T-shirt, Tommy Hilfiger windbreaker, Oakley shades.

"Hey there, Snowman," Sampson said in his deep voice. "You're melting away to nothing."

Even Snow's hustler friends laughed. Darryl was around five-eleven, and I doubt he weighed a hundred and twenty pounds with his clothes on, designer labels and all.

"Walk and talk with me, Darryl," I told him. "This is not open to discussion."

His head shook like a dashboard doll's, but he reluctantly went along. "I don't wanna talk to you, Cross."

"Errol and Brianne Parker," I said, once we were far enough away from the others.

Darryl looked at me and frowned heavily as his head continued to bob. "You the one was married to his sister or whatever? Why you askin' me? Why you always prosecutin' me, man?"

"Errol doesn't spend a lot of time with the family anymore. He's too busy robbing banks. Where is he, Darryl? Sampson and I don't owe you any favors right now. That's a dicey place to be."

"I can live with it," Darryl said, and looked away into the streetlights.

My hand shot out and grabbed some windbreaker and shirt. "No, you can *not.* You know better, Darryl."

Snow sniffled and cursed under his breath. "I hear Brianne be over the old First Avenue projects. Rat-shit buildings on First? I don't know she still at that place, though. That's all I got." He held out his hands, palms up.

Sampson came rolling up behind Snow. *"Boo,"* he said, and Darryl's sneakered feet almost left the ground.

"Is Darryl being helpful?" he asked me. "Seems a little jumpy."

"Are you being helpful?" I asked Snow.

He whined pathetically. "I told you where Brianne Parker be seen, din't I? Why don' you just go over there? Check it out, man. Leave me the hell alone. You two like the *Blair Witch Project* or somethin'. Scary, man."

"Much scarier," said Sampson, and he grinned. "*Blair Witch* is just a movie, Darryl. We're for real."

Chapter 13

"I HATE THIS nasty, eerie, middle-of-the-night shit," Sampson said as we approached the First Avenue project on foot. What we saw up ahead were abandoned tenement buildings where junkies and homeless people lived, if you could call it living, in America's capital city.

"*Night of the Living Dead* all over again," Sampson muttered. He was right; the hangarounds outside the buildings did look like zombies.

"Errol Parker? Brianne Parker?" I said in a low voice as I walked past badly strung-out men with hollow, unshaven faces. Nobody answered. Most of them wouldn't even look at me or Sampson. They knew we were police.

"Errol? Brianne Parker?" I continued, but still no one answered.

"Thanks for the help. God loves you," Sampson said. He was mimicking the rap of the more irritating panhandlers around town.

We began to walk through each of the buildings, floor

by floor, basement to the roof. The final building we came to looked deserted and for a good reason: It was the most squalid and broken down.

"After you, Alphonse," Sampson growled. It was late and he was getting grumpy.

I had the flashlight, so I led the way. As we'd done in the other buildings, we started in the cellar. The floor was potholed, heavily stained cement. Dusty cobwebs wove from one end of the basement to the other.

I came to a closed wooden door and pushed it open with my foot. I could hear rodents of various sizes scurrying around inside the walls, scratching furiously as if they were trapped. I waved my flashlight around. Nothing but a couple of glaring rats.

"Errol? Brianne?" Sampson called to them. They chittered back at us.

He and I continued the floor-to-floor search. The building was damp and smelled of urine, feces, mildew. The stench was unbearable.

"I've seen better Holiday Inns," I said, and Sampson finally laughed.

I shoved open another door, and knew by the putrescent odor that we'd found dead bodies. I waved the flashlight and saw Brianne and Errol. They no longer looked human. The building was warm and decomposition began fast. I calculated they'd been dead for at least a day, probably more.

I shone the Maglite flashlight at Errol first, then at his wife. I sighed and felt a little sick inside. I thought of Maria and how she had liked something about Errol. When he was little, my son Damon had called him Uncle Errol.

The corneas of Brianne's eyes were cloudy, as if she had cataracts. Her mouth was wide open, the jaw slack. Errol looked pretty much the same. I thought of the family that had been executed in Silver Spring. What kind of killers were we dealing with? Why had they killed the Parkers?

Brianne's top had been removed, and I didn't see it anywhere in the room. Her jeans were pulled down, exposing red panties and her thighs.

I wondered what it meant. Had the killer taken Brianne's top? Had someone else been in here since the murders? Had they played around with Brianne after she was dead? Was it the killer?

Sampson looked troubled and puzzled. "Doesn't look like an overdose," he said. "Too violent. These two suffered."

"John," I finally spoke in a quiet voice, "I think they might have been poisoned. Maybe they were *supposed* to suffer."

I made a call to Kyle Craig and told him about the Parkers. Had we solved part of the Silver Spring robbery? Was at least one killer still out there?

Chapter 14

A RUSH-RUSH AUTOPSY confirmed my suspicion that Errol and Brianne Parker had been poisoned. The ingestion of a massive dose of Anectine had caused rapid muscle contractions and led to cardiac arrest. The poison had been mixed into a bottle of Chianti. Brianne Parker had been sexually violated after she was dead. What a mess.

Sampson and I spent another couple of hours talking to the hangarounds, the homeless, the junkies living in the abandoned project buildings on First Avenue. No one admitted knowing Errol or Brianne; no one had seen any unusual visitors at the building where the couple had been hiding.

I finally drifted home for a few hours' sleep, but I was restless in my bedroom. I got up and hobbled downstairs around five. I was thinking about Christine and little Alex again.

Nana's latest refrigerator note was posted. It read: "Never once / did she wanna be white / to pass / dreamed only of being darker." I opened the fridge and took out a Stewart's root beer, then I wandered out of the kitchen. The poem from the refrigerator door drifted through my head.

I flicked the television on, then off. I played the piano in the sunroom — "Crazy for You" and then some Debussy. I played "Moonglow," which reminded me of the best times with Christine. I imagined ways that we might fix the relationship. I'd tried to be there for her every day since her return to Washington. She kept pushing me away. Tears finally welled in my eyes and I wiped them away. *She's gone. You have to start over again.* But I wasn't so sure that I could.

The floorboards squeaked. "I heard you playing 'Clair de Lune.' Very nicely, I might add." Nana was standing in the doorway with a tray in her hands. There were two steaming coffee mugs on it.

She pushed one of them toward me and I took it. She then sat in the old wicker rocker near the piano, quietly sipping her brew.

"This instant?" I kidded her.

"You find any instant coffee in my kitchen, I'll give you this house."

"I own the house," I reminded her.

"So you say, sonny boy. Sunrise concerto, Alex? What's the occasion?"

"Presunrise concerto. I couldn't sleep. Bad night, bad dreams. Bad morning so far." I sipped the delicious coffee, which was laced with chicory. "Good coffee, though."

Nana continued to sip hers. "Mmm-hmmm. Tell me something I don't know. What else?"

"You remember Maria's stepbrother Errol? Sampson and I found his body in the First Avenue projects last night," I told her.

Nana made a low clucking sound, and she gently shook her head. "That's so sad, such a shame, Alex. They're a good family, nice people."

"I have to go and tell the family this morning. Maybe that's why I'm up so early."

"What else?" Nana asked again. She knew me so well, and in a way that was comforting now. "Talk to me, Alex. Tell your Nana."

"It's Christine," I finally said. "I think it's over between us. She doesn't want to see me. She told me, made it official. I don't know where that leaves little Alex. Nana, I have tried everything in my power. I swear I have."

She put down her coffee mug and slid one skinny arm around me. She still has a lot of strength in her body. She held me tight. "Well then, you've done what you can, haven't you? What else can you do?"

"She hasn't gotten over what happened in Bermuda," I whispered. "She doesn't want to be with a homicide detective. She can't do it. She doesn't want to be with me."

Nana whispered back at me, "You're taking too much on your shoulders. You're taking on blame you shouldn't. It's bending you, Alex. You can break. You listen to Nana now."

"I'm listening. I always do."

"Do not."

"Do too."

"*Do not,* and I can keep this up longer than you," she snapped. "Besides, it proves my point."

Nana always has the last word. She is the best psychologist in the house, or so she tells me constantly.

Chapter 15

THE SECOND BANK ROBBERY went off like a time bomb early that morning in the town of Falls Church, Virginia, about nine miles outside Washington.

The bank manager's house was a well-maintained colonial in a sweet neighborhood where the people seemed to genuinely like one another. There was evidence of well-loved children everywhere: Tyco toys, bikes, a basketball net, dueling swings, a makeshift lemonade stand. There was a beautiful garden filled with flowering shrubs. Birds perched on a whimsical weathervane — a witch on a broom — up on the garage roof. That morning you could almost hear the witch's cackle.

The Mastermind had told his new crew *what they would find* and *how they should proceed*. Every move was carefully planned and rehearsed.

The new crew was superior to the Parkers. It had taken half of the money from the Citibank job to interest them, but it was worth it. They called one another Mr. Red, Mr. White, Mr. Blue, and Ms. Green. They had long hair and looked like a heavy metal rock band, but they were an efficient team, very high-tech.

Mr. Blue was at the First Union branch when it opened in downtown Falls Church. Ms. Green was there with him. They both had semiautomatic weapons in shoulder holsters underneath their windbreakers.

Mr. Red and Mr. White went to the manager's house. Katie Bartlett heard the door chimes and thought it was the baby-sitter. When she opened the front door, she turned pale and her legs buckled at the sight of an armed, masked man wearing a headset with a microphone jutting under his chin. Behind him was a second armed man.

"Back inside! Move it!" Red screamed loudly through his mask. He held his gun inches from her face.

Red and White herded the mother and her three small children into the family room on the main floor. The room featured a home entertainment center, and a Tae Bo video was playing. A picture window looked out on a small, still lake, but no one could see them unless they had a boat, and there were no boats on the lake that morning.

"Now, we're going to make a home movie," Mr. Red explained to Mrs. Bartlett and the kids. He talked to them in a matter-of-fact, almost friendly way.

"You don't have to hurt anyone," Katie Bartlett told him. "We'll cooperate with you. Please put the guns away. I beg you."

"I hear you, Katie. But we have to show your husband that we're serious and that I'm actually here in the house with you and the kids."

"They're two, three, and four," the mother said. She started to cry, but then she seemed to will herself to stop. "They're just little babies. My babies."

Mr. Red slid his gun inside his holster. "There, there. I don't want to hurt the kids. I promise I don't."

He was pleased with the job so far. Katie seemed smart, and the kids were well behaved. They were a nice family, the Bartletts. Just as the Mastermind had said.

"I want you to be the one to put this duct tape on the kids' mouths," Mr. Red told Katie Bartlett. He handed over a thick roll of tape.

"They won't make any noise. I *promise*," she said. "They're good kids."

Mr. Red felt sorry for her. She was pretty, and an okay lady. He thought of the couple and the kid in the movie *Life Is Beautiful*. Mr. Red spoke directly to the kids. "This is duct tape, and we're going to play a game with it. It'll be cool," he said.

Two of the kids glared at him, but the three-year-old grinned. "Duck tape?"

"That's right. Duck tape. *Quack, quack, quack, quack.* Now Mommy's going to put the duck tape on everybody's mouth. Then we make a home movie for Daddy to see how you look."

"Then what?" asked Dennis, the four-year-old, who now seemed interested in the game. "We quack up Daddy."

Mr. Red laughed. Even Mr. White managed a smirk. The kids were cute. He hoped he wouldn't have to kill them in a few minutes.

Chapter 16

SOMEBODY was going to be murdered in just a few minutes. It was 8:12. The Falls Church robbery was on the clock and it couldn't be stopped.

Ms. Green had a rapid-fire weapon aimed in the direction of two frightened women tellers; both of them were in their mid- to late twenties.

Mr. Blue was already in the manager's office at the First Union branch. He was explaining the rules of the game of "truth or consequences" to James Bartlett and his assistant manager.

"Nobody has any panic buttons on them?" Mr. Blue asked in a fast, high-pitched voice that was *intended* to communicate that he was tense and maybe close to losing it. "That would be a serious mistake, and there can be *no* mistakes."

"We don't have panic buttons," said the bank manager, who seemed smart enough and eager to please. "I would tell you if we did."

"You ever listen to the training tapes put out by the American Society for Industrial Security?" Blue asked.

"N-no, I haven't," the bank manager answered with a nervous stutter. "I'm — I'm — s-sorry."

"Well, their number one recommendation during a robbery is cooperation so that no one gets hurt."

The manager nodded his head rapidly. "I agree with that. I hear you. I'm cooperating, sir."

"You're a pretty smart guy for a bank manager. Everything I told you about your family being held as hostages is the absolute *truth*. I want you to always tell me the truth, too. Or there will be unfortunate *consequences*. That means *no* trip alarms, *no* bait money, *no* dye packs, *no* hidden cameras. If Sonitrol has a device in here that's recording me now, tell me."

"I know about the job at the Citibank in Silver Spring," the manager said. His wide, square face was beet red. Perspiration dripped from his forehead in large drops. His blue eyes blinked repeatedly.

"Watch your computer screen," Mr. Blue said, and pointed with his gun. "Watch it."

A film sequence came up, and the manager saw his wife putting black tape on the mouths of his three children.

"Oh, God! I know that the manager in Silver Spring was late. Let's get going," he said to the ski-masked man in his office. "My family is everything to me."

"We know," Blue said. He turned to the assistant manager. He pointed the gun at her. "You're not a hero, are you, Ms. Collins?"

She shook her head of soft red curls. "No, sir, I'm not.

The bank's money is not my money. It isn't worth dying for. It isn't worth Mr. Bartlett's children dying for."

Mr. Blue smiled under his mask. "You took the words right out of my mouth."

He turned back to the manager. "I have children, you have children. We don't want them to be fatherless," he said. It was the Mastermind's line and an effective one, he thought. "Let's get going."

They hurried to the main vault, which had a dual combination and needed both Bartlett and his assistant manager to open it. In less than sixty seconds, the vault was open.

Mr. Blue then held up a silver metal device for all to see; it looked like a TV remote control. "This is a police scanner," he said. "If the police or the FBI are alerted and come our way, I'll know as soon as they do. And then you two, and also the two tellers, die. Are there any trip alarms inside the vault?"

The manager shook his head. "No, sir. There are no secret alarms. You have my word."

Mr. Blue smiled again behind his mask. "Then let's go get my money. Move it!"

Blue had just about finished loading up the cash when his police scanner suddenly picked up an alert. *"Robbery in progress at First Union Bank, downtown Falls Church."*

He swiveled toward James Bartlett and shot the bank manager dead. Then he turned and shot Ms. Collins through the forehead.

Just the way it had been planned.

Chapter 17

THE SIREN ON THE ROOF OF MY CAR was screaming.

So was my body.

And my brain.

I arrived at the First Union Bank in Falls Church, Virginia, at almost the same time that Kyle Craig and his FBI team got there.

A black helicopter was just settling into the mostly empty shopping-mall parking area directly behind the bank. Kyle and three other agents climbed out of the chopper and headed toward me at a fast trot. They were stooped over and looked like monks hurrying to chapel. All four wore blue FBI windbreakers, which meant the Bureau wanted the public to know the FBI was involved with the investigation. The murders so far were gross and chilling for everyone. People needed to be reassured, to have their hands held.

"You been inside the bank already?" Kyle huffed as he

came jogging up to me. He, too, looked as if he hadn't slept.

"I just got here myself. Saw the big bad Bell Jet sputtering in. Figured it had to be you, or Darth Vader. Let's go in together."

"This is Senior Agent Betsey Cavalierre," Kyle said, indicating a smallish woman with lustrous black hair and eyes almost as dark. She wore her oversized FBI windbreaker over a white T-shirt, khaki trousers, running shoes. She was probably in her mid-thirties. Intense looking and also pretty, though certainly not glamorous.

"This is the rest of the first team. Agents Michael Doud and James Walsh," Kyle continued with the introductions. "This is Alex Cross. He's the VICAP liaison with the D.C. police. Alex found the bodies of Errol and Brianne Parker."

There were quick, polite hellos and handshakes all around. Senior Agent Betsey Cavalierre seemed to be sizing me up. Maybe it was because her boss and I were friends. Or maybe because I was VICAP, the official liaison between the FBI and the Metro police. Kyle took me by the elbow and steered me away from his agents.

"If the original two bank robbers are dead, who the hell did this job?" Kyle asked as we walked past ribbons of yellow crime tape snapping loudly in a crisp breeze from the southeast. "This is as bad as it gets. You see why I brought you in?"

"Because misery likes company," I said.

The FBI ADIC, or assistant director in charge, walked with me into the bank lobby. My stomach fell. Two female tellers were lying on the floor. They were dressed in dark blue business suits, now stained with their blood.

Both were dead. Their head wounds indicated they had been shot at close range.

"Executed. Goddamnit. *Goddamnit*," Agent Cavalierre said as we stopped at the bodies. An FBI crime scene unit immediately began videotaping the scene and taking still photographs. We headed toward the open bank vault.

Chapter 18

IT GOT WORSE IN A HURRY. Two more victims were inside the vault, a man and a woman. They had been shot several times. The business suits and bodies were riddled with bullets. *Had they been punished, too?* I wondered. *What were their sins? Why the hell was this happening?*

"This makes no goddamn sense to me," Kyle said, rubbing his face with both hands. It was a familiar tic of his and instantly reminded me of the many cases we had worked together on in the past. We complained about it sometimes, but we'd always been there for each other.

"Bank robbers don't usually kill anybody. Not pros," Agent Cavalierre spoke. "So why do this sick stunt?"

"Was the family of the manager held hostage as in the Silver Spring robbery?" I asked. I almost didn't want to hear the answer.

Kyle looked my way, nodded. "Mother and three kids. We just got word on them. Thank God, they were released. They weren't harmed. So why were these four butchered and the family released? Where's a pattern?"

I didn't know yet. Kyle was right: The robbery-murders didn't make any sense. Or rather, *we weren't thinking like the killers. We didn't get it, did we?*

"There might have been a screwup here at the branch. If this is connected to the bank in Silver Spring."

"We have to assume it is," said Agent Cavalierre. "The father, the nanny, and child were killed in Silver Spring because the manager was warned that the crew had to be out of the bank at a certain time or the *hostages died.* According to the video monitor at the bank, they missed by seconds."

As usual, Kyle had information the rest of us didn't. He shared it now. "An alarm went to the police here in Falls Church. I think that's what prompted the four murders. We're trying to run down where the warning call came from."

"How would the crew know the alarm went to the police?" I asked.

"They probably had a police scanner," Agent Cavalierre said.

Kyle nodded. "Agent Cavalierre is very smart about bank robberies," he said, "and just about everything else."

"I'm after Kyle's job," she said, and smiled thinly. I took Agent Cavalierre at her word.

Chapter 19

I ACCOMPANIED KYLE and his first-team entourage to FBI headquarters in downtown Washington. We were all feeling a little sick about the murder scene we'd witnessed. Agent Cavalierre did know a great deal about bank robberies, including several committed in the Midwest that resembled the Citibank and First Union jobs.

At headquarters, she pulled up as much relevant information as she could get in a hurry. We read printouts about a pair of desperadoes named Joseph Dougherty and Terry Lee Connor. I wondered if their exploits might have served as some kind of model for the two recent robberies. Dougherty and Connor had hit several banks in the Midwest. They would usually kidnap the manager's family first. Before one robbery, they held the manager and his family for three days over a holiday weekend, then robbed the bank on a Tuesday.

"There's a big difference, though. Dougherty and Connor never hurt a soul in any of the robberies," Cavalierre said. "They weren't killers like the scum we're dealing with now. What the hell do they want?"

I made myself go home around seven that night. I had a home-cooked dinner with Nana and the kids: shallow-fried chicken, cheese grits, and steamed broccoli. After we did the dishes, Damon, Jannie, and I trooped down to the basement for the kids' weekly boxing lesson. The boxing lessons have been going on for a couple of years and aren't really necessary for Damon and Jannie anymore. Damon is a clever ten, Jannie's eight, and they can both defend themselves. But they like the exercise and the camaraderie, and so do I.

What happened that night came out of the blue. It was unannounced and totally unexpected. Afterward, once I knew what had happened, I understood why.

Jannie and Damon were fooling around, showing off a little, strutting their stuff. Jannie must have walked into a punch from Damon.

The looping blow struck her squarely in the forehead, just above the left eye. *That much I'm certain about.* The rest was a blur to me. A complete shock. It was as if I were seeing life as a series of stop-motion photos.

Jannie tilted to the left and she went down in a frightening collapse. She hit the floor hard. Her movements suddenly became jerky, and then her limbs went completely stiff. There was absolutely no warning.

"Jannie!" Damon yelled, aware that he'd hit and hurt his sister, though it was an accident.

I hurried to her side as Jannie's body began to shake and spasm uncontrollably. Soft, gagging moans came from her throat. She obviously couldn't speak. Then her eyes rolled way back until only the whites showed.

Jannie began to choke horribly. I thought she was going to start swallowing her tongue. I yanked off my belt. I folded it and wedged it into Jannie's mouth to keep her from swallowing her tongue or possibly lacerating it with a hard bite. My heart was pounding as I held the tightly folded belt in her mouth. I kept telling her, "It's okay, it's okay, Jannie. Everything is okay, baby."

I tried to be as soothing as I possibly could be. I tried not to let her see how scared I was. The violent spasms wouldn't stop. I was pretty sure Jannie was having a seizure.

Chapter 20

EVERYTHING IS OKAY, baby. Everything is going to be fine.

Two or three horrifying minutes passed like that. Everything wasn't okay, though, not even close; everything was as terrible as it could be, as terrible as it had ever been.

Jannie's lips had turned bluish, and she was drooling. Then she lost control of her bladder and peed on the floor. She still couldn't speak.

I had sent Damon upstairs to call for help. An ambulance arrived less than ten minutes after Jannie's seizure ended. So far, there hadn't been another one. I prayed there wouldn't be.

Two EMS attendants hurried down to the basement, where I still knelt on the floor beside Jannie. I held one of her hands; Nana held the other. We had propped a pillow from the couch under her head and covered her with a blanket. *This is crazy,* I kept thinking. *This can't be happening.*

"You're okay, sweetie," Nana hummed softly.

Jannie finally looked at her. "No, I'm not, Nana."

She was fully conscious now, scared and confused. She was also embarrassed because she'd wet herself. She knew something strange and terrible had happened to her. The EMTs were gentle and reassuring. They checked Jannie's vital signs: temperature, pulse, and blood pressure. Then one of them inserted an IV in her arm while the other brought out an intubation box / breathing aid.

My heart was still pounding, racing terribly. I felt as if I might stop breathing, too.

I told the EMS workers what had happened. "She had violent spasms for about two minutes. Her limbs were stiff as boards. Her eyes rolled back." I told them about the shadowboxing and the punch that had landed above her left eye.

"It does sound like a seizure," the lead person said. Her green eyes were sympathetic, reassuring. "It could have been the blow she took, even if it was a light hit — the angle of attack. We should take her to St. Anthony's."

I nodded agreement, then watched in horror as they strapped my little girl on a stretcher and carried her out to the waiting ambulance. My legs were still unsteady. My whole body was numb and my vision tunneled.

"You *have* to use the siren," Jannie whispered to the EMS techs as they lifted her into the back of the ambulance van. "Please?"

And they did — all the way to St. Anthony's Hospital. I know — I rode with Jannie.

Longest ride of my life.

Chapter 21

AT THE HOSPITAL, Jannie had an EEG, then she underwent as thorough a neurological exam as they could give her at that time of the day. Her cranial nerves were tested. She was asked to walk a straight line, then to hop on one foot to determine the presence of any ataxia. She did as she was told, and seemed better now. Still, I watched her as if she might suddenly shatter.

Just as she was finishing the exam, Jannie had a second seizure. It lasted longer and was more violent than the first one. It couldn't have been any worse if it had happened to me. When the attack finally stopped, Jannie was given a Valium IV. The hospital staff was right there for her, but their concern was also frightening. A nurse asked me if there had been any symptoms before the seizure, such as blurred vision, headaches, nausea, loss of coordination. I hadn't noticed anything unusual.

When she had finished her examination of Jannie, Dr.

Bone from the emergency room took me aside. "We'll keep her here overnight for observation, Detective Cross. We'd like to be extra careful."

"Extra careful is good," I said. I was *still* shaking a little. I could see it in my hands.

"She might be here longer than that," Dr. Bone then added. "We need to do more tests on Jannie. I don't like the fact that there was a second seizure."

"All right. Of course, Doctor. I don't like that there was a second seizure either."

There was a bed available on the fourth floor, and I went up there with Jannie. Hospital policy required that she be taken up on a gurney, but I got to push it. She was groggy and unusually quiet in the elevator going up; she didn't ask me any questions until we were alone behind a curtain in the hospital room.

"Okay," she said then. "Tell me the truth, Daddy. You have to tell me everything. The *truth*."

I took a deep breath. "Well, you probably had what's called a grand mal seizure. Two of them. Sometimes they just happen, sweetheart. Out of the blue, like tonight. Damon's punch might have had something to do with it."

She frowned. "He barely touched me." Jannie stared into my eyes, trying to read me. "Okay," she said. "That's not so bad, is it? At least I'm still here on planet Earth for now."

"Don't talk like that," I told her. "It isn't funny."

"Okay. I won't scare you," she whispered.

Jannie reached out and took my hand and we held on tight. In a few minutes she was fast asleep, still holding on to my hand.

Part Two

HATE MAIL

Chapter 22

NO ONE COULD FIGURE OUT what was happening, or why.

He just loved that. The feeling of superiority it bred. They were all such dithering fools.

On a numerical scale of 9.9999 out of 10, things were going very well. The Mastermind was certain that he hadn't made a meaningful mistake. He took particular satisfaction in the Falls Church robbery and especially the four puzzling murders.

He relived every moment of the bloody crime as if he had been there instead of lucky Messrs. Red, White, and Blue, and Ms. Green. He visualized the scene at the manager's house, and then the murders at the bank, with intense pleasure and satisfaction. The Mastermind re-created it in his mind again and again and never tired of the scenario, especially the killings. The artistry and symbolism of them infused him with confidence in the cleverness of his thinking — the rightness of it.

He found himself smiling at the thought of the phone call to the police: the tip that a robbery was in progress. He'd made the call. He wanted the First Union employees killed. *That was the whole goddamn point. Didn't anybody see that yet?*

He had another team to recruit now, the most important one, and the hardest to find. The final crew had to be extremely capable and self-sufficient, and, because of that self-sufficiency, they would pose a danger to him. He understood very well that clever people often had large and uncontrollable egos. *He* certainly did.

He brought up the names of potential candidates on his computer screen. He read lengthy profiles and even criminal records, which he thought of as their résumés. Then suddenly that dreary, rainy afternoon, he came across a crew that was as different from the others as he was from the rest of humanity.

The proof? They had no criminal record. They had never been caught, never even been suspected. It was why they'd been so hard for him to find. They seemed perfect — for his perfect job — for his masterpiece.

No one could figure out what was going to happen.

Chapter 23

AT 9:00 A.M., I met with a neurologist named Thomas Petito, who patiently explained the tests Jannie would go through that same morning. He wanted first to eliminate some possible causes of the seizures. He told me that worrying would do no good, that Jannie was in excellent hands — *his* — and that for the moment the best thing I could do was to go to work. "I don't want you worrying needlessly," Petito said. "And I don't want you in my way."

I drove I-95 South to Quantico that afternoon after I had lunch with Jannie. I needed to visit with the FBI's best technicians and profilers, and they were at Quantico. I didn't like leaving Jannie at St. Anthony's but Nana was with her now, and there weren't any major tests scheduled until the following morning.

Kyle Craig had called me at the hospital and asked about Jannie. He was genuinely concerned. Kyle then told me that the Justice Department, the banking industry, and the media were all over him like a cheap suit. The FBI dragnet now covered most of the East Coast, but it wasn't delivering results. He'd even flown in one of the agents from the team that had tracked down master bank robber Joseph Dougherty in the mid-eighties.

Kyle also said that Senior Agent Cavalierre was running the task force. I wasn't too surprised. She had struck me as one of the brightest and most energetic of the Bureau agents I'd met, other than Kyle himself.

The agent from the original Dougherty team was named Sam Withers. Kyle, Agent Cavalierre, and I met with him in Kyle's conference room at Quantico. Withers was in his mid-sixties now; he was retired and told us he played a lot of golf in the Scottsdale area. He admitted he hadn't given much thought to bank robbers in several years, but the horror of these robberies had caught his attention.

Betsey Cavalierre got right down to business. "Sam, did you get a chance to read our write-ups of the Citibank and First Union robberies?"

"Sure did. I read them a couple of times on my way here," Withers said, running the palm of his hand over his buzz cut. He was a beefy man, probably two hundred forty pounds or more, and reminded me of retired baseball sluggers like Ted Klusewski and Ralph Kiner.

"First impressions?" she asked the former agent. "What do you think, Sam? Is there any connection to the current mess?"

"Big, big differences between these jobs and the ones I worked on. Neither Dougherty nor Connor was violent by nature. Those guys were basically small-town, small-time criminal minds. 'Old school,' like those commercials you see on ESPN. Even the hostages spoke of them as 'congenial' and 'pleasant.' Connor always carefully explained that he didn't want to steal anything in the hostages' homes. Said he didn't want to harm anyone. He and Dougherty both despised banks, and they despised insurance companies. That might be the hookup with your perps."

Withers continued to reminisce and conjecture in a soft, sleepy Midwestern drawl. I sat back and thought about what he had said. Maybe somebody else out there despised banks and insurance companies, too. Or possibly they hated bankers and their *families* for some reason. Someone with a deep enough grudge could be behind the robberies and murders. It made some sense, as much as anything else we had.

After Sam Withers left the conference room we talked about other cases that might relate to this one. One in particular caught my attention. A major robbery had occurred outside Philadelphia in January. Two men had kidnapped a bank executive's husband and infant son. They said they had a bomb and threatened to blow up their hostages unless the bank vault was opened.

"They kept in touch with walkie-talkies. Used police scanners, too. Kind of like the First Union job," Betsey reported from her extensive notes. "It might be the same people who did the First Union."

"Any violence in the job outside Philly?" I asked her.

She shook her head, and her shiny black hair flipped to one side. "No, none."

With all the resources of the FBI and hundreds of local police departments, we were still nowhere on the robbery-murders. Something was very wrong with this picture. We still weren't thinking like the killers.

Chapter 24

I GOT BACK TO ST. ANTHONY'S around four-thirty in the afternoon. Jannie wasn't in her room, which surprised me. Nana and Damon were sitting and reading. Nana said she had been taken for tests ordered by her neurologist, Dr. Petito.

Jannie returned at quarter to five. She looked tired. She was so young to be going through this kind of ordeal. She and Damon had always been healthy, even as babies, which made this even more of a shock.

When Jannie rolled into the room in a wheelchair, Damon suddenly choked up. So did I.

"Give us a big bear hug, Daddy," Jannie looked at us and said, "like you used to when we were little."

The vivid image came flooding back to me. I remembered the feeling of holding them both in my arms when they were much smaller. I did what Jannie asked: I bear-hugged my two babies.

As the three of us embraced, Nana came back from a walk down the hall. She had someone tagging along.

Christine Johnson entered the room behind Nana. She wore a silver-gray blouse with dark blue skirt and matching shoes. She must have come to the hospital from school. She seemed a little distant to me, but at least she was there for Jannie.

I would ask Nana later who was taking care of Alex.

"Here's everybody," Christine said. She never made eye contact with me. "I wish I had my camera."

"Oh, we're always like this," Jannie said to her. "This is just our family."

We talked some, but mostly we listened to Jannie describe her long, scary day. She seemed so vulnerable suddenly, so small. She was brought dinner at five. Rather than complain about the bland hospital food, she compared it favorably to her favorite dishes prepared by Nana.

That got a laugh out of everybody except Nana, who pretended to be miffed. "Well, we can just order out from the hospital when you get home," Nana said as she gave Jannie the evil eye. "Save me a lot of aggravation and work."

"Oh, you like to work," Jannie told Nana. "And you *love* aggravation."

"Almost as much as you love to tease me," Nana countered.

As Christine was getting up to leave, the nurse brought a phone from the nurses' station. She announced that there was an important call for Detective Cross. I groaned and shook my head. Everybody stared at me as I took the phone.

"It's okay, Daddy," Jannie said.

Kyle Craig was on the line. He had bad news. "I'm on my way to the First Virginia branch in Rosslyn. They hit another bank, Alex."

Nana shot poisoned darts at me with her eyes. Christine wouldn't look at me. I felt guilty and ashamed, and I hadn't done anything wrong.

"I have to go for an hour or so," I finally said. "I'm sorry."

Chapter 25

THE BANK ROBBERIES were coming too fast, one after the other, like dominoes tumbling. Whoever was behind them didn't want to give us a chance to think, to catch a breath, or to organize ourselves.

Rosslyn was only about fifteen minutes from St. Anthony's Hospital. I didn't know what I would find there: the possible brutalities, the number of dead bodies.

The branch of First Virginia was only a block away from Bell Atlantic headquarters. It was another freestanding bank. Did that mean something to the perps? Probably. What, though? The few clues we had so far weren't adding up to anything. Not for me, anyway.

I noticed a Dunkin' Donuts and a Blockbuster Video directly across the street. People were going in and out. The suburban neighborhood was busy and operating as if nothing had happened.

Something had definitely happened.

I spotted four dark sedans clustered together in the

bank parking lot. I suspected they were FBI cars and pulled in beside them. There were no police cars on the scene yet. Kyle had called me, but he hadn't called in the Rosslyn police. Not a good sign.

I showed my detective's badge to a tall, lanky agent posted at the back door. He looked to be in his late twenties. Nervous and scared.

"The ADIC is inside. He's expecting you, Detective Cross," the agent said in a soft Virginia accent not unlike Kyle's.

"Casualties in there?" I asked.

The agent shook his dark, crew-cut, bullet-shaped head. He was trying not to show that he was nervous. "We just arrived, sir. I don't know the casualty situation inside. I was told to wait out here by Senior Agent Cavalierre. It's her case."

"Yes, I know."

I opened the glass door. I paused for a beat alongside the ATMs in the vestibule. Focused. Prepared myself a little. I saw Kyle and Betsey Cavalierre across the lobby.

They were talking to a silver-haired man who seemed to be the bank's manager, or possibly the assistant manager. *It didn't look as if anyone had been hurt. Jesus. Was that possible?*

Kyle saw me and immediately walked my way. Agent Cavalierre stayed close at his side, so close she looked glued to Kyle.

"It's a miracle," Kyle said. "No one's hurt here. They took the money and got away clean, though. We're going to the manager's house. His wife and daughter were held hostage, Alex. The phones at the house are dead."

"Call the Rosslyn police, Kyle. They'll have squad cars there."

"We're three minutes away. Let's go!" Kyle barked. He and Agent Cavalierre were already headed toward the door.

Chapter 26

THE MESSAGE FROM KYLE was loud and clear. *The FBI* was in charge of the bank robbery-murders investigation. I was welcome to join up, or leave. For the moment, I went along. It was Cavalierre and Kyle's case and their huge headache, their time in the pressure cooker.

No one spoke as we rode through Rosslyn in one of the FBI sedans. One pattern of the robberies had been clear so far: *Somebody died when a robbery took place.* It almost seemed that a serial killer was robbing banks.

"The bank alarm went directly to the FBI?" I finally spoke up about something that had bothered me since I got Kyle's call at St. Anthony's.

Betsey Cavalierre turned toward me from the front seat. "First Union, Chase, First Virginia, and Citibank are all connected to us for the time being. It was their decision — we didn't pressure them. We've moved several dozen extra agents into the D.C. area so we'd be ready when and if another bank was hit. We arrived at the branch in Rosslyn in less than ten minutes. They got out, anyway."

"You call the Rosslyn PD yet?" I asked.

Kyle said, "We called, Alex. We don't want to step on anybody's toes if we don't have to. They're on their way to the bank branch."

I shook my head and rolled my eyes. "Not to the bank manager's house, though."

"We want to check the house ourselves first," Agent Cavalierre answered for Kyle. "The killers aren't making any mistakes. Neither can we." She was brusque and impatient with me. I didn't much like her tone, and she didn't seem to care what I thought.

"Rosslyn has a very good police force," I told her. "I've worked with them before. Have you?" I felt I had to defend some of the people I knew and respected.

Kyle sighed. "You know it depends on who responds first. That's the problem. Betsey's right — we can't make mistakes on this one. They don't."

We turned onto High Street in Rosslyn. The neighborhood looked peaceful, serene, thriving: nicely groomed lawns, two-car garages, large homes both new and old.

They always kill somebody, I couldn't help thinking. *They've done it to a family before.*

We parked in front of a house with a big red number 315 on a pale yellow mailbox. A second dark sedan edged into the curb behind us — more agents. The more the scarier.

"The crew is probably gone," Kyle spoke into his walkie-talkie. "But remember, you never know. These guys are killers. They seem to like it, too."

Chapter 27

YOU NEVER KNOW, I thought. How true that was, and
how thoroughly frightening it could be sometimes.

Was it part of what kept me on the job? The adrenaline
spike that wasn't like anything else I'd ever experienced?
The uncertainty of each new case? The thrill of the hunt?
A dark side of myself? What? Good occasionally triumphing over evil? Evil often triumphing over good?

As I unholstered my Glock, I tried to clear my mind of
anything that would interfere with my timing or reflexes
in the next few moments. Kyle, Betsey Cavalierre, and I
hurried toward the front door. We had our guns drawn.
Everyone looked solid, professional, appropriately nervous.

You never know.

The house was deadly quiet from the outside. Somewhere in the neighborhood a dog howled. A baby bawled.
The baby's cry hadn't come from the bank manager's
house.

Somebody had died at each of the first two robberies. That was the only pattern so far. The killer's ritual? The warning? The *what?* Could this be a pattern murderer robbing banks? What in the name of God was happening?

"I go in first," I said to Kyle. I wasn't asking his permission. "We're in Washington. We're close, anyway."

Kyle chose not to argue with me. Agent Cavalierre was silent. Her dark eyes studied my face. Had she been on the front line before? I wondered. What was she feeling right now? Had she ever used her gun?

The door of the house was unlocked. *They had left it open.* On purpose? Or because they'd departed in a hurry?

I moved inside. Quickly, silently, hoping for the best, expecting the worst. The foyer, living room, and kitchen beyond were all dark. Except for the stuttering red glow of a blinking digital clock on the stove. The only sound was the refrigerator humming.

Agent Cavalierre motioned for the three of us to split off. There wasn't so much as a whisper inside the house. This wasn't good. Where was the family?

I moved in a low crouch toward the kitchen. I took a look inside. *No one there.*

I opened a wooden door at the rear of the kitchen: *closet. The pungent odor of spices and condiments.*

I opened a second door: *back stairs leading to the second floor.*

A third door: *stairs leading down to the cellar.*

The cellar had to be checked out. I flicked on the light switch. No light came on. *Damnit.*

"Police," I called out. No answer.

I took a deep breath. I didn't see any immediate danger to myself, but I feared what I might find down there. I hesitated a second or two, then I stepped on creaking wooden stairs. I hate cellars, always have.

"Police," I repeated. Still no answer from down there. Checking out dark places in a house isn't fun. Not even when you have a gun and know how to use it pretty well. I flicked on my Maglite flashlight. *Okay, here we go.*

My heart was beating wildly as I hurried down the flight of stairs. My gun was at the ready. I lowered my head and took a good look around. Jesus!

I saw them as soon as I cleared the wooden overhang. I felt the adrenaline spike.

"I'm Detective Cross. I'm the police!"

The wife and the baby girl were there. The mother was bound and gagged with black tape over different-colored cloths. Her eyes were wide and as bright as searchlights. The baby had black tape over her mouth. The infant's chest was heaving with silent sobs.

They were alive, though. No one had been hurt either here or at the bank.

Why was that?

The pattern had changed!

"What's going on down there? You all right, Alex?" I heard Kyle Craig call. I flashed the light up and saw Kyle and Agent Cavalierre standing at the top of the stairs.

"They're here. They're safe. Everyone's alive."

What in hell was going on?

Chapter 28

THE MASTERMIND — what a quaint, totally absurd name. It was almost perverse. He liked it for just that reason.

He actually watched the scene at the bank manager's house, and he felt as if he were standing outside of his own body. He remembered an old TV show from his youth: *You Are There.* He was, wasn't he?

He found it quite thrilling to see the FBI technicians enter the house with their magic black boxes. He knew all about them, the VCU, or Violent Crime Unit.

He closely observed the somber, serious-faced agents come and go.

Then the Rosslyn police arrived en masse. Half a dozen squad cars with their turret lights blazing. Sort of pretty.

Finally, he saw Detective Alex Cross leave the house. Cross was tall and well built. He was in his early forties, resembled the fighter Muhammad Ali at his best. Cross's face wasn't flat, though. His brown eyes sparkled constantly. He was better looking, actually, than Ali had ever been.

Cross was one of his prime opponents, and this was a fight to the death, wasn't it? It was an intense battle of wits, but even more than that, a battle of wills.

The Mastermind was confident that he would win against Cross. If anything, this was a mismatch. The Mastermind always won, didn't he? And yet, he felt a little unsure. Cross exuded confidence, too, and that made him angry. *How dare he? Who did the detective think he was?*

He watched the house for a while longer, and knew it was perfectly safe for him to be there.

Perfectly safe.

On a numerical scale of 9.9999 out of 10.

He had a crazy thought then, and he knew where it came from. When he was just a boy, he absolutely loved cowboy-and-Indian movies and TV shows. He always rooted for the Indians. And he particularly loved one extraordinary trick that they had — they would sneak into an enemy's camp and simply touch the enemy while he slept. It was called, he believed, *counting coup*.

The Mastermind wanted to count coup on Alex Cross.

Chapter 29

AS SOON AS WE KNEW that everyone in the house was safe, I called St. Anthony's Hospital to check on Jannie. Guilt, paranoia, and duty were all pulling hard at me. The furies had me in a terrible vise. The bank manager's family was safe. What about my own?

I was put in contact with the nurses' station on Jannie's floor. I spoke to an RN, Julietta Newton, who sometimes stopped by Jannie's room when I came to visit. Julietta reminded me of an old friend, a nurse who had died the year before, Nina Childs.

"This is Alex Cross. I'm sorry to bother you, Julietta, but I'm trying to reach my grandmother. Or my daughter, Jannie."

"Nana isn't on the floor at the moment," the nurse told me. "Jannie just went down for an MRI. A spot opened up and Dr. Petito wanted her to take it. Your grandmother accompanied her downstairs."

"I'm on my way. Is Jannie all right?"

The nurse hesitated, then she spoke. "She had another seizure, Detective. She's stabilized, though."

I rushed back to the hospital from Rosslyn and got there in about fifteen minutes. I hurried down to B-1 and found an area marked DIAGNOSTIC TESTING. It was late, almost ten o'clock. No one was at the front desk, so I walked right past and down a light blue corridor that looked eerie and forbidding at that time of night.

As I approached a room with COMPUTERIZED TOMOGRAPHY and MRI lettered on the door, a technician appeared from a doorway across the hall. He startled me — I was walking in a fog. Thinking, worrying about Jannie.

"Can I help you? Are you supposed to be down here, sir?"

"I'm Jannie Cross's father. I'm Detective Cross. She's having an MRI. She had a seizure tonight."

The man nodded. "She's down here. I'll show you the way. I believe she's about halfway through the test. Our last patient for the night."

Chapter 30

THE HOSPITAL TECH showed me into the MRI room, where Nana was sitting vigil. She was trying to keep up a calm exterior, trying to maintain her usual self-control. For once, it wasn't working. I saw the fear lighting up her eyes, or maybe I was projecting my own feelings.

I looked over at the MRI machine, and it was state-of-the-art. It was more open and less restraining than others I'd seen. I'd had two MRIs, so I knew the drill. Jannie would be lying flat inside. Her head would be immobilized on either side by "sandbags." The image of Jannie alone inside the imposing machine was disturbing. But so was her third seizure in two days.

"Can she hear us?" I asked.

Nana cupped her hands to her ears. "She's listening to music in there. But you can hold her hand, Alex. She knows your touch."

I reached out and took one of Jannie's hands. I

squeezed gently, and she squeezed back. *She knew it was me.*

"What happened while I was gone?" I asked Nana.

"We were lucky, so lucky," she said. "Dr. Petito stopped by on his rounds. He was talking to Jannie when she had another grand mal. He ordered the MRI, and they had an opening for her. Actually, they stayed open for her."

I sat down because I needed to. It had been a long and stressful day and it wasn't over yet. My heart was still racing; so was my head. The rest of my body was struggling to catch up.

"Don't start blaming yourself," Nana told me. "Like I said, we're very lucky. The best doctor in the hospital was right there in her room."

"I'm not blaming anybody," I muttered, knowing it wasn't true.

Nana frowned. "If you had been there during the seizure, she'd still be here having the MRI. And in case you think it could have been the boxing, Dr. Petito said there's almost no chance. The contact was too minimal. It's something else, Alex."

That was exactly what I was afraid of. We waited for the test to be over, and it was a long, hard wait. Finally, Jannie slowly slid out of the machine. Her little face brightened when she saw me.

"Fugees," she said, then took off the earphones for me to hear. *"Killing me softly with his song,"* she sang along with the music. "Hello, Daddy. You said you'd come back. Kept your promise."

"I did." I bent down to kiss her. "How are you, sweetie?" I asked. "You feeling okay now?"

"They played some really nice music for me," she said. "I'm hanging in there, hanging tough. I can't wait to see the pictures of my brain, though."

Neither could I, neither could I. Dr. Petito had waited around for the pictures. He never seemed to leave the hospital. I met with him in his office at a little past eleven-thirty. I was beyond tired. We both were.

"Long day for you," I said. Every day seemed to be like that for Petito. The neurologist had office hours starting at seven-thirty in the morning, and he was still around the hospital at nine and ten o'clock at night, sometimes later. He actually encouraged patients to call him at home if they had a problem or just got scared at night.

"This is my life." He shrugged. "Helped get me divorced a few years back." He yawned. "Keeping me single now. That and my fear of attachment. I love it, though."

I nodded and thought that I understood. Then I asked the question that was burning in my mind. "What did you find? Is she all right?"

He shook his head slowly, then he spoke the words I hadn't wanted to hear. "I'm afraid there's a tumor. I'm pretty certain that it's a pilocytic astrocytoma, a kind of tumor that strikes the very young. We'll confirm that after the surgery. It's located in her cerebellum. The tumor is large, and it's life threatening. I'm sorry to have to give you that news."

I spent another night at the hospital with Jannie. She fell asleep holding my hand again.

Chapter 31

EARLY THE NEXT MORNING my beeper went off.
I made a call and got bad news from Sandy Greenberg,
a friend who worked at Interpol headquarters in Lyon,
France.

A woman named Lucy Rhys-Cousins had been savagely murdered in a London supermarket. She was killed
while her children looked on. Sandy told me the police in
London suspected that the killer was her husband, Geoffrey Shafer, a man I knew as the Weasel.

I couldn't believe it. Not now. Not the Weasel. "Was it
Shafer or not?" I asked Sandy. "Do you know for certain?"

"It's him, Alex, though we won't confirm it for the
press vermin. Scotland Yard is positive. The children recognized him. Their mad-hatter daddy! He killed their
mother right before their eyes."

Geoffrey Shafer had been responsible for Christine's
kidnapping. He had also committed several grisly mur-

ders in the Southeast section of Washington. He'd preyed on the poor and defenseless. The news that he might be alive, and killing again, was like a swift, sudden punch below the belt. I knew it would be even worse for Christine to learn about Shafer.

I called her at home from St. Anthony's but got her answering machine. I talked calmly to the machine. "Christine, pick up if you're there. It's Alex. Please, pick up. It's important that I talk to you."

Still, no one picked up at Christine's. I knew that Shafer couldn't be here in Washington — and yet I worried about the possibility that he could be. His pattern was to do the unexpected. The goddamn Weasel!

I checked my watch. It was 7:00 A.M. Sometimes Christine went to the school on Saturday. I decided to head over to the Sojourner Truth School, anyway. It wasn't far.

Chapter 32

AS I DROVE THERE, I was thinking, *Don't let this be happening. Not again! Please, God, don't do this to her. You can't do this. You wouldn't.*

I parked near the school and dashed out of the car. Then I found myself running down the hall to Christine's corner office. My heart pounded dully in my chest. My legs were unsure. I could hear the clicking of the word processor before I reached the door.

I peered inside.

I was relieved to see Christine there in her warm and fuzzy, thoroughly cluttered office. She was always intensely focused when she worked. Not wanting to startle her, I stood and watched for a moment. Then I knocked gently on the doorjamb.

"It's me," I said in a soft voice.

Christine stopped typing and turned. For just an instant, she looked at me like she used to. It melted me. She had on a pair of navy blue trousers and a tailored yellow silk blouse. She didn't look as if she were going through a bad time, but I knew that she was.

"What are you doing here?" she finally asked. "I already heard it on CNN this morning," she continued. "I saw the glorious murder scene at the market in London." She shook her head, closed her eyes.

"Are you all right?" I asked.

Christine snapped out an answer. "I'm not all right! I'm a million miles from all right. This news doesn't help. I *can't sleep* nights. I have nightmares all the time. I can't concentrate during the day. I imagine terrible things happening to little Alex. To Damon and Jannie and Nana, and to you. I can't make it stop!"

Her words cut right through me. It was a terrible feeling not to be able to help. "I don't think he'll come back here," I said.

Anger flashed in Christine's eyes. "You don't know that for sure."

"Shafer considers himself beyond us. We aren't that important in his fantasy world. His wife was. I'm surprised that he didn't murder the kids, too."

"You see, you're *surprised*. Nobody knows for sure what these insane, pathetic maniacs will do! And now you're involved with more of them: depraved men who murder innocent hostages for no reason. *Because they can.*"

I started to walk into the office — but she raised her hand. "Don't. Please stay away from me."

Christine then rose from her chair and walked past me

toward the teacher's washroom. She disappeared inside without looking back.

I knew she wouldn't come out — not until she was sure I was gone. As I finally walked away, I was thinking that she hadn't asked about Jannie.

Chapter 33

I STOPPED AT ST. ANTHONY'S HOSPITAL again before I went to work. Jannie was up and we had breakfast together. She told me that I was the best dad in the world, and I said she was the best daughter. Then I told her about the tumor and that she needed to have surgery. My little girl cried in my arms.

Nana arrived, and Jannie was taken away for more tests. There was nothing I could do at the hospital for several hours. I went off to meet with the FBI again. The job *was* always there. Christine had told me, *Your work is chasing insane, pathetic maniacs.* There didn't seem to be any end in sight.

Special Agent in Charge Cavalierre arrived precisely at eleven for her briefing of the team at the Bureau's field office on Fourth Street in Northwest. It looked to me as if half the Bureau were there, and it was an impressive sight, somewhat reassuring.

I was reminded that the bank-robbing crew demanded

exactness. Maybe that was the reason Kyle Craig felt
Agent Cavalierre was right for this case. He'd told me that
she was exacting and precise, one of the most professional agents he'd seen in his years at the Bureau. My
thoughts kept going back to the high-profile bank jobs
and the murders. Why did they want publicity, even in-
famy? Were the robbers preconditioning other bank employees and corporations for future robberies? Scaring
the shit out of everyone so there would be no resistance?
Or did the murders have to do with revenge? It made
sense that one or more of the killers might have worked at
a bank. We were chasing that lead with everything we
had.

I peered around the overcrowded crisis room inside the
FBI field office. Several partitions on one wall had been
allotted to write-ups and photos of suspects and wit-
nesses. Unfortunately, none of the suspects were particularly hot. Not even lukewarm. The partitions were titled
"Fat Man," "Manager's Wife," "Husband's Girlfriend,"
"Mustache."

*Why didn't we have a single good suspect? What
should that be telling us? What were we all missing?*

"Hi and good morning. I want to thank everyone in ad-
vance for giving up your weekend," Agent Cavalierre said
with just the right amount of irony and humor. She was
wearing khakis and a light purple T-shirt. There was a tiny
purple barrette in her hair. She looked confident and surprisingly relaxed.

"If you don't come in on Saturday," an agent with a
droopy mustache spoke up from the back of the room,
"don't bother to come in on Sunday."

"You ever notice how the wiseasses always sit in the

back?" Cavalierre cracked, and then smiled convincingly. She was as cool as they come.

She held up a thick blue folder. "Everybody has a big bad file like this one, containing past cases that might relate. The Joseph Dougherty robberies through the Midwest in the eighties were similar in some ways. There's also material on David Grandstaff, who masterminded the largest single bank robbery in American history. Of some interest, Grandstaff was caught by the Bureau. However, in our zealous efforts to take him down, questionable tactics were used. After a six-week trial, a jury deliberated for all of ten minutes, then let Grandstaff off. To this day, the three million from the Tucson First National Bank job hasn't been recovered."

There was a hand wave and a question from the front of the room. "Where is Mr. Grandstaff now?"

"Oh, he's gone underground," said Agent Cavalierre. "About six feet. He isn't involved in these robberies, Agent Doud. But he may have helped inspire them. The same goes for Joseph Dougherty. Whoever did these jobs might be aware of their handiwork. As I've heard them say in the movies, 'He's a student of the game.'"

About half an hour into the meeting, Agent Cavalierre introduced me to the other agents.

"Some of you already know Alex Cross from the D.C. police. He's Homicide, with a Ph.D. in psychology. Dr. Cross is a forensic psychologist. He is a *very good* friend of Kyle Craig, by the way. The two of them are tight. So whatever you might think of the Metro police, or ADIC Craig, you'd better keep it to yourself."

She looked over at me. "Actually, Dr. Cross discovered the bodies of Brianne and Errol Parker in D.C. That's as close as we have to a break in the case. Notice how I'm careful to kiss Dr. Cross's butt."

I stood up and looked around the conference room as I spoke to the agents. "Well, I'm afraid the Parkers have gone underground, too," I said, and got a few laughs. "Brianne and Errol were small-timers, but had served time for bank jobs. We're checking on anyone they knew at Lorton Prison. So far, nothing has come of it. Nothing much has come of anything we've done, and that's disturbing.

"The Parkers were competent thieves, but not as organized as whoever brought them in — and then decided to kill them. The Parkers were poisoned, by the way. I think the killer watched them die, and the deaths were gruesome. The killer may have had sex with Brianne Parker after she was dead. This is just a guess right now, but I don't think this mess is just about bank robberies."

Chapter 34

THE MASTERMIND COULDN'T SLEEP! Too many unwelcome thoughts were buzzing around like a swarm of angry wasps invading his already overwrought brain. He had been severely victimized, driven to this intolerable state. He needed revenge. He'd dedicated his life to it — every waking moment of the past four years.

The Mastermind finally rose up from bed. He sat slumped over his desk, waiting for the waves of nausea to pass, waiting for his goddamn hands to stop trembling. *This is my pitiful life,* he thought. *I despise it. I despise everything about it, every breath I take.*

Finally, he began to write the hate mail that had been on his mind as he lay in bed.

Attention of the Chairman, Citibank

> *This is a wake-up call, and it's serious. The consequences to Citibank are dire.*

*You think that you're safe from the little people,
but you're not safe.*

*My hand is shaking as I write this. My whole
body trembles with outrage.*

*My banker is asleep at the switch. For a
"personal banker," she is about as impersonal as
one of the gray partitions in her cubicle office. I
had always thought bankers were smart, and
buttoned-up. How is it possible, then, that on
numerous occasions I have had annoying, insane,
egregious errors made on my account?*

*I requested a simple transfer of money between
Funds: IMMA to checking. It didn't get done in a
timely manner.*

*When I recently moved, my change of address
was not handled properly. Three months have
passed, and I still haven't received any of my
statements. It turns out the address was never
changed and my statements are going to the
wrong address.*

*After all of these insults, after all of these
mistakes by your busy-doing-nothing employees,
your bank has the nerve, the gall, to deny me a
personal loan. The most intolerable part is to
have to sit there and listen to little Miss Princeton
Priss turning me down with insincerity and
condescension dripping in her voice.*

*I judge service organizations on a ten scale. I
expect 9.9999 out of 10. Your bank fails
miserably.*

The little people will have their day.

He reread the letter and thought it wasn't too bad — not for two-something in the morning. No, actually the letter was good.

He would do an edit, then sign, and finally deposit it in his file cabinet — as he did with all the other letters. They were far too dangerous and incriminating to actually send through the federal mail system.

Goddamnit, he hated the banks with a passion! Insurance companies! Self-important investment houses! Cheeky Internet firms! The government! The big boys and girls had to go down. And they would. The little people would finally have their day.

Chapter 35

I HAD PROMISED JANNIE something when I left her that morning. My most solemn oath was that I would stop at Big Mike Giordano's for pizza takeout.

I was juggling a hot box in my hands when I entered her room at the hospital. She wouldn't be able to eat much, but Dr. Petito said a slice would be fine.

"Delivery," I said as I waltzed into the room.

"Hoo-ray! Hoo-ray!" she cheered from her bed. "You saved me from this awful, dreadful hospital food. Thank you, Daddy. You are the greatest."

Jannie didn't look sick; she didn't look as if she needed to be at St. Anthony's. I wished that were so. I already had the essential information on her operation. The total time for prep and the surgery would be between eight and ten hours. The surgeon would dissect the tumor and a piece would be used for a biopsy. Until the surgery, her condition was stabilized with Dilantin. The operation was set for 8:00 A.M. tomorrow.

"You wanted olives and anchovies, right?" I teased her as I opened the pizza box.

"You got that wrong, Mr. Delivery Man. Better take that nasty pie right back to the store if it has those slimy little anchovies on it," she said, giving me the evil eye she must have learned from her great-grandmother.

"He's just teasing you," Nana said, and gave me a softer version of the squinty-eyed look.

Jannie shrugged. "I know it, Nana. I'm teasing him back. *It's our thing, doo, doo. Do what you wanna do,*" she sang the old pop tune and smiled.

"I like anchovies," Damon said, just to be controversial. "They're real salty."

"You would." She frowned at her brother. "I think you might have been an anchovy in another life."

We were laughing, just like always, as we dug into the extra-cheese pizza and milk. We exchanged news of our days. Jannie held center court again, elaborately describing her second CT scan, which had lasted half an hour. Then she proclaimed: "I've decided to become a doctor. My decision is final. I'll probably go to Johns Hopkins like Daddy did."

Nana and Damon finally got up to leave around eight. They'd been at the hospital since just after three.

Jannie announced: "Daddy's staying for a while extra because he had to work and I didn't see enough of him today." She motioned for Nana to give her a hug and they held on to each other for a long moment. Nana whispered something private in Jannie's ear, and she nodded that she understood.

Then Jannie waved Damon over to her bedside. "Give me a big hug and a kiss," she commanded.

Damon and Nana Mama left with a lot of bye-byes, and extra waves, and see-you-tomorrows, and brave smiles. Jannie sat there with her cheeks wet and shiny, crying and smiling at the same time.

"Actually, I sort of like this," she told them. "You know that I *have* to be the center of attraction. And everybody stop worrying — I am going to be a doctor. In fact, from now on, you all can call me Dr. Jannie."

"Good night, Dr. Jannie. Sweet dreams," Nana spoke softly from the doorway. "I'll see you tomorrow, darling girl."

"Night," Damon said. He turned away, then turned back. "Oh, all right — *Dr. Jannie.*"

She and I were quiet for a few moments after Nana and Damon left. I came over and put my arm around her. I think that the parting scene had been too much for both of us. I sat on the edge of the hospital bed, and I held her as if she would break. We stayed like that for a long time, talking a little bit, but mostly just holding on to each other.

I was surprised when I saw that Jannie had fallen fast asleep in my arms. That's when the tears finally started to roll from my eyes.

Chapter 36

I STAYED IN THE HOSPITAL with Jannie all night. I was as saddened and afraid as I'd ever been; the fear was a living thing constricting my chest. I slept some, but not much. I thought about the bank robberies a little — just to put my mind somewhere else. Innocent people had been savagely murdered, and that hit home with me and everybody else.

I also thought about Christine. I loved her, couldn't help it, but I believed she had made up her mind about the two of us. I couldn't change it. She didn't want to be with a homicide detective, and I probably couldn't be anything else.

Jannie and I were both awake around five the next morning. Her room looked out on an expansive sunroof and a small, flowering garden. We sat quietly and watched the sunrise through the window. It looked so stunningly beautiful and serene that it made me sad all over again.

What if this was our last sunrise together? I didn't want to think like that, but I couldn't help it.

"Don't worry, Daddy," Jannie said, reading my face like the little necromancer she could be sometimes. "There'll be lots of pretty sunrises in my life. . . . I am a little scared, though. Truth be told."

"Truth be told," I said. "That's the way it always has to be between us."

"Okay. So I'm very scared," Jannie said in a tiny voice.

"Me, too, little girl."

We held hands and stared at the glorious orangish-red sun. Jannie was very quiet. It took all of my willpower to keep from breaking up. I started to choke and hid it with a false yawn that I was sure didn't fool her.

"What happens this morning?" Jannie finally asked in a whisper.

"The rest of the pre-op workup," I told her. "Maybe another blood test."

She wrinkled her nose. "They're vampires here, you know. It's why I made you stay the night."

"Good thinking on your part. I fought off a few dastardly attacks in the wee hours. Didn't want to wake you. They'll probably give you your very first shave."

Jannie put both hands over her head. *"No!"*

"Just a little in the back. It will look cool."

She continued to look horrified. "Yeah, right. You think so? Why don't you get a shave on the back of your head, too? Then we can both look cool."

I grinned at her. "I will if you want me to."

Dr. Petito walked into Jannie's room and heard us trying to cheer each other up.

"You're number one on our list," he told her, and smiled.

Jannie puffed up her little chest. "See that? I'm number one."

They took Jannie away from me at five minutes past seven in the morning.

Chapter 37

I HELD A SPECIAL IMAGE in my mind of Jannie dancing with Rosie the Cat, singing "Roses are red." I let it play over and over again that long, terrible day at St. Anthony's. I suspect that waiting in hospitals is as close as we get to being in hell before our time, or at least in purgatory. Nana, Damon, and I didn't talk much the whole time. Sampson and Jannie's aunts came by for short stints. They were devastated, too. It was just awful. The worst hours of my life.

Sampson took Nana and Damon to the cafeteria to get something to eat, but I wouldn't leave. There was no word of how Jannie was doing. Everything at the hospital felt unreal to me. Images of Maria's death came flashing back to me. After my wife was wounded in a senseless drive-by shooting, she had been brought to St. Anthony's, too.

At a few minutes past five, the neurologist, Dr. Petito, walked into the waiting room where we were gathered. I saw him before he saw us. I felt ill. Suddenly, my heart was racing, thudding loudly. I couldn't tell anything from his face, other than that he looked tired. He saw us, waved a hand, and walked our way.

He was smiling, and I knew it was good.

"We got it," Dr. Petito said as soon as he reached us. He shook my hand, then Nana's, and Damon's. "Congratulations."

"Thank you," I whispered as I held his hand tightly, "for all your sacrifices."

About fifteen minutes later, Nana and I were allowed into the recovery suite. Suddenly I was feeling buoyant, pleasantly light-headed. Jannie was the only patient in there. We walked quietly to her bedside, almost on tiptoe. A gauze turban covered her little head. She was hooked up to monitors and an IV.

I took one hand. Nana Mama took the other. Our girl was okay; *they got it*.

"I feel like I *lived* and went to heaven," Nana said to me, and smiled. "Don't you?"

Jannie stirred and began to wake up after about twenty-five minutes in the recovery room. Dr. Petito was called and returned moments later. He asked her to take some deep breaths, then try to cough.

"You have a headache, Jannie?" he asked.

"I think so," she said.

Then she looked over at Nana and me. She squinted first, then she tried to open her eyes wide. She was obviously still groggy. "Hello, Daddy. Hello, Nana. I knew you'd be in heaven, too," Jannie finally said.

I turned around then, so that she could see what I'd done.

I had shaven a spot back there. It was just like hers.

Chapter 38

TWO DAYS LATER, I returned to the robbery-murders, a case that both fascinated and repulsed me. Work was still there, wasn't it? The investigation had survived without me. On the other hand, no one had been caught. One of Nana's favorite sayings came to mind: *If you're going around in circles, maybe you're cutting corners.* Perhaps that was the problem with the investigation so far.

I saw Betsey Cavalierre at the FBI office on Fourth Street. She wagged a finger at me, but she also smiled in a friendly way. She had on a tan blazer, blue T-shirt, jeans, and she looked good. I was glad to see her. That first smile of hers seemed to finally break the ice between us.

"You should have told me about your little girl — the operation. Everything okay, Alex? You haven't slept much, have you?"

"The doctor said he got it all. She's a tough little girl.

This morning she asked me when we could start our boxing lessons again. I'm sorry I didn't tell you before. I wasn't myself."

She waved off my last few words. "I'm just happy that your daughter is fine," she said. "I can see the relief on your face."

I smiled. "Well, I can feel it. It brought lots of things into focus for me. Let's go to work."

Betsey winked. "I've been here since six."

"Show-off," I said.

I sat down at the desk I was using and started to look through the mountain of paperwork that had already accumulated. Agent Cavalierre was at the desk across from mine. I was glad to be back on the line. One or more killers were out there murdering bank tellers, managers, families. I wanted to help stop it if I could.

An hour or so later, I looked up and saw Agent Cavalierre staring my way with a blank look on her face. She'd been lost in her thoughts, I suppose.

"There's someone I need to see," I said. "I should have thought of him before today. He left Washington for a while. Went to Philly, New York, Los Angeles. Now he's back. He's robbed a lot of banks, *and he's violent.*"

Betsey nodded. "I'd love to meet him. Sounds like a swell guy."

It probably had something to do with our scarcity of solid leads that she went with me that morning. We rode in her car to a fleabag hotel on New York Avenue. The Doral was a decrepit, paint-peeling flophouse. A trio of skinny, shopworn prostitutes in miniskirts were just leaving the hotel as we arrived. A retro-looking pimp in a gold lamé zoot suit leaned against a yellow Cadillac convertible, picking at his teeth.

"You take me to all the nicest places," Agent Cavalierre said as she climbed out of the car. I noticed she was wearing an ankle holster. Dressed for success.

Chapter 39

TONY BROPHY was living the *vida loca* up on the fourth floor of the Doral. The hotel desk clerk said he'd been staying here for a week, and that he was "a very troubled dude, not a nice person, and a serious asshole."

"I don't think this place is connected with the Doral in Miami," Betsey said as we took the back stairs. "What a dump."

"Wait until you meet Brophy. He fits right in here."

We arrived unannounced at his room and unholstered our guns. Brophy was a legitimate suspect in the robbery-murders. He fit the profile. I rapped my knuckles on a scarred, bare wood door.

"What?" a gruff voice called from inside. "I said *what*?"

"Washington PD. Open up," I called out.

I heard movement, then someone snapped a few locks on the other side. The door slowly opened and Brophy filled the narrow doorway. He was six-four and close to two sixty, a lot of it bulging muscle. His dark hair was shaved with neat razor lines to the scalp.

"Asshole D.C. cop," he said, a nonfilter cigarette hanging from his lips. "And who's this lovely asshole with you?"

"Actually, I can talk for myself," Betsey said to Brophy.

Tony Brophy grinned down at her. He apparently liked to get a response to his rudeness. "Okay. Speak. *Woof.*"

"I'm Senior Agent Betsey Cavalierre. FBI," Betsey said.

"*Senior* agent! Let's see, what's the line from all the cop shows on TV? We can do this the hard way — or we can do it the easy way," he said, and showed off surprisingly even white teeth. He was wearing black paramilitary pants, off-white shower thongs, no shirt. His arms and upper torso were covered with jailhouse tats and curled black hair.

"I vote for the hard way. But that's just me," Betsey said.

Brophy turned to a skinny blond who was sitting on a lime green retro couch propped in front of a TV. She wore a loose-fitting FUBU shirt over her underwear.

"You like her as much as I do, Nora?" Brophy asked the blond.

The woman shrugged, apparently uninterested in anything but Rosie O'Donnell on TV. She was probably high. Her hair was stringy, with the bangs gelled down to her forehead. She had barbed-wire tattoos on both ankles, wrists, and around her throat.

Brophy looked back at Betsey Cavalierre and me. "I take it we have business to discuss. So, the mystery lady is FBI. That's very good. Means you can afford any information I might have."

Betsey shook her head. "I'd rather beat it out of you."

Tony Brophy's dark eyes came alive again. "I *really* like her."

We followed Brophy to a lopsided wooden table in a tiny kitchen. He sat straddled on a chair, the backrest wedged against his hairy stomach and chest. We had to arrive at a financial agreement before he would give up anything. He was right about one thing — Betsey Cavalierre's budget was a lot bigger than mine.

"This has to be good information, though," she warned.

He nodded confidently, smugly. "This is the best you can buy, baby. Top of the line. Y'see, I *met* with the man behind those nasty jobs in Maryland and Virginia. Want to know what he's like? Well, he's one cold motherfucker. And remember who's telling you that."

Brophy stared hard at Betsey and me. He definitely had our interest.

"He called himself *Mastermind*," Brophy said in a slow Florida drawl. "He was dead serious about it. *Mastermind!* You believe it?

"The two of us met at the Sheraton Airport Hotel. He contacted me through a guy I know from New York," Brophy went on. "The so-called Mastermind knew things about me. He ticked off my strengths, then weaknesses. He had me down to a T. He even knew about the lovely Nora and her habit."

"Think he was a cop? All the information he had about you?" I asked Brophy.

Brophy grinned broadly. "No. *Too smart.* He might have talked to some cops, though, considering he knew everything. That's why I stayed and listened to the dude. That, plus he told me this was a high-six-figure opportunity for me. *That* caught my interest."

All Agent Cavalierre and I had to do now was listen. Once Brophy got started there was no stopping him.

"What did he look like?" I asked.

"You want to know what he looked like? That's the million-dollar question, Regis Philbin. Let me set the scene for you. When I walked into the room at his hotel, there were bright lights shining at me. Like Hollywood premiere movie lights. I couldn't see shit."

"Not even shapes?" I asked Brophy. "You must have seen something."

"His silhouette. He had long hair. Or maybe he was wearing a wig. Big nose, big ears. Like a car with both doors open. We talked and he said he'd be in touch — but I never heard from him again. Guess he didn't want me for his crew."

"Why not?" I asked Brophy. It was a serious question. "Why wouldn't he want someone like you?"

Brophy made a pistol with his hand and shot me. "He wants *killers,* dude. I'm not a killer. I'm a lover. Right, Betsey?"

Chapter 40

WHAT BROPHY HAD TOLD US was scary and it couldn't get out to the press. Someone who called himself the Mastermind was out there interviewing and hiring professional killers. *Only killers*. What was he planning next? More bank-hostage jobs? What the hell was he thinking?

After I finished work that night, I went to St. Anthony's. Jannie was doing fine, but I stayed another night with her, anyway. My home away from home. She had begun calling me her "roomie."

The next morning I waded through files on disgruntled former employees of Citibank, First Union, and First Virginia; and also records of anyone who had made any kind of serious threat against the banks. The mood in the FBI field office was one of quiet desperation. There was none of the buzz and excitement that went along with leads, clues, progress of any kind. We still didn't have a single good suspect.

Threats and crank communications to banks are usually handled by an in-house investigative department. General hate mail is most often from people who are denied loans or have had their homes foreclosed. Hate mail is as likely to come from a woman as from a man. According to the psychological profiles I read that morning, it was usually someone having work, financial, or domestic problems. Occasionally, there were serious threats because of a bank's labor practices or its affiliations with foreign countries such as South Africa, Iraq, and Northern Ireland. Mail at the major banks was X-rayed in the mail room, and there were frequent false alarms. Musical Christmas cards sometimes set off the system.

The process was exhausting but necessary. It was part of the job. I glanced over at Betsey Cavalierre around one. She was right there with the rest of us, seated at a plain metal desk. She was nearly hidden behind stacks of paper.

"I'm going to run out again for a while," I told her. "There's a guy I want to check out. He's made some threats against Citibank. He lives nearby."

She put down her pen. "I'll go with you. If you don't mind. Kyle says he trusts your hunches."

"Look where it got Kyle," I said, and smiled.

"Exactly," Betsey said, and winked. "Let's go."

I had read and reread Joseph Petrillo's file. It stood out from the others. Every week for the past two years, the chairman of Citibank in New York had received an angry, even vicious letter from Petrillo. He had worked in security for the bank from January of 1990 until recently. He'd been fired because of budget cuts that affected every department in the bank, not just his. Petrillo didn't accept the explanation, or anything else the bank tried to make him go away.

There was something about the tone of the letters that alarmed me. They were well-written and intelligent, but the letters showed signs of paranoia, possibly even schizophrenia. Petrillo had been a captain in Vietnam before he worked for the bank. He'd seen combat. The police had been to see him about the crank mail, but no charges had been filed.

"This must be one of those famous feelings of yours," Betsey said as we rode to the suspect's house on Fifth Avenue.

"It's one of those famous *bad* feelings," I said. "The detective who interviewed him a few months ago had a bad feeling, too. The bank refused to go any further with the complaint."

Unlike its namesake in New York, Fifth Avenue in D.C. was a low-rent area on the edge of gentrifying Capitol Hill. It had originally been mostly Italian American but was now racially mixed. Rusted, dated cars lined the street. A BMW sedan, fully loaded, stood out from the other vehicles. Probably a drug dealer.

"Same old, same old," Betsey said.

"You know the area?" I asked as we turned onto the street where Petrillo lived.

She nodded and her brown eyes narrowed. "A certain number of years ago, that number not to be disclosed at this time, I was born not far from here. Four blocks, to be exact."

I glanced over at Betsey and saw a grim look on her face as she stared out the windshield. She had let me in on a little piece of her past. She'd grown up on the wrong side of the tracks in Washington. She didn't look like it.

"We don't have to follow up on this hunch," I told her. "I can check it out later. It's probably nothing, but Petrillo lives so close to the field office."

She shook her head, shrugged. "You read a lot of files today. This is the one that popped for you. We should follow up on it. I'm fine being here."

We stopped in front of a corner deli, where local kids had probably been hanging out for the past few decades. The current group looked a little retro in their choice of loose-fitting jeans, dark T-shirts, slicked-back hair. They were all white.

We crossed the street and walked toward the end of the block. I pointed out a small yellow house. "That's Petrillo's."

"Let's go talk to the man," she said. "See if he's robbed any banks lately."

We climbed pockmarked concrete steps to a gray metal screen door. I knocked on the door frame and called out, "D.C. police. I'd like to talk to Joseph Petrillo."

I turned to Betsey, who was standing to my left, down one of the stone stairs. I'm not even sure what I was going to say to her.

Whatever it was — *I never got it out.*

There was a tremendous gun blast — probably a shotgun. Very loud, deafening, scarier than a bolt of lightning. It came from inside the house, not far from the front door.

Betsey screamed.

Chapter 41

I DIVED HEADFIRST OFF THE PORCH, taking Betsey with me. We lay on the lawn, scrambling to get our guns, breathing hoarsely.

"Jesus Christ! *Jesus!*" she gasped. Neither of us had been hit, but we were scared shitless. I was also angry at myself for being careless at the door.

"*Damn it!* I wasn't expecting him to shoot at us."

"Last time I ever doubt your gut feelings," she whispered. "I'll call for backup."

"Call Metro *first,*" I told her. "This is our city."

We crouched beside an untrimmed hedge and several out-of-control rose bushes. Both of us had our pistols ready. I held mine pointed upward alongside my face. Was this the Mastermind in here? Had we found him?

Across the street, the teens in front of the deli were brazenly checking out the action, more specifically, where the gunshot had come from. They had wide-eyed expressions and were watching us as if we were characters in an episode of *NYPD Blue* or *Law & Order.*

"Crazy fuckin' Joe," one of them held his hands cupped around his mouth and shouted loudly.

"At least he stopped shooting for the moment," Betsey whispered. "Crazy fucking Joe."

"Unfortunately, he still has his scattergun. He can shoot some more if he wants to."

I shifted around on the ground so I could see the front of the house a little better. There was no hole in the door. Nothing.

"Joseph Petrillo!" I shouted again.

No response came from inside the house.

"D.C. police!" I called out. *You waiting for me to show my face again, Crazy Joe? You want a little better target this time?*

I inched up closer to the porch, but I stayed down below the railing.

The kids across the street had started mimicking me. *"Mr. Petrillo? Crazy Mr. Petrillo?* You okay in there, you nutso asshole?"

Help arrived minutes later. Two cruisers with their sirens wailing. Then two more. Then a couple of FBI sedans. Everybody was armed to the gills and ready for big trouble. Blockades were set up and down the street. The houses across the way were vacated, as was the corner store. A TV news helicopter dropped by for an unexpected and unwelcome visit — a flyby.

I had participated in this kind of shoot-'em-up scene more times than I liked to think about. Not good. We waited another twenty minutes before a SWAT team arrived. The blue knights. They wore full body armor and used a battering ram to take down the front door. Then we went inside.

I didn't have to go, but I entered the house behind the primary. I had on a Kevlar vest and so did Agent Cavalierre. I kind of liked that she went in with us.

It was weirder than weird inside. The living room of the house looked like the attic of a library: musty, coverless books, tattered magazines, and old newspapers were piled as high as seven feet and took up most of the room. There were cats everywhere, dozens of them. They *meowed* loudly, pathetically. The cats looked half starved.

Joseph Petrillo was there, too. He lay in a pile of old copies of *Newsweek, Time, Life,* and *People* magazines. He must have toppled them when he fell backward. His mouth was open in what looked like a smile — half a smile, anyway.

He had blown himself away with a shotgun. It was on the floor near his bloodied head. Most of the right side of his face was gone. Blood was splattered on the wall, an armchair, some of the books. One of the cats was fastidiously licking his hand.

I looked down at the overturned books and papers near the body. I noticed a brochure for Citibank. Also several of Petrillo's bank statements. The statements showed a balance of $7,711 three years before, but now was down to $61.

Betsey Cavalierre was crouched near the wasted body. I sensed that she was trying hard not to be sick. A couple of the mangy cats were rubbing against her leg, but she seemed oblivious to them.

"This couldn't be the Mastermind," she said.

I looked into her eyes and saw fear, but mostly sadness there. "No, I'm sure it isn't, Betsey. Not poor Petrillo and his starving cats."

Chapter 42

I FINALLY GOT TO GO HOME to my own bed for a night. Jannie took pity on me for the sore back I was developing sleeping in the chair in her room. I was fast asleep at home when the phone rang. I picked up after a couple of loud rings.

It was Christine.

"Alex, there's someone in the house. I think it's Shafer. He's come here to get me. Please help me!"

"Call the police. I'm on my way," I said into the phone. "You and Alex get out of there *now!*"

It usually takes me close to half an hour to get out to Mitchellville. I got there in less than fifteen minutes that night. Lights were blazing all over the street. Two police cruisers were parked in front of Christine's town house. It was raining hard.

I jumped out of the Porsche and ran to the porch. A burly patrolman in a dark blue rain slicker raised his hand to stop me.

"I'm Detective Alex Cross, Metro D.C. I'm a good friend of Christine Johnson."

He nodded and didn't make me show my badge. "She's inside with the other officers. Ms. Johnson's fine, Detective. So is the little boy."

I could already hear little Alex crying in there. As I entered the living room I saw two patrolmen with Christine. She was crying, but also talking loudly to the policemen.

"He's here! I'm telling you. Geoffrey Shafer — the Weasel! He's here somewhere!" she yelled, and ran both hands through her hair.

The baby was wailing in his Pack 'N Play. I went over and picked him up. The Boy quieted down as soon as he was in my arms. I walked over to Christine and the two patrolmen.

"Tell them about Geoffrey Shafer," Christine pleaded with me. "Tell them what's already happened. *How crazy he is!*"

I told the officers who I was and then the story of Christine's horrific kidnapping more than a year before in Bermuda. I tried to give a short version, and when I was finished they nodded. They got it, understood.

"I remember the case from the newspapers," one of them said. "Trouble is, there's no evidence that anyone was here tonight. We've checked all the doors, windows, and the grounds."

"Would you mind if I took a look around?" I asked.

"Not at all. We'll wait here with Ms. Johnson. Take your time, Detective."

I gave the baby over to Christine and then I checked the house very carefully. I looked everywhere, but I didn't find any sign of entry. I walked the grounds and even though it was wet, saw no evidence of fresh footprints. I doubted that Shafer had been there that night.

When I returned to the living room, Christine and the baby were cuddled up quietly on the couch. The two patrolmen were waiting outside on the front porch. I went out and talked to them.

"Can I be honest?" one of them asked me. "Could Ms. Johnson have had a bad dream? It sounds like some kind of nightmare or something. She's sure this guy Shafer was in her house. In the bedroom. We saw nothing to support that, Detective. The doors were locked. The alarm was still on. Does she have nightmares?"

"Sometimes she does. Lately. Thank you for your help. I'll take it from here."

After the squad cars drove off, I went back inside to be with Christine. She seemed a little calmer now, but her eyes were so damn sad.

"What's happening to me?" she asked. "I want my life back. *I can't get away from him.*"

She wouldn't let me hold her, not even then. She didn't want to hear that she might have been dreaming about Geoffrey Shafer, the Weasel. Christine did thank me for coming, but then she told me to go home.

"There's nothing you can do for me," she said.

I kissed the baby, and then I went home.

Chapter 43

AT PRECISELY 7:00 A.M. Mr. Blue took up his position in the thick fir woods behind a house in the Woodley Park section of Washington.

As he'd done for the past three mornings, the bank manager, Martin Casselman, left his home at around twenty past seven. Casselman peered around the neighborhood before he got into his car. It was possible he was spooked by the recent bank robberies in Maryland and Virginia. Still, most people never really thought it could happen to them.

Casselman's wife was a teacher at Dumbarton Oaks High School. She taught English, which Mr. Blue had always hated. Mrs. C. would be leaving for work sometime closer to eight. The Casselmans were both organized and predictable, which made the job simpler.

Mr. Blue crouched beside an old elm that was dying; he waited for a call on his cell phone. Everything was on schedule so far, and he felt relaxed. Approximately eight minutes after Martin Casselman left, the phone rang. He pushed the *Talk* button.

"Mr. Blue. Talk to me."

"C. has arrived for our meeting. He's in the parking lot as we speak. Over."

"Roger that. Everything looks good for my meeting with Mrs. C."

No sooner had Mr. Blue pushed *End* on the phone than he saw Victoria Casselman step out the front door of the house and lock up. She had on a pink suit and reminded him of Farrah Fawcett in her glory days.

"Where the hell is she going?" he said, surprised. There weren't supposed to be any surprises on this job. The Mastermind had supposedly scoped everything out perfectly. *This wasn't perfection.* Mr. Blue started to walk fast through the tangle of woods and high weeds separating him from the Casselman house. He could already see that he wasn't going to make it in time.

Mistake.

Mine, or hers?

Both of ours! She's leaving too early this morning; I'm out of position!

He began to run toward Hawthorne Street, but she was already inside her black Toyota and backing out of the driveway. If she turned right, everything was completely screwed. If she turned left, he still had a chance to save the day. *C'mon Farrah, honey, go left!*

Mr. Blue was trying to think of something to shout to her — something that would stop her cold. What, though? *Think. Think.*

Good girl! She had turned left, but he still didn't think he could get to the freaking road in time to stop her.

He started to sprint, head down. He felt a burst of sudden, deep heat roaring through his chest. He couldn't remember the last time he'd had to run at full tilt like this.

"Hey! Hey! Can you help me?" he called at the top of his voice. "Please help me! Help!"

Victoria Casselman's head of teased blond hair turned when she heard the shouts. She slowed the car a little, but she still didn't stop completely.

He had to stop her.

"My wife's having a baby!" Mr. Blue shouted. "Please help. My wife's having a baby."

He sighed with incredible relief when he saw the black sedan stop in the middle of the road. He hoped that no busybody neighbor was watching from one of the houses lined up and down the street. It didn't matter, though. He had to stop her one way or the other. He was still gasping as he ran up to the car.

"What's the matter with you? Where's your wife?" Victoria Casselman called to him through the open window.

Mr. Blue continued to wheeze until he was right up beside the car. Then he pulled out a Sig Sauer pistol and whacked her jaw with the barrel. Victoria Casselman's head snapped to the side and she cried out in pain.

"We're going back to the house!" he shouted as he jumped into the car. He held the gun to her forehead.

"Where the hell were you going at seven-forty? Oh, just shut up. I don't really care. You made a mistake, Victoria. You made a bad mistake." It was all Mr. Blue could do not to shoot her dead in the front seat of her car.

Chapter 44

A ROBBERY WAS IN PROGRESS at the Chase Manhattan Bank branch near the Omni Shoreham Hotel in Washington. Betsey Cavalierre and I didn't talk much on the ride from the FBI offices to the bank. We were both dreading what we might find.

Betsey was all business. She'd placed a siren on the roof and we raced through Washington. It was raining again, and streaks of water hammered the car's roof and windshield. The city of Washington was crying. This nightmare was deepening and seemed to be accelerating. It was as scary and unpredictable as any multiple-murder case I had worked before. It didn't make sense to me. A bank-robbing crew, or possibly a couple of crews, was operating like a gang of mass killers. The press coverage was massive and overwhelming; the public was terrified, and had a right to be; the banking industry was up in arms that the robberies and murders hadn't been stopped.

I was shaken from my reverie by the sound of police sirens wailing up ahead. The shrill chorus made the hairs on the back of my neck stand up. Then I saw the blue-and-white sign of the Chase Bank branch.

Betsey stopped about a block away on Twenty-eighth Street. It was as close as we could get. Even with the heavy rain, there were a hundred spectators, dozens of ambulances, police cruisers, even a fire truck had arrived on the scene.

We ran through the hissing downpour toward a modest red-brick building on the corner of Calvert. I was a few strides ahead of Betsey, but she was moving.

"Metro police. Detective Cross," I said, and flashed my badge at a patrolman who tried to block the way into the bank parking lot. The patrolman saw the gold shield and stepped aside.

The assorted police and emergency sirens continued to wail loudly, and I wondered why. The moment I walked inside the bank lobby, I knew. I counted five bodies. Tellers and executives: three women, two men. All had been shot dead. It was another massacre, possibly the worst one so far.

"Why? Jesus!" Agent Cavalierre muttered at my side. For a second she held on to my arm, but then realized what she had done and let go.

An FBI agent hurried up to us. His name was James Walsh, and I remembered him from the first meeting at the field office. "Five are dead here. They're all on staff, bank employees."

"Hostages at home?" Betsey asked.

Walsh shook his head. "The manager's wife is dead,

too. Shot at close range. Executed for no reason we can figure out. . . . Betsey, they left a survivor at the bank. He has a message for you and Detective Cross. It's from someone called the Mastermind."

Chapter 45

THE SURVIVOR'S NAME was Arthur Strickland, and he was being kept in the slain manager's office, as far away as possible from the press. He was the bank's security guard.

Strickland was a tall, slender, well-built man in his late forties. Although physically impressive, he looked to be in a state of shock. Beads of perspiration covered his face, his thick mustache. His light blue uniform shirt was entirely soaked through.

Betsey went up to the bank guard and spoke very softly, compassionately. "I'm Senior Agent Cavalierre from the FBI. I'm in charge of this investigation, Mr. Strickland. This is Detective Cross from the D.C. police. I hear that you have a message for us?"

The powerful-looking man suddenly broke down. He sobbed into his hands. It took him a minute or so before he pulled himself together and was able to talk.

"They were nice people that got killed here today. They were my friends," he said. "I was supposed to protect them, and our customers, of course."

"It's a terrible thing that happened, but it's not your fault," Betsey said to the guard. She was trying to be kind, to calm him, and she was doing a good job. "Why did the gunmen kill them? How did you get away?"

The guard shook his head in dismay. "I didn't get away," he said. "They held me in the lobby with the others. Two of 'em did the job. All of us were told to stay facedown on the floor. They said they had to be out the bank quarter past eight. No later than that. No mistakes, they said several times. No alarms. No panic buttons."

"They were late getting out of the bank?" I asked Arthur Strickland.

"*No, sir,*" the guard said to me. "That's just it. They could have made it on time. They didn't seem to want to. They told me to stand up. I thought they was going to shoot me right then. I was in Vietnam, but I was never this afraid."

"They gave you a message for us?" I asked him.

"Yes, sir. A message for both of you. *'You like this bank?'* one of them asked me. I said that I liked my job. He called me a dumb spade asshole. Then he said that I was to be their messenger. I should tell FBI Agent Cavalierre and Detective Cross that there was a mistake made at the bank. He said there could be no more mistakes. He repeated that several times. *No more mistakes.* He said, 'Tell them the message is from the Mastermind.' Then they shot everybody else. They shot them where they lay on the floor, in cold blood. It's all my fault. I was the guard on duty at the bank. I let it happen."

"No, Mr. Strickland." Betsey Cavalierre spoke softly to the bank guard. "You didn't. We're the ones at fault, not you."

Chapter 46

THERE CAN BE NO MORE MISTAKES.

The Mastermind knew all about the FBI's Betsey Cavalierre and Detective Cross. He was on top of everything, even the police officers assigned to the case. They were part of his plan now.

It was a gorgeous day for his excursion into the countryside outside Washington. The lilies were in bloom, and the sky was clear; it was bright china blue, with just a couple of cloud puffs placed symmetrically to the east and west.

The current bank-robbing crew was staying in a farmhouse just south of Hayfield, Virginia. It was a little more than eighty miles southwest of Washington, almost in West Virginia.

He rounded a bend on an unpaved road and saw the rear end of Mr. Blue's van jutting out of a faded red barn. A pair of dogs were roaming in the yard, biting at horseflies. He didn't see any of the gang yet, or their girlfriends, but he did hear their loud rock-and-roll music: guitar-heavy, Southern-flavored rock that they played constantly, morning and night.

He walked into the farmhouse living room, which had been remodeled to resemble a loft. He saw Mr. Blue, Mr. Red, Mr. White, and their girlfriends, including Ms. Green. He could smell coffee brewing. A broom was leaning against one wall, which meant they had cleaned up a little before he arrived. Next to the broom was a Heckler and Koch Marksman's rifle.

"Hello, everybody," he said, and waved shyly, *his way.* He smiled, but knew that they considered him a geek. So be it. Ms. Green was looking at him as if he were *a geek with the hots for her.*

"Hey, mon professor," Blue said, and gave him a light-hearted grin that was so insincere it hurt. The Mastermind wasn't fooled. Mr. Blue was a stone-cold killer. That was why he had been chosen for the First Union, First Virginia, and Chase robberies. They were all killers, even the three girls.

"Pizza." He held up two boxes and a paper bag. "I bought pizza. And some excellent Chianti."

Chapter 47

KILLJOY, he was thinking.

> *Killing machine.*
> *Killing time.*
> *Killer idea.*
> *Killing fields.*

The Mastermind smiled thinly at his own obsessive wordplay. It was the kind of half smile that didn't feel good on his face, though. It felt false and a little forced. It was just past four o'clock, and it was still brightly sunny outside. He'd gone for a nice walk in the fields. He'd thought everything through. Now he was returning to the farmhouse.

He entered through the front screen door and let his eyes crawl over the bodies. The crew members were dead, all six of them. Their bodies were strangely twisted and contorted, the way metal can get in a firestorm. He had seen that phenomenon once, after a fire that raged through the hillsides outside Berkeley, in California. He'd loved that: the sheer beauty of a natural disaster.

He stopped and studied the dead. They were murderers, and they'd suffered for it. He'd used Marplan as the poison this time. Interestingly, the antidepressant was most potent when ingested with cheese or red wine, especially Chianti. The odd chemical combination induced a sharp increase in blood pressure followed by cerebral hemorrhage, and finally circulatory collapse. *Voilà.*

He looked more closely at the dead, and it was extraordinarily fascinating. Their pupils were dilated. The mouths were open in horribly twisted screams. Bloated bluish tongues hung out of the sides of the mouths. Now he had to get them out of here. He had to make the bodies disappear, almost as if they had never existed.

A girl named Gersh Adamson was sprawled on the floor near the front door. She'd tried to run outside, hadn't she? Good for her. She was Ms. Green, a tiny blond lady who said she was twenty-one, but who looked no more than fifteen. Her mouth was frozen in an anguished scream that he simply loved. He almost couldn't tear his eyes away from Gersh Adamson's lips.

He figured that she was the lightest to carry; she probably weighed no more than a hundred pounds.

"Hello, Ms. Green. I've always liked you, you know. I'm a little diffident, though. I should say that I *used* to be shy. I'm getting over it."

He reached out and touched her small breasts. He was surprised to find that Ms. Green wore a push-up bra under her blouse. Not quite the little dippie-hippie she seemed to be. He unbuttoned her blouse, then pulled it off and stared at her breasts.

He unbuttoned the dead girl's jeans. Then he inserted a finger inside her panties. The flesh was a little cool. She had a silver ring in her belly button. He touched it. Pulled on it like a pop-top.

She was wearing satiny gray platforms with high heels, and he carefully took those off her feet. He pulled the tight jeans down and then wriggled them off, too. Ms. Green's toenails were painted bright blue.

The Mastermind unclasped the lacy push-up bra and kneaded her smallish breasts. He rubbed them together with his palms. Then he pinched the tiny, perfect nipples hard. He'd wanted to do that from the first time he saw her. He'd wanted to hurt her a little, or maybe a lot.

He looked out the farmhouse window, then around at the dead bodies again. "I'm not grossing any of you out, am I?" he asked.

He dragged Ms. Green by her bare feet to the faded rug at the center of the room. Then he took off his own trousers. He was getting hard. He never got this way anymore. Maybe the FBI was right: He might be a pattern killer, after all. Maybe he was just beginning to understand who he really was.

"I'm a ghoul," the Mastermind said, then he pulled aside her panties and thrust himself inside the dead woman's vagina. "I'm crazy, Ms. Green, and that's the biggest joke of all. *I'm the one who's crazy.* If the police only knew. What a great clue."

Part Three

HANGING WITH THE BIG DOGS

Chapter 48

THREE DAYS PASSED without another robbery. One of them was a Saturday, and I got to spend the afternoon with the Boy. At around six, I finally brought him back to Christine's.

Before we went inside, I carried little Alex around the flower garden behind her apartment in Mitchellville. Her "country estate," I liked to call it. The garden was glorious. Christine had planted and nurtured it herself. It was filled with a variety of roses: hybrid teas, floribunda and grandiflora. It reminded me of how she had been before the kidnapping in Bermuda. Everything about the garden was visually pleasing. Which was probably why it felt so damn sad to be there without her.

I carried the Boy easily on my hip, talking to him, pointing out the manicured lawn, a weeping willow tree, the sky, the setting sun. Then I showed him the similarity in our faces: nose to nose, eyes to eyes, mouth to mouth.

Every few minutes I'd stop to kiss Alex's cheek or neck or the top of his head.

"Smell the roses," I whispered.

I saw Christine hurrying out of the house a few minutes later. I could tell she had something on her mind. Her sister Natalie trailed close behind her. For protection? I had the feeling that they were about to gang up on me.

"Alex, we have to talk," Christine said as she came up to me in the garden. "Natalie, could you take care of the baby for a few minutes?"

Reluctantly, I handed Alex over to Natalie. It didn't sound like I had much of a choice. Christine had changed so much in the past months. Sometimes, I felt as if I didn't even know her. Maybe it all had to do with her nightmares. They didn't seem to be getting any better.

"I have to get out some things. Don't say anything, please," she began.

Chapter 49

I BIT DOWN ON MY TONGUE. This was the way it had been between us for months. I noticed that Christine's eyes were red rimmed. She'd been crying.

"You're off on another murder case now, Alex. I suppose that's good — it's your life. You're obviously very skilled at it."

I couldn't keep silent. "I've offered to leave the police department, to go into private practice. I'd do that, Christine."

She frowned and shook her head. "I'm so honored."

"I'm not trying to fight you," I said. "I'm sorry, go ahead. I didn't mean to interrupt."

"I have no life here in Washington anymore. I'm always afraid. *Petrified* is a better word. I hate going into the school now. I feel as if my life has been taken away from me. First George, and then what happened in Bermuda. I'm afraid that Shafer is coming back for me."

I had to speak. "He's not, Christine."

"Don't say that!" She raised her voice. *"You don't know. You can't!"*

The air in my lungs was slowly being sucked away. I wasn't sure where Christine was going with this, but she seemed on the edge. It was like the night she'd had a nightmare that Geoffrey Shafer was in her house.

"I'm moving away from the Washington area," she said. "I'll leave after the school year. I don't want you to know where I'm going. I don't want you looking for me. Please don't try to be a detective with me, Alex. *Or a shrink.*"

I couldn't believe what I'd heard. I hadn't expected anything like this. I stood there speechless, just staring at Christine. I don't think I'd ever felt so devastated, so saddened and alone in my life. I felt hollowed out and empty.

"What about the baby?" I finally said in a whisper that came out hoarse and strangled.

Tears suddenly welled in her beautiful eyes. Christine began to sob, and to shake. Uncontrollably. "I can't take Alex with me. Not the way I am. Not like *this*. The baby has to stay with you and Nana for now."

I started to speak, but nothing came out, not a word. Christine held eye contact with me briefly. Her eyes were so sad, so hurt and confused. Then she turned away and walked back to her house. She disappeared inside.

Chapter 50

I WAS ANGRY AND SAD and I was holding it all inside. I knew better than to do that, which only made it worse. *Physician, heal thyself.*

I happened to see my psychiatrist, Adele Finally, in church on Sunday morning. We were attending the nine o'clock service with our families. We moved to the rear vestibule to talk. Adele must have seen something in my eyes. She doesn't miss much and knows me well, since I've been seeing her for almost four years.

"Did Rosie the Cat die or something?" she asked, and smiled.

"Rosie's just fine, Adele. So am I. Thanks for your concern."

"Uh-huh. Then why do you look like Ali the morning after he fought Joe Frazier in Manila? Can you please explain that for me? Also, you didn't shave for church."

"That's a nice dress," I told her. "The color looks good on you."

Adele frowned and would have none of it. "Right. Gray is definitely my color, Alex. What's wrong?"

"Not a thing."

Adele lit a votive candle. "I just love magic," she whispered, and smiled mischievously. "I haven't seen you in a while, Alex. That's either very good or very bad."

I lit a votive candle myself. Then I said a prayer. "Dear Lord, continue to watch over Jannie. I also wish that Christine wasn't moving away from Washington. I know you must be testing me again."

Adele winced as if she'd been burned. She looked away from the flickering votive flame and into my eyes. "Oh, Alex, I'm so sorry. You don't need any more tests."

"I'm all right," I told her. I didn't want to get into it now, not even with Adele.

"Oh, Alex, Alex." She shook her head back and forth. "You know better than that. I know better."

"I'm fine, really."

Adele looked completely exasperated with me. "Fine, then. That will be one hundred for the visit. You can put it in the collection basket."

Adele walked back to her family, who were already seated about halfway down the center aisle. She turned, and looked at me. She wasn't smiling now.

When I got to our pew, Damon asked me who the pretty lady was that I'd been talking to in the back of the church.

"She's a doctor. A friend of mine," I said, which was true enough.

"Is she your doctor? What kind of doctor is she? She looks like she's kind of mad at you," he whispered. "What did you do wrong?"

"I didn't do anything wrong," I whispered back. "Don't I get any privacy?"

"No. Besides, we're in church. I'm hearing your confession."

"I don't have any confession for you to hear. I'm all right. I'm fine. I'm at peace with the world. I couldn't be happier."

Damon gave me the same look of exasperation that Adele had. Then he shook his head and turned away. He didn't believe me, either. When the collection basket came, I put in a hundred dollars.

Chapter 51

THE MASTERMIND was keeping everything on a tight schedule. The clock inside his head was ticking loudly, always ticking.

The best of the bank-robbing crews, the crème de la crème, was scheduled to meet with him in his suite at a Holiday Inn near Colonial Village in Washington. They were on time, of course. He had made it a formal condition of the meeting.

Brian Macdougall swaggered into the suite ahead of the others. The Mastermind smiled at the absurdly cocksure way Macdougall carried himself. He knew that Macdougall would lead the way into the room. He was followed by his subordinates, B. J. Stringer and Robert Shaw. *The three of them look like anything but high-level thieves,* he thought. Two of the three wore royal-blue-and-white T-shirts from the same Long Island softball league.

"Mr. O'Malley and Mr. Crews?" the Mastermind

asked from behind the screen of lights that prohibited them from seeing him. "Where are they, might I ask?"

Macdougall spoke for the group. "They have to work today. You gave us kind of short notice, partner. Three of us took off this morning. It'd look suspicious if we all called in sick."

The Mastermind continued to observe the three New York men sitting behind the lights. Each looked like your average Joe. In truth, they were the most dangerous of the bank-robbing crews he'd used. They were exactly what he needed for the next test.

"So this is what, an audition?" Macdougall asked. He had on a black silk shirt, black trousers, and loafers. He had slicked-back black hair and a goatee.

"An audition? No, not at all. The job is yours, if you want it. I know how you work. Know all about you. I know your track record."

Macdougall stared ahead at the bright lights, almost as if his gaze could penetrate them. "This needs to be a face-to-face meeting," he said stonily. "That's the *only* way we'll do the job."

The Mastermind rose quickly. He was stunned and angry. The legs of his chair made a loud scraping noise against the floor. "You were told from the beginning that wasn't possible. This meeting is *over.*"

A heavy silence filled the hotel room. Macdougall looked over at Stringer and Shaw. He scratched his goatee a few times, then he laughed out loud. "I was just testing, partner. I guess we can live without seeing your face. If you have our payment with you?"

"I have the money, gentlemen. Fifty thousand dollars. Just for meeting with me. I always keep my promises."

"And we walk away with the payment if we don't like your plan for the job?"

Now it was the Mastermind's turn to smile. "You'll like the plan," he said. "You'll especially like the part about your share. It's fifteen million dollars. I'll contact you later."

Chapter 52

"DID HE SAY FIFTEEN MILLION?"

"That's what the man said. What the hell are we supposed to rob?"

Vincent O'Malley and Jimmy Crews weren't at work that day. They were waiting inside a Toyota Camry and an Acura Legend, respectively. They were in contact with each other by headset. Their cars were parked on opposite sides of the Holiday Inn in Washington. They were watching for the Mastermind to appear outside, so that maybe they could follow him, find out who the hell he was.

O'Malley and Crews listened to the meeting through Brian Macdougall, who was wired for sound. They heard *fifteen million* mentioned and they wondered what the hell the job could be. The guy who called himself the Master mind was something else. He talked, or rather lectured and he made the mind-boggling job sound like a walk in the park. Six to eight hours of work; thirty million to split

The most impressive thing of all was that he answered all of Brian Macdougall's tough questions.

O'Malley stayed in contact with Crews in the other car. "You listening to this shit, Jimmy? You believe it?"

"He has my rapt attention. I'd love to see the fricking look on Macdougall's face right about now. This asshole has his number. It's like he *knows* everything about Brian. Hey, I think the meeting's breaking up."

O'Malley and Crews remained silent for the next few minutes. Then O'Malley spoke. "He's outside the hotel. I see him, Jimmy. He's on foot. He's walking south on Sixteenth Street. Doesn't seem concerned about being followed. I got him!"

"Maybe he's not so fucking smart, after all," Crews said.

O'Malley laughed. "Shit. I was kind of hoping he *was* this smart."

Crews said, "I'll go parallel down Fourteenth. What's he look like? What's he wearing?"

"Tall, over six feet. White guy. Beard, maybe a fake one. Long hair. Pretty nondescript clothes: dark sport coat and slacks, blue shirt . . . He's picking up the pace. He's starting to jog now. He's going off the main street, Jimmy. He's headed back through a yard. He's *running!* Son of a bitch is on the run! Here we go!"

Vincent O'Malley jumped out of his car and followed the Mastermind. He ran close to the maple and oak trees that lined the street. He continued to report in to Crews. "He's going into the woods off Shepherd Park. Motherhumper is trying to get away from us. Imagine that."

O'Malley followed the Mastermind as best he could, but he couldn't keep up. The guy was a runner. He didn't look like it, but he could move real well.

Then O'Malley lost him! "He's gone. Fuck me in the heinie. I lost him, Jimmy. I don't see him anymore. This is not good."

Crews picked him up again. "*I got him.* I'm on foot, too. He's still running like some pickpocket with my wallet."

"You keep up with him?"

"Hope so. We'll see. For fifteen million dollars I'll keep up with him somehow."

The Mastermind finally came out of the woods and onto a side street filled with brick town houses. Crews was panting as he spoke into the mike on his headset. "Thank God I run every day. He runs, too. He's out on Morningside Drive. . . . Awhh shit, he's heading back into the goddamn woods. He's picking up the pace again. The bastard must train on the Appalachian Trail."

It became an incredible game of cat and mouse. Even though they were good at it, O'Malley and Crews lost their prey twice more in the next twenty minutes. They were miles from the Holiday Inn, somewhere south of Walter Reed Army Medical Center.

Then Crews spotted him on a narrow side street called Powhatan Place. The Mastermind had turned into a back driveway or something. Crews followed. He saw a metal sign, and he almost couldn't believe what it said.

Crews reported back to O'Malley. Then he talked to Brian Macdougall, who'd joined the merry chase.

Crews couldn't keep the irony out of his voice. "I know where the hell he is, fellas. Get this — he's inside a nuthouse. He's on the grounds of a mental institution called Hazelwood. And now I've lost him again!"

Chapter 53

MONDAY MORNING, I got a call to meet Kyle Craig and Betsey Cavalierre at the Hoover Building on Tenth Street and Pennsylvania Avenue. They wanted me to be at the director's office at eight o'clock. An "emergency" meeting had been called.

The Hoover Building is sometimes called the "Puzzle Palace," and for obvious reasons. Kyle and Betsey were waiting when I arrived in the FBI director's conference room. Betsey looked tense for her. Her small hands were clenched into fists, the knuckles white.

I pretended to be annoyed that Director Burns wasn't there yet. "He's late," I muttered. "Let's get out of here. We've got better things to do."

Just then, one of two polished oak doors into the room opened. I knew both of the men who walked in. Neither of them looked very happy. One was FBI Director Ronald Burns, whom I'd met during the Casanova killings in Durham and Chapel Hill, North Carolina. The second man was Secretary of Justice Richard Pollett. I had met him when I'd worked on a case involving the president.

"We're getting an awful lot of heat on these robbery-murders. The big banks, Wall Street," Pollett said to Kyle. He nodded in my direction. "Hello, Detective." Then he looked at Betsey. "I'm sorry, we haven't met."

"I'm Senior Agent Cavalierre," she said, and rose to shake the secretary's hand. I'm the SAC."

"Ms. Cavalierre is the agent in charge of the investigation?" Pollett asked Director Burns.

"Yes, she is," Kyle answered the question. "This is her case."

Secretary Pollett turned his unwavering gaze on her. "All right, you're the SAC. Where are some results, Ms. Cavalierre? I walked into this room ready to make heads roll. Tell me why I shouldn't." Richard Pollett had run a large and successful Wall Street investment house before he came to Washington. He knew nothing about law enforcement but believed he was smart enough to figure out anything once he had some facts.

"Have you ever been part of a national manhunt?" Betsey stared right back into his eyes.

"I don't think that's a relevant question," he answered dryly. "I've run some very important investigations, and I've always gotten results."

"The robberies have been coming fast," I found myself saying to Pollett. "Obviously, we were starting from nowhere. Here's what we know now. A single man planned the Citibank, First Union, First Virginia, and Chase robberies and murders. We know he's selecting crew members that are willing to kill. *He's only interested in recruiting killers.*

"Our profile tells us he's a white male between thirty-five and fifty. He's probably well educated, with a thorough knowledge of banks and their security systems. He may have worked for a financial institution in the past, or even more than one, and might have a grudge against them. He robs banks for the money, but the murders are probably for revenge. *That* we're not sure about yet."

I looked around the room. Everyone was listening instead of bickering. "A few days ago we located and questioned a man named Tony Brophy. He was recruited for one of the jobs but was turned down. He wasn't cold-blooded enough. He wasn't a killer."

Betsey spoke. "We have over two hundred agents in the field. We were only a couple of minutes behind them at the Chase robbery in D.C.," she said. "We know that he calls himself the Mastermind. There's been a lot of progress in a relatively short time."

Pollett turned to the FBI director and nodded curtly. "I'm not satisfied, but at least I finally got a few answers. It's your job to get this Mastermind, Ron. Do it. What's happening makes all our financial systems appear vulnerable. The polls say confidence in the banks is down. And that's a disaster for this country. I assume your *Mastermind* has figured that out already."

Ten minutes later, Betsey Cavalierre and I rode the elevator down to the FBI's underground garage together. Kyle had stayed behind with Director Burns.

When we got to the basement floor, she finally spoke. "I owe you one for upstairs. You saved me. Big time. I was *this* close to unloading on that pompous Wall Street asshole."

I looked at her and a smile broke on my face. "You definitely have a temper. I hope *you* don't have a grudge against Big Business or the banking system?"

She finally grinned. "Of course I do. Who doesn't?"

Chapter 54

I SPENT THE NEXT COUPLE OF HOURS at the hospital with Jannie. She told me again that she was going to be a doctor and she sounded ready to take her med boards. She took delight in using terms like *pilocytic astrocytoma* (her tumor), *prothrombin* (a plasma protein used in the clotting of blood), and *contrast material* (dye used in the CT scan she'd had just that morning).

"I'm back," Jannie finally announced, "and the new and improved model is better than ever."

"Maybe you better go into the public relations or the advertising field when you grow up," I teased her. "Work for J. Walter Thompson or Young and Rubicam in New York."

She puckered her mouth and looked as if she'd just bitten into a lemon. "*Dr.* Janelle Cross. Remember where you heard it first."

"Don't worry," I told her, "I won't forget any of this."

Around one o'clock I went over to the crisis center at

the FBI field office on Fourth. After the meeting with Pollett and Burns, I knew we'd be working late. A conference room had been commandeered on the third floor. More than a hundred agents were working out of there. Also, about sixty detectives from D.C. and the surrounding areas.

We had a few more suspects up on the walls now. They were all bank robbers with the skills and experience to pull off big jobs. I studied the list and made notes on a few of them.

Mitchell Brand was a suspect in several unsolved robberies in and around D.C. Stephen Schnurmacher was the person behind at least two successful bank heists in the Philadelphia area. Jimmy Doud was a bartender in Boston who'd never been caught but who had robbed dozens of banks up in New England. Victor Kenyon had been concentrating his efforts in central Florida. They all did banks, and they hadn't been caught yet. They were smart, and good at what they did. But were they masterminds?

Everything about the long session on Fourth Avenue was intense, and intensely frustrating. I made some calls about the suspects, particularly Mitchell Brand, since he worked out of D.C. It was nearly eleven-thirty when I looked at my watch for the first time all night.

Betsey Cavalierre and I hadn't gotten the chance to talk since I'd arrived that afternoon. I drifted her way to say good night before I left the building. She was still going at it. She was talking to a couple of agents but gestured for me to wait.

Finally, she walked over. She still managed to look fresh and alert, and I wondered how she did it.

"Metro has a couple of leads on Mitchell Brand," I told

her. "He's violent enough to be involved in something like this."

Suddenly, she yawned. "Longest day of my life. *Whew!* How's Jannie doing?" she asked. I was surprised and also pleased by the question.

"Oh, she's doing good; *great,* actually. Hopefully, she'll come home soon. She wants to be a doctor now."

"Alex," she said, "let's go have a drink. This is a shot in the dark, but I get the feeling that you need to talk to somebody. Why won't you talk to me?"

I must admit, the offer caught me completely off guard. I stammered out a response. "I'd like to, but not tonight. I have to go home. Rain check?"

"Sure, I understand. It's okay. Rain check," she said, but not before a look of hurt had passed over her face.

I never expected that from Agent Betsey Cavalierre. She had shown concern about my family. And she was *vulnerable.*

Chapter 55

THIS WAS THE PLACE, the time, the opportunity.

The Renaissance Mayflower Hotel, on Connecticut Avenue near Seventeenth.

It was as busy as ever that morning, busy and important looking. The Mayflower has been the site of every presidential inaugural ball since Calvin Coolidge. The hotel had been completely renovated in 1992, with architects and historians working together to restore it to its earlier grandeur. It was a popular place for corporate conferences and board of directors meetings. That was how the Mastermind knew about it.

A blue-and-gold chartered tour bus had been waiting in front of the Mayflower since a little before nine. It was scheduled to leave at nine-thirty and would be making scheduled stops at the Kennedy Center, the White House, the Lincoln and Vietnam memorials, the Smithsonian Institution, and other favorite tourist spots around Washington. The bus company was called Washington on Wheels.

The corporate group on board was from the MetroHartford Insurance Company.

Sixteen women and two children were on the bus when the driver, Joseph Denyeau, finally shut the door at nine-forty. "All aboard for various museums, historic sites, and *lunch,*" he announced into his microphone.

A corporate assistant named Mary Jordan stood up in front and addressed the group. Jordan was in her early thirties, attractive and likable, supremely efficient. She was courteous to the important women on the bus without fawning over them or sounding obsequious. Her nickname at MetroHartford was Merry Mary.

"You all know the itinerary for this morning," she said. Then she smiled brilliantly. "But maybe we should scrap the whole plan and go drinking. Just kidding," she added quickly.

"Boo," said one woman. "That sounds like fun, Mary. Let's go to a real drinking bar. Where does Teddy Kennedy go for his morning wake-up shot?" Up and down the aisle everyone laughed.

The tour bus proceeded down the driveway of the hotel at a leisurely pace, then turned onto Connecticut Avenue. A few minutes later, the bus turned onto Oliver, which was a residential street. It was a shortcut drivers often took from the Mayflower.

A dark blue Chevy van backed out of a driveway about halfway down the block. The van's driver obviously didn't see the bus, but the bus driver saw the Chevy. He braked smoothly and stopped in the middle of the street.

The driver of the van wouldn't move even after Joe Denyeau sounded his horn. Denyeau figured that the man must have been fed up with all the trucks and buses that used the side street as a shortcut. What other reason could there be for the guy to just sit there, staring angrily at him?

Two masked men suddenly appeared from behind a high hedge. One of them stepped directly in front of the tour bus; the other thrust an automatic weapon inside the open side window, inches from the driver's head.

"Open the door or you're dead, Joseph," he shouted at the driver. "No one gets hurt if you obey. You have three seconds to follow directions. One —"

"It's open, it's open," Denyeau said in a high-pitched, very frightened voice. "Take it easy."

Several of the wives stopped in the middle of their conversations and peered up toward the front of the bus. Mary Jordan slid down in the bus seat behind the driver, where she was riding alone. She could see the man with the gun, and then he winked at her.

"Do what he says, Joe," Jordan whispered. "Don't play the hero."

"Don't worry. It didn't even cross my mind."

The armed, masked man suddenly boarded the bus. He held a Walther double automatic pointed at them. Some of the passengers began to scream.

The masked man shouted out, "This is a hijacking! We're only interested in getting money from MetroHartford. I promise you, no one will be hurt. I have children, you have children. Let's make sure all of our children get to see us tomorrow morning."

Chapter 56

THE TOUR BUS became strangely silent. Even the small children were quiet.

Brian Macdougall had the floor and he immensely enjoyed being the center of attention. "There are a few rules of order. *One,* no more screams. *Two,* nobody cries, not even the kids. *Three,* nobody yells for help. Okay so far? Understood?"

The passengers stared openmouthed at the man with the gun. Another man had climbed onto the bus roof and was changing the alphanumeric indicator, which was the easiest way police aircraft could spot it on the road.

"I said — *okay so far?*" Brian Macdougall yelled.

The woman and children nodded and answered him in muffled voices.

"Next piece of business. Everyone with a cell phone pass it forward — right now. As we all know, the police can track cell phones. Not easily, but it can be done. Anyone still holding a phone when we do body searches will be killed. Even if it's a kid. Simple as that. Understood? Okay so far? We still crystal clear on everything?"

The cell phones were hurriedly passed to the front. There were nine of them. The gunman threw them outside the bus, into the hedges. He then used a small hammer and smashed the bus's two-way radio beyond repair.

"Now, everybody, put your heads way down below the level of the windows. Everybody stay very quiet down there. That includes the kids. Put your heads down now and don't look up again until you're told. Do it."

The women and the children on the bus obeyed.

"Big Joe," the gunman turned and addressed the bus driver, "you have only one instruction — *follow the blue van*. Do not fuck around in any way or you will die instantly. You are worth nothing to us, alive or dead. Now, Joe, what do you do?"

"Follow the black van."

"Very good, Joe. Excellent. Except the van is *blue*, Joe. See the *blue* van? Now follow it, and drive carefully. We don't want any vehicular violations on our trip."

Chapter 57

THERE WERE THREE EXECUTIVE ASSISTANTS busily answering phones and collecting mail and faxes for the thirty-six MetroHartford directors working in the famed Chinese Room at the Mayflower Hotel. The assistants loved being out of the office, especially since the home offices were in Hartford, Connecticut.

Sara Wilson, the youngest assistant, saw the fax from the kidnappers first. She quickly read it, then passed it on to the two more-senior assistants. Her face was beet red and her hands were trembling badly.

"Is this some kind of a sick joke?" Betsy Becton asked when she saw the fax. "This is crazy. What is this?"

Nancy Hall was the executive assistant to the group CEO, John Dooner. She barged into the board meeting without knocking and called clear across the room. Actually, she needn't have raised her voice. The Chinese Room at the Mayflower has an acoustic problem. The ceiling is a sweeping dome. Even a whisper on one side of the large room can be heard on the other.

"Mr. Dooner, I have to see you *right now,*" she said. She was more agitated and upset than her boss had ever seen her.

The departure of the CEO brought a general lightening of the mood around the room, but the small talk and smiles were short-lived. He was back in less than five minutes. His face was pale as he hurriedly walked to the podium.

"Time is of the essence," said Dooner in a trembling voice that shocked the other board members. "Please listen carefully. The chartered tour bus carrying my wife and many of your wives has been hijacked. The men responsible claim to be the same sick bastards who've been robbing banks and taking hostages in Maryland and Virginia during the past few weeks. They claim that the robberies and murders were committed as 'object lessons' for the people in this room. They want us to know they are deadly serious about their demands being met — and met on time. To the second."

The CEO continued, his face dramatically lit by the podium lamp. "Their demands are simple and clear. They want thirty million dollars to be delivered to them in exactly five hours, or all the hostages will be murdered. We don't know how the tour bus was taken. Steve Bolding from our Control Risks Group is on his way over here. He's deciding which police agency to involve. It will probably be the FBI."

Dooner stopped to take a breath. The color in his face was returning slowly. "As you know, we have a kidnapping insurance policy that covers up to fifty million in ransom. I suspect that the kidnappers already know this. They seem to be thorough and organized. They're also clearheaded, which gives them an advantage. I think they know that we are the underwriters on the policy ourselves. Therefore, we can get the money and we can get it fast.

"Now, ladies and gentlemen, please, we have to talk about our alternatives. *If* there are any alternatives. The kidnappers have made one thing very clear — there can be no mistakes or people will die."

Chapter 58

I WAS AT THE FBI FIELD OFFICE on Fourth Street when we got the emergency call.

A Washington on Wheels tour bus with eighteen passengers and the driver had been hijacked soon after it left the Renaissance Mayflower Hotel. Minutes later, a thirty-million-dollar ransom had been demanded from the MetroHartford Insurance Company.

The instructions from the kidnappers stated that police agencies were not to be involved, but there was no way we could back off and trust them. We set up at the Capitol Hilton, which was close to the Mayflower, on Sixteenth and K. We had four mobile command units in addition to the dozen agents already operating inside the Mayflower. It was dangerous, but Betsey felt we needed primary surveillance at the hotel. The technical penetration involved concealed listening devices and a limited amount of video surveillance. The entire Metropolitan Field Office of the FBI was put on alert.

High-tech helicopters, Apaches, were in the air searching for the Washington on Wheels bus. The Apaches had heat monitors for tracking purposes, if and when the kidnappers attempted to hide the bus and its passengers. The alphanumeric indicator on the bus's roof had been given out to aerial police, military, city, state, and even civil aircraft. None of the groups were told why they were looking for the bus.

The Capitol Hilton was close enough for us to get to the Mayflower in about ninety seconds if necessary. We hoped it was far enough away so that the crew wouldn't know we were there. We now had exactly two hours until the money was to be dropped. The schedule was incredibly tight. For them and for us.

Then the job got harder.

Jill Abramson from the insurance company's internal security committee and Steve Bolding from the security firm itself arrived at the Hilton. Abramson was a heavyset woman in a yellow pinstriped business suit. She looked to be in her late forties. Bolding was tall and in good shape, probably in his early fifties. He had on a blue blazer, white shirt, and jeans. They had come to the Hilton to tell us how to do our jobs.

Betsey opened her mouth to speak, but Bolding abruptly waved her off. He had something to say first. It was clear that he wanted to take control of the meeting.

"This is how it's going to be. I let you in on this, but I can also shut you right out again. I'm a former SAC with the Bureau so I know all the right moves — and all the wrong ones. We don't have time for niceties here. Agent Cavalierre, are there any leads on the identity of the

UNSUBs? It's eleven forty-six. Our zero hour is one-forty-five. *Precisely.*"

Betsey took a short breath before she answered Bolding's question. She was keeping her cool better than I would have done with the private security expert.

"Suspects, yes, but nothing we can use to help the hostages. A neighbor saw the hijacking of the bus. Two males were involved. They wore ski-style masks. The bus was spotted on DeSales Street, but we don't know if that was before or after the hostages were taken. It's now eleven forty-*seven*, Mr. Bolding."

Ms. Abramson said something that surprised all of us. "We have the money coming to the Mayflower right now. The ransom will be paid."

"On schedule," said Bolding. "We're waiting for further instructions from the hijackers. They have been incommunicado since their first contact. Our people will make the drop, and we'll make it alone."

Betsey Cavalierre finally went off on Bolding. "I listened to you, now you listen to me, mister. You *were* a SAC. I *am* a SAC. I would have been your superior if you had stayed at the Bureau, and I'm your superior now. My people will make the money drop. I'll be there — you won't. That's how it will be done!"

Both Abramson and Bolding started to argue with her, but Betsey cut them off instantly.

"That's enough bullshit out of both of you. Everything will be handled with the full knowledge of how dangerously predictable the hijackers are. If you don't like my terms, then *you're* out. I'll arrest you right here, Bolding. That goes for you, too, Ms. Abramson. We have lots of work to do — *in exactly one hour and fifty-seven minutes.*"

Chapter 59

HE WALKED AMONG THE PEOPLE in the crowded lobby and the vast *corridors to nowhere* inside the Capitol Hilton hotel. None of them had any idea what was happening, which was just as he liked it. Only he had the answers, and the questions as well.

He had already spotted the FBI agents and Metro Detective Cross as they arrived. They hadn't seen him, of course, but even if they did, there was no chance that he would be stopped and apprehended. It just couldn't happen.

This was such an incredible mismatch — his mind and experience against theirs. Sometimes, it didn't even seem like a challenge to him. That was the rub, the only problem he could see: *If he got too bored and careless, then maybe they had a chance to catch him.*

He noticed a small entourage, nervous and worried looking, cross through the lobby and head toward the hotel's cramped nest of meeting rooms. That was where the FBI had set up camp. MetroHartford had violated his warning, but he'd known they would. It really wasn't important. Not this time. He had wanted the FBI and Cross brought in on this.

Finally, he decided to leave the Hilton. He walked to the Renaissance Mayflower — *the scene of the horrific crime.* That was where the real action would be.

And that's where the Mastermind wanted to be as well. He wanted to watch, to be right there.

Chapter 60

THE KIDNAPPERS finally called MetroHartford's board of directors at ten past one. There were only thirty-five minutes left until the deadline.

We knew what would happen if we missed the deadline. Or if the kidnappers did, even if they did it on purpose.

Betsey and I hurried to the Mayflower Hotel. We caught two small breaks, but given the direction of things so far, they felt much larger. The first was that the service door of the kitchen led to a small loading dock and alley. During the Clinton inaugural, the Secret Service had parked there. We used the alley to get inside without being seen. The second break was that the FBI agents in the hotel had learned that the room where the MetroHartford board was meeting, the Chinese Room, had a unique feature that would be useful to us. There was a narrow metal staircase directly behind it. The stairs led to a cat-walk above the rotunda. There were small viewing holes there so we could watch and listen but not be seen.

Betsey and I hurried up to the catwalk and crouched high over the meeting room. We needn't have bothered.

The kidnappers were still on the line.

"We *assume* that the FBI and possibly the Washington police are involved at this point," the voice of one of the kidnappers said over the speakerphone in the Chinese Room. "We have no objection. We fully expected it. In fact, we welcome the Bureau. We've written you into the plan."

Betsey and I shared looks of exasperation. The Mastermind was making us look bad. Why? We hurried downstairs and joined the others in the Chinese Room. My head was spinning with questions. The Mastermind was good at keeping us off balance. Too good.

"First, I'm going to repeat our demands for the money," the distorted voice on the speakerphone said. "This is important. Please follow the instructions. As you know, five million of the thirty should be in uncut diamonds. The diamonds must be packed in one duffel bag. There should be no more than eight other duffels. The cash must be in twenties and fifties. No hundred-dollar bills. No dye packs. No tracking devices of any kind. Now, who am I speaking to?"

Betsey moved close to the speakerphone. So did I. "This is Special Agent Elizabeth Cavalierre. I'm Special Agent in Charge with the FBI."

"I'm Alex Cross, Washington police and liaison with the Bureau."

"Good for you. I'm familiar with both your names, your reputations. Is our money ready as requested?"

"Yes, it is. The money and the diamonds are here at the Mayflower," Betsey answered.

"Excellent! We'll be in touch."

We heard a *click* as he hung up the phone.

The CEO of MetroHartford exploded in anger. "They knew you were here! Oh Christ, what have we done! They'll kill the hostages!"

I put a firm hand on his shoulder. "Take it easy. Please. Is the payoff arranged exactly as they've requested?" I asked.

He nodded. "Exactly. The diamonds will be here any minute. The money has already arrived. We're doing our part, everything that we can. What are you people doing?"

I continued to speak in a soft voice. "And no one at MetroHartford has heard a word about where the money and diamonds are to be dropped? This is an important question."

The insurance executive was frightened, and with good reason. "You heard the man on the phone. He said they'd be in touch. *No,* we haven't heard anything about where to drop the money and diamonds."

"That's good news, Mr. Dooner. They're acting in a professional way. So are we. I don't believe they've harmed anyone yet. We'll wait for the next call. The exchange is the hardest part for them."

"My wife is on that bus," the chief executive said. "So is my daughter."

"I know," I told him. "I know."

And I also knew that the Mastermind seemed to like hurting families.

Chapter 61

IT WASN'T as if we weren't doing everything we could, but we were at their mercy so far, and our time was running out. The clock was ticking. Very fast.

No aircraft had spotted the tour bus, and that meant that the bus had gotten off the road quickly, or possibly that they'd changed the alphanumeric indicator on the roof. The heat-seeking army helicopters hadn't found anything, either. At twenty past one, another call came to the Chinese Room at the Mayflower. It was the same disturbing, machine-distorted voice.

"It's time to move. There's a delivery at the front desk for Mr. Dooner. Inside you'll find Handie-Talkies. Bring all of them."

"Where are we going?" Betsey asked.

"*We're* going to be rich. *You're* going to load the money and diamonds into a van and head north on Connecticut Avenue. If you deviate from the route I give you, a hostage will be shot."

The line went dead again.

We had a van parked in the alley outside the hotel kitchen. The kidnappers knew we did. How, though? What did that tell us? Betsey Cavalierre and I and two other agents rushed outside to the van, then headed onto Connecticut Avenue.

We were still on Connecticut when the Handie-Talkie went off. FBI agents call walkie-talkies "Handie-Talkies." So had the kidnappers on the phone. What did that clue mean? Was it a clue? Was the caller simply communicating that he knew everything about us?

"Detective Cross?"

"I'm right here. We're on Connecticut Avenue. Now what?"

"I knew you would be. Listen closely. If we see any surveillance planes or helicopters flying above your prescribed route — *a hostage will be shot*. Understand?"

"I understand perfectly," I said. I looked over at Betsey. She had to cut off air surveillance immediately. The kidnappers seemed to know everything we were doing.

"Proceed as fast as possible to the Baltimore-Washington Airport rail station. You and the FBI agents are to be on board the five-ten P.M. Northeast Corridor train from Baltimore to Boston. Bring the money duffels with you. Bring the diamonds. The five-ten to Boston! We are aware that all FBI agents in the Northeast are available to you. Get ready to use them. It doesn't matter to us. We dare you to stop the payoff. It can't be done!"

"Is this the Mastermind I'm speaking to?"

The Handie-Talkie went dead.

Chapter 62

FBI AGENTS AND LOCAL POLICE were dispatched to all the train stations along the route of the Northeast Corridor train, but blanketing the entire route would be next to impossible. The kidnappers knew that. They had everything working for them now.

Agents Cavalierre, Walsh, and Doud and I were on board the train out of Baltimore. We stationed ourselves at the front of the second car.

The rumbling train was a noisy place to be; we couldn't think straight, or even talk among ourselves very well. We waited for the next contact from the kidnappers. Every passing minute seemed longer than it really was.

"Sometime soon they're going to tell us to toss the duffel bags off the moving train," I said. "That how you figure it? Any other ideas?"

Betsey nodded. "I don't think they'll chance meeting the train in one of the stations. Why should they? They know we can't cover all of the territory between here and Boston. The ban they put on planes flying anywhere near the train was the clincher."

"They seem to have solved the tricky problem of the drop, the exchange. He is a smart son of a bitch," Agent Walsh said.

Betsey said, "He, or maybe it's a she."

I reminded her. "Tony Brophy said he met with a male, if we can believe him."

"And if the person he saw was really the Mastermind," she countered.

Agent Doud said, "The name bothers me. Makes him sound like a geek. A loser. The *Mastermind*."

"Brophy said as much. He said the man he spoke to was an asshole. But he still wanted the job," said Betsey.

"Yeah, well, the pay is good," Doud said.

Betsey shrugged. "Maybe he is a geek, maybe some kind of computer genius. I wouldn't be all that surprised. Geeks are running the world now, right? Getting even for what happened to them in high school. I sure am."

"I was reasonably cool in high school," I said, and winked.

The Handie-Talkie crackled again.

"Hi there, law-enforcement stars. The real fun's about to start. Remember, if we see any choppers or planes near the train, *a hostage will be shot*," the familiar male voice instructed. Was it the Mastermind?

"How do we know the hostages are still alive?" Betsey asked. "Why should we trust you to tell the truth? You've murdered innocent people before."

"You *don't*. You *shouldn't*. We *have*. The bus hostages

are alive, though. All right — open the train doors now! Get ready for my next signal. Get the duffel bags up to the door! Now, now, now! Move it! Don't make us kill somebody."

Chapter 63

THE FOUR OF US rushed to get the heavy bags of money to the nearest train door. I was already starting to sweat. My face and scalp felt flushed.

"Get ready! Get ready!" The voice on the Handie-Talkie yelled out frantic commands. *"This is it."*

Betsey was already on another two-way alerting her people. The countryside was flashing by in bright greens and muddy browns. We were somewhere near Aberdeen, Maryland, having passed through the last station about seven minutes earlier.

"Get ready! Are you ready? Don't disappoint me!" the voice squawked loudly.

So far, the only trick we had come up with was to try to spread out the area where the money bags would fall. We had even considered keeping one bag on board, which might force them to search for a while. But we agreed that was too dangerous for the hostages.

The Handie-Talkie went dead again.

"Fuck!" Doud exclaimed.

"Do we throw the money bags out?" Walsh yelled over the rumble of the train and the rushing wind.

"No! Wait!" I yelled at him and Doud, who was leaning precariously over the train's edge. "Wait for their instructions! He would have told us to throw the money off. Don't throw the bags!"

"Son of a bitch!" Betsey shouted as she swung her arm around in a fast, hard arc. "They're messing with us. They're laughing at us right now."

"Yes, they probably are," I said. "Let's keep our cool. We have to keep it together."

The FBI was going crazy trying to track the channel the kidnappers were using for the two-way radios. It wasn't working. The two-ways were state-of-the-art, the kind the military used. The scrambler chips in them were encoded to change the frequency each time they were used. It was even possible that the kidnappers had several two-ways and were discarding them after each call.

Betsey was still incensed. Her brown eyes flashed. "He's thought of everything, including not giving us time to plan. Who is this bastard?"

The Handie-Talkie crackled again.

"Open the door! Get ready to heave the bags out," the radio voice suddenly commanded again.

I grabbed two bags full of twenty- and fifty-dollar bills. My heart was in my throat as I rushed to the open door a second time. The wind outside roared.

The train was hurtling through deep woods now, elms and pines and thick brush. I saw no houses — or anyone lurking in the woods. It seemed like a good spot for the drop-off.

The Handie-Talkie went dead again!

"Assholes!" Agent Doud yelled at the top of his voice. The rest of us groaned and dropped to the floor.

The voice repeated the drill eleven times in the next hour and a quarter. Three times we were made to move all the money to different cars on the train.

We were sent all the way to the last car — then we were immediately ordered back to the front again.

"You guys are good. Very obedient," said the radio voice.

Then the two-way was silent again.

Chapter 64

"I CAN'T STAND THIS!" Betsey yelled. "Goddamn him to hell! I want to kill that bastard." The money bags were oversized and heavy; we were exhausted from lugging them through the train. We were covered with perspiration and dirt and soot. Jumpy and on edge. The constant rattle of the train was noisier than ever.

The Amtrak train was rushing through deep woods again. Its horn blared loudly. Agent Walsh was keeping track of the stations we'd passed.

Then the Handie-Talkie came to life again. "Get those bags of money and diamonds ready. Open the doors now! And when you toss them — throw them out close together. If you don't, a hostage will be shot! We're watching every move you make. You're very pretty, Agent Cavalierre."

"Yeah, and you're a geek," Betsey muttered to herself. Her pale blue T-shirt was stained darker with sweat. Her black hair stuck close to her scalp. If she'd had an ounce of fat on her before, she'd lost it during the jarring train ride.

"False alarm," the voice on the radio said with obvious glee. "As you were. That's all for the moment."

The two-way went dead again.

"Shit!"

Everyone collapsed onto the duffel bags and lay there breathing heavily. I was trying to keep my brain working in straight lines, but it was getting harder after each false alarm. I really wasn't sure if I could make another run to the other end of the train.

"Maybe we should get off the train with the money bags," Walsh spoke from his perch on the bags. "Screw up their timing, at least. Do something they don't expect."

"It's an idea, but too dangerous for the hostages," Betsey told him.

Walsh and Doud cursed loudly when the two-way came on again. We had almost reached our limit. What *was* our limit?

"No rest for the wicked," the voice said. We could hear the pop of a soft drink or beer can being opened. Then a sigh of refreshment. "Or maybe the line should be, rest for the wicked?"

The radio voice screamed at us. "Throw out the bags now! Do it! We're watching the train. We see you! Throw the bags or we kill all of them!"

We had no choice; no options had been left open to us. It was all we could do to try to throw the bags off close to one another. We were too tired to move as fast as we might have. I felt as if I were moving in a dream. My clothes were soaking wet, my arms and legs sore.

"Throw the bags faster!" the voice commanded. "Let's see those muscles, Agent Cavalierre."

Could he see us? Probably. It sounded like it. No doubt he was in the woods with his two-way. How many of them were there?

When the nine bags were gone, the train rushed around a sharp bend in the tracks. We couldn't see what was happening fifty yards behind us. We fell to the floor, cursing and moaning.

Betsey gasped. "Goddamn them. They did it. They got away with it. Oh, goddamn them to hell."

The Handie-Talkie came on again. He wasn't finished with us. "Thanks for the help. You guys are the best. You can always get a job bagging groceries at the local A&P. Might not be a bad career option after this."

"Are you the Mastermind?" I asked.

The line went dead.

The radio voice was gone and so were the money and diamonds, and they still had the nineteen hostages.

Chapter 65

SEVEN MILES AHEAD, Agents Cavalierre, Doud, and Walsh and I stumbled off the train at the next available station.

Two black Suburbans were waiting for us. Standing around the vehicles were several FBI agents with rifles. A crowd of people had gathered at the station. They were pointing at the guns and agents as if they'd spotted the Washington Redskins fresh from a hunting trip.

We were given up-to-the-minute information. "It appears they're already out of the woods," an agent told us. "Kyle Craig is on his way here now. We're setting up roadblocks, but they'll be hit-and-miss. There is some good news, though. We might have caught a break on the tour bus."

Moments later, we were being patched in to a woman from Tinden, a small town in Virginia. Supposedly, the woman had information on the whereabouts of the bus.

She said she would only talk to "the police," and that she didn't much care for the FBI and their methods.

Only after I identified myself was the elderly woman willing to talk to me. She sounded nervous.

Her name was Isabelle Morris and she had sighted a tour bus in the farmlands out in Warren County. She'd become suspicious because she owned the local bus company and the bus wasn't one of hers.

"The bus was blue with gold stripes?" Betsey asked without identifying herself as FBI.

"Blue and gold. Not one of mine. So I don't know what the tour vehicle would be doing here," Mrs. Morris said. "No reason for a bus like that to be out in these parts. This is redneck territory. Tinden isn't on any tours that I know of."

"Did you get the license number, or at least a part of it?" I asked her.

She seemed annoyed by the question. "I had no earthly reason to check the license number. Why would I do that?"

"Mrs. Morris, then why *did* you report the bus to the local police?"

"I told you, if you were listening before. There's no reason for a tour bus out here. Besides, my boyfriend is on the local citizens' patrol hereabouts. I'm a widow, y'see. He's the one actually called the police. Why are *you* so interested, may I ask?"

"Mrs. Morris, when you saw the tour bus, were there any passengers on board?"

Betsey and I glanced at each other while we waited for her to answer.

"No, just the driver. He was a large fellow. I didn't see anyone else. What about the police? And the infernal FBI? Why are you all so interested?"

"I'll get to that in a minute. Did you notice *any* identification on the bus? A destination sign? A logo? Anything you might have seen would be a help to us. People's lives are in danger."

"Oh, my," she said then. "Yes, there was a sticker on the side: *Visit Williamsburg.* I remember seeing it. You know what else? I think the bus might have said Washington on Wheels on the side panel. Yes, I'm almost sure it did. Washington on Wheels. Is that any help to you?"

Chapter 66

BETSEY WAS ALREADY on another line talking to Kyle Craig. They were making a plan to get us to Tinden, Virginia, in a hurry. Mrs. Morris continued to talk my ear off. Bits and pieces were coming back to her. She told me that she had seen the tour bus turn onto a small country road not far from where she lived.

"There are only three farms on the road, and I know 'em all very well. Two of the farms border a deserted army base built in the eighties. I've got to check this funny business out for myself," she said.

I interrupted her right there. "*No, no.* You sit tight, Mrs. Morris. Don't move a muscle. We're on our way to you."

"I know the area. I can help you," she protested.

"We're on our way. Please stay put."

One of the FBI helicopters searching the nearby woods was brought over to the railroad station. Just as it was arriving — so did Kyle. I'd never been so glad to see him.

Betsey told Kyle exactly what she hoped to do in Virginia. "We take the chopper in as close as we can without being spotted. Four or five miles from the town of Tinden. I don't want too large a ground force involved. A dozen good people, maybe less."

Kyle agreed to the plan, because it was a good one, and we were off in the FBI chopper. He knew the agents at Quantico he wanted involved and he dispatched them to Tinden.

Once we were on board the helicopter we reviewed everything we had learned during the previous bank robberies. We also began to receive information on the area where Mrs. Morris had seen the bus. The army base she mentioned had been a nuke site in the 1980s. "ICBMs were kept underground at several nuke bases outside Washington," Kyle said. "If the tour bus is on the site, a concrete silo could shield it from heat-seeking search helicopters."

Our chopper began to settle down onto an open area near a regional high school. I glanced at my watch. It was just past six o'clock. Were the nineteen hostages still alive? What sadistic game was the Mastermind playing?

Bright green athletic fields stretched out behind an idyllic-looking two-story redbrick school. The entire area was deserted except for two sedans and a black van waiting for us. We were four or five miles from the state road where Mrs. Morris had seen the Washington on Wheels bus.

Isabelle Morris was sitting in the first sedan. She looked to be in her late seventies, a stout woman with an inappropriately cheery, false-teeth smile. Somebody's nice grandmother.

"Which farm should we go to first?" I asked her. "Where might somebody be hiding?"

The old woman's bluish-gray eyes narrowed to slits as she thought. "Donald Browne's farm," she finally said. "Nobody lives there these days. Browne died last spring, poor man. Someone could hide out there easy."

Chapter 67

"KEEP GOING. DRIVE BY," I told our driver as we reached the Browne farm on State Road 24. He did as I asked. We curled around a bend in the road about a hundred yards farther on. Then the car eased to a stop.

"I saw somebody on the grounds. He was leaning against a tree. Up near the house. He was watching the road, Kyle. Watching us go by. *They're still here.*"

Up ahead, I could see the remains of the old missile site that had once been in operation out here. I figured we would find the tour bus hidden in a missile silo, safe from the Apache search helicopters. I wasn't so optimistic about the nineteen hostages from MetroHartford. The Mastermind hated insurance companies, didn't he? Was this about revenge?

I was flashing lurid images of the hostages who'd been killed during the bank robberies; I was afraid of finding a massacre scene at the farm. We had been warned. No errors, no mistakes. The rules had been enforced during the bank jobs. Had anything changed?

Kyle said, "Let's go in through the woods. We don't have time to be choosy."

He made contact with the other units. Then he, Betsey, and I ran due north through the dense woods. We couldn't see the farmhouse yet, but we couldn't be seen, either.

The woods came up close to the main house, which was fortunate for us. The brush was mostly overgrown, almost all the way to the driveway. The lights were off inside the house. There was no movement that I could make out. No sound.

I could still see the sentry for the kidnappers. He wasn't too far away and he had his back to us. Where were the others? Where were the hostages? Why weren't any lights on in the house?

"What the hell is he doing?" Kyle muttered. He was just as mystified as I was.

"Not much of a lookout," Betsey whispered. "I don't like it."

"Me, either," I said. It made no sense. Why put out a single sentry? And why would the kidnappers still be here?

"Let's take him down first. Then we move on the house," Kyle whispered.

Chapter 68

I GESTURED TO KYLE AND BETSEY that I was going after the sentry. I got to him quickly and with a minimum of noise. I swung out hard with the butt of my pistol. There was a satisfying crunch, and the kidnapper crumpled to the ground. He never made a sound. *It was too easy. What the hell was going on?*

Betsey was crouched low, coming up to me fast. She whispered, "What the hell kind of lookout was that? They've always been careful before."

A half dozen agents appeared out of the woods behind us. Betsey signaled for them to stop. There still were no lights in the farmhouse and no movement. The scene was eerie and unreal.

Then Kyle gave the order to go, to move on the house. We were quiet as we ran forward. There didn't seem to be any more sentries or guards. Was this some kind of trap? Were they expecting us to break inside? What about Mrs. Morris? Could she be part of this?

I got to the farmhouse with the first wave of agents and I was filled with a sense of dread. I raised my Glock and kicked the front door open. I couldn't believe my eyes. I had to stop myself from shouting out loud.

The hostage group was there in the farmhouse living room. They were staring at me, clearly frightened, but no one was hurt. I did a quick count: sixteen women, two children, and the driver. All alive. No one punished because we'd broken the rules.

"The kidnappers?" I asked in a low voice. "Are any of them still here?"

A dark-haired woman stepped forward and spoke. "They left sentries around the house. There's one man by the elm tree in front."

"Not anymore. We didn't see any others," Betsey told the group. "Everybody stay right here while we look around."

FBI agents were inside and spreading out all over the house. Some of the hostages began to cry when they realized they weren't going to die, that they'd finally been rescued.

"They said we'd be killed if we tried to leave the house before tomorrow morning. They told us about the Buccieri and Casselman families," a tall, dark-haired woman said between sobs. Her name was Mary Jordan and she'd been in charge of the tour group.

We did a careful search of the house — no one else was there. There wasn't any obvious evidence, but the technicians would be here soon. The tour bus had already been found in a shed on the former army base.

After half an hour or so, Mrs. Morris came waddling through the front door. A couple of agents were futilely trying to stop her. The local woman's appearance was an almost comical punctuation to the stress of the last several hours. "Why did you hit old Bud O'Mara? He's just a nice fella, works at the truck stop. Bud said he was paid to stand around and wait. Got all of a hundred bucks for the dent in his skull. He's harmless, Bud is."

An odd and exhilarating thing happened as several rescue vehicles finally arrived. The hostages started to clap and to cheer. We'd come for them; we hadn't let them die.

But I knew otherwise: For some reason, the Mastermind hadn't wanted them to die.

Part Four

HIT AND RUN

Chapter 69

OF COURSE, the case continued to be a full-blown knock-down-drag-out media event. The press had learned about the existence of a "Mastermind," and it made for sensational headlines. A picture of the Buccieri boy, one of the first victims, was the featured art in story after story. I had begun seeing the little boy's face in my dreams.

I was working twelve- and sixteen-hour days. The Washington bank robber named Mitchell Brand was still high on the list of FBI suspects. He had been up on the wall of suspects for over a week. We hadn't been able to locate Brand, but he fit the profile. Meanwhile, crime-scene investigators covered the money pickup site, combing it for evidence. FBI technicians went over every square inch of the Browne farmhouse. Traces of theatrical makeup were found in the sink of the farmhouse. I talked to several hostages, and they supported the idea that the kidnappers might have worn makeup, wigs, and possibly lifts in their shoes.

Sampson and I worked in Washington the first two days. MetroHartford had offered a million-dollar reward for information leading to the capture of the men involved in the crime. The reward was aimed at the general public, but also at anyone involved in the robbery whose take was less than the reward being offered.

The search for the bank robber Mitchell Brand was also centered in Washington. Brand was a thirty-year-old black man who was suspected in half a dozen robberies, but who had never been officially charged and suddenly had gone underground. Once upon a time he had been an army sergeant in Desert Storm. Brand was known to be violent. According to his army records, he had an IQ over one-fifty.

A mountain of evidence was being collected, but the notoriety of the case was also working against us. The phone calls and faxes offering tips never stopped coming at the FBI field office. Suddenly, there were hundreds of leads to follow up. I wondered if the Mastermind was still working against us.

The second night after the MetroHartford kidnapping, Sampson showed up at the house around eleven. I had just gotten there myself. I grabbed a couple of cold beers and we talked out on the sunporch more or less like civilized adults.

"I was hoping to see the little prince tonight," Sampson said as we sat down.

"He's coming here to live with us." I told John the latest news. Some of it, anyway.

He broke into a broad smile, his teeth as large and

white as piano keys. "That's great news, sugar. I assume Ms. Christine is coming as part of the package."

I shook my head. "No, she isn't, John. She's never gotten over what happened with Geoffrey Shafer. She's still afraid for her life, for all of our lives. She doesn't want to see me anymore. It's over between us."

Sampson just stared at me. "You two were so good together. I don't buy it, sugar."

"I didn't, either. Not for months. I offered to leave police work and I guess I would have. Christine told me it wouldn't matter."

I stared into my friend's eyes. "I've lost her, John. I'm trying to move on. It breaks my heart."

Chapter 70

MY BEEPER went off late the following night at the house. It was Sampson. "All hell is breaking loose," he said. "Seriously, Alex."

"Where are you?" I asked.

"I'm with Rakeem Powell right now. We're over at the East Capitol Dwellings. One of his snitches gave us something good. We might have located Mitchell Brand."

"What's the problem, then?" I asked.

"Rakeem called his lieutenant. The lou called the Jefe. Chief Pittman has half of D.C. on the way here now."

I think I actually saw red at that moment. "It's still my goddamn case. Pittman didn't contact me."

"That's why I'm calling you, sugar. Better burn on over here."

I met Sampson at the East Capitol Dwellings housing project. According to the snitch, Brand was holed up there. East Capitol Dwellings are what I've heard called a "subsidized human warehouse." Actually, the project looks like a failed prison. Cold, white cinder-block fences surround bunkerlike buildings. It's thoroughly depressing and not atypical of housing in much of Southeast. The poor people who live here do the best they can under the circumstances.

"This has gotten out of control, Alex," Sampson complained once we were together in one of the dirt-patch yards separating the project buildings. "Way too much firepower here. Too many cooks in the kitchen. The chief of detectives strikes again."

I looked around, shook my head, and cursed under my breath. It was a goddamn zoo. I saw SWAT personnel and several homicide detectives. Plus the usual neighborhood looky-loos. *Mitchell Brand. Jesus. Could he possibly be the Mastermind?*

I quickly put on a Kevlar vest. I checked my Glock. Then I went and talked to the chief of detectives. I reminded Pittman that this was my case, and he couldn't argue with that. I could tell he was surprised that I was at the scene, though.

"I'll take it from here," I said.

"We've got Brand all set up. Just don't fuck it up," Pittman finally snarled, then walked away from me.

Chapter 71

SENIOR AGENT JAMES WALSH arrived on the scene after I did. No Betsey Cavalierre, though. I went up to Walsh. He and I had gotten friendly over the past couple of weeks, but he seemed distant tonight. He didn't like what was going on here, either. He'd been called late, too.

"Where's Senior Agent Cavalierre?" I asked.

"She had a couple days off. I think she's visiting a friend in Maryland. You know this Mitchell Brand?" he asked.

"I know enough about him. He'll probably be heavily armed if he's up there. He apparently has a new girlfriend named Theresa Lopez. She lives in the project. Lopez has three kids. I know her by sight."

"That's really great," Walsh said, and shook his head, rolled his eyes. "Three kids, their mommy, and an armed bank-robbing suspect."

"You got it. Welcome to D.C., Agent Walsh. Anyway, Brand could have been part of the team that struck Metro-

Hartford. He could be the Mastermind. We have to go get him."

I met with the raid team at an OP, an observation point, in a nearby building. The OP was a studio apartment used by Metro narcotics detectives assigned to the East Capitol Dwellings project. I had been in the apartment a few times before. This was my neighborhood.

A team of eight of us would go into the sixth-floor apartment to take down Mitchell Brand. Eight was more than enough; there's only safety in numbers up to a point.

As the team checked weapons and put on Kevlars, I stared out onto the streets. Sodium-vapor streetlights created a yellow fuzziness down below. What a bad scene. Even with this much police presence in the neighborhood, the drug game continued. Nothing could stop it. I watched a brazen team of lookouts and steerers selling crack on the far corner, beyond the projects. An addict approached, quick-stepping, his head down. A local foolio, a familiar sight to me. I turned away from the drug deal as if it weren't happening.

I began to talk to the team. "Mitchell Brand is wanted for questioning in the robbery of a Union Trust in Falls Church. He could definitely be our link to whoever is behind the robberies. This is the best suspect we've come up with so far. He *could* be the Mastermind.

"As best we can tell, Brand is up in the girlfriend's apartment. She's a new honey for him. Detective Sampson will pass around a standard layout for a one-bedroom in the building. You should know that inside the one-bedroom we may find Brand, his girlfriend, and her three children, aged two to six."

I turned to Agent Walsh. Two of his agents were part of

the go team. He had nothing to add, but he told his men, "The Washington police will act as the primary at the apartment. We will be backup in the hallway and going into the girlfriend's apartment. That's about it," he said.

"Okay, let's move out," I said. "Everybody use extreme care. Everything we know about Brand says he's dangerous and will be heavily armed."

"He was Special Forces, Army," John Sampson added. "How's that for whipped cream on shit?"

Chapter 72

ARMED AND DANGEROUS — it is a common enough catchphrase, but with real meaning to police officers.

We entered Building Three single file through the dingy, underlit basement, then we hurriedly marched up several flights of stairs toward the sixth floor. The stairway was dirty and stained the color of bad teeth. There might have been a serious fire in the building at one time. Heavy soot caked the walls, the floor, and even the metal banister. Could the Mastermind be hiding up here? Was he a black man? That seemed unthinkable to the FBI. Why?

Suddenly, we surprised a pair of pathetic, bone-thin crackheads lighting up on the fourth-floor stairwell. We had our guns out, and they stared at us bug-eyed, afraid to be there, afraid to move.

"We didn't do nothin' to nobody," one of the men

finally said in a scratchy gargle. He looked well past forty but was probably only in his twenties.

"As you were," I said in a low voice. I sternly pointed a finger at them. "Not even a whisper."

The paranoid junkies must have thought that we were coming for them. The two crackheads couldn't believe it when we hurried right past them. I heard Sampson say, "Get the fuck out of here. It's your *last* lucky day."

I could hear infants crying and small children shouting, the babble of several TV sets, and jazz and hip-hop and salsa music leaking through the thin walls. My stomach was knotted up. Moving in on Brand in a crowded building was a very bad deal, but everybody wanted results now. Brand *was* an excellent suspect.

Sampson lightly touched my shoulder. "I'll go in with Rakeem," he said. "You *follow*, sugar. Don't argue with me."

I frowned but nodded. Sampson and Rakeem Powell were the best marksmen we had. They were careful and smart and experienced, but this was a tough, scary bust. *Armed and dangerous*. Anything could happen now.

I turned to a detective who held a heavy metal ram with two hands. It looked like a small, blunt missile. "Take the door right the hell down, officer. I'm not asking you to knock first."

I looked back at the lineup of tense and anxious men behind me. I held up one fist. "We're going on four," I said.

I gestured with my fingers — one — two — three!

The battering ram hit the door with all the shattering force of an NFL blocking fullback. The door locks blew right off. We were inside. Sampson and Powell were a step ahead of me. No shots had been fired yet.

"Mom-mee!" One of the small children screeched an alarm. I had an instant of fear about the families that had been hurt already because of the Mastermind. We didn't need any blood to flow here.

Armed and dangerous.

Two kids were watching *South Park* on TV. Where was Mitchell Brand? And where was the kids' mother, Theresa Lopez? Maybe they weren't even home. Sometimes kids got left alone in apartments for days.

The bedroom door in front of us was closed. Music was playing somewhere in the apartment. If Mitchell Brand was here tonight, he wasn't too security conscious. That didn't track very well for me. I didn't like anything about this so far.

I yanked open the bedroom door and peered inside. My heart was thundering. I was in a crouched shooting stance. A third small child was playing with a teddy bear on the floor. "Blue Bear," she told me.

"Blue Bear," I whispered.

I stepped back fast into the hallway. I saw Sampson kick another door open. *The apartment layout we'd been given was wrong! This was a two-bedroom apartment.*

Suddenly, Mitchell Brand came out into the hallway. He was dragging along Theresa Lopez. He had a .45-caliber handgun pressed up against her forehead. She was a pretty, light brown–skinned woman, shaking badly. Both Brand and Lopez were naked except for gold chains around his thick neck, wrist, and left ankle.

"Put down the gun, Brand," I shouted above the din in

the apartment. "You're not going anywhere. You can't get out of here. You're smart enough to know that. *Put down the gun.*"

"Just get out of my way!" he shouted. "I'm smart enough to put a hole in your face first."

I stood my ground in front of Brand. Sampson and Rakeem Powell came up on either side. "The First Union Bank job in Falls Church. If you're not involved, you've got no problem," I said, lowering my voice some. "Put down the gun."

Brand yelled again. "I didn't rob the First Union Bank! I was in New York City the whole week! I was at a weddin', Theresa's sister. *Somebody set me up. Somebody did this to me!*"

Theresa Lopez was starting to sob uncontrollably. Her children were crying and calling out for their mother. Detectives and FBI agents held them back, kept them safe.

"He was at my sister's wedding!" Theresa Lopez screamed at me. Her eyes were pleading. *"He was at a wedding!"*

"Mommee! Mommee!" the kids cried.

"Put the gun down, Brand. Get some clothes on. We need to talk to you. I *believe* you were at a wedding. I believe you and Theresa. *Put the gun down.*"

I was aware that my shirt was soaked through to the skin. One of the children was still lurking behind Brand and Lopez. In the line of fire. *Oh, God, don't make me shoot this man.*

Then, slowly, Mitchell Brand lowered his gun from the forehead of Theresa Lopez. He kissed the side of her head. "Sorry, baby," he whispered.

I was already thinking we'd made a mistake. I felt it in

my gut. When he lowered his gun, I *knew* it. Maybe somebody had set up Mitchell Brand. We'd wasted a lot of time and resources to capture him. We had been distracted for days.

I felt the cold breath of the Mastermind on the back of my neck.

Chapter 73

I CAME HOME VERY LATE from the East Capitol
Dwellings project. I wasn't feeling too hot about a lot of
things: working too much, Christine, the arrest that night
of Mitchell Brand.

I needed to wind down, so I played Gershwin and Cole
Porter on the piano until I couldn't keep my eyes open
any longer. Then I climbed upstairs. I fell fast asleep as
soon as my head collided with the pillow.

I actually slept in the next morning. I finally joined
Nana and Damon for breakfast around seven-thirty. This
was a big day for the Cross family. I wouldn't even be
going in to work. I had better things to do.

We left the house at eight-thirty. We were on our way
to St. Anthony's Hospital. Jannie was coming home.

She was waiting on us. Jannie was all packed up
and dressed in blue jeans and a "Concern for the Earth"
T-shirt when we arrived at her room. Nana had brought
her clothes the day before, but of course Jannie had told
Nana exactly what to bring.

"Let's go, let's go. I can't wait to get home," she giggled and motormouthed as soon as we walked in the door. "Here's my suitcase, what's the hurry?" She handed her little pink American Tourister to Damon and he rolled his eyes, but he took the overnighter from her anyway.

"How long is this special treatment supposed to last?" he asked.

"Rest of your life." She set her brother straight about men and women. "Maybe even longer than that."

Suddenly, a storm cloud of fear crossed Jannie's face. "I can go home, can't I?" she asked me.

I nodded and smiled. "You sure can. But what you *can't* do is walk out of here by yourself. Hospital rules, little sister."

Jannie looked a little crestfallen. "Not in a wheelchair. My grand exit."

I reached down and picked her up. "Yes, in a wheelchair," I said. "But you're all dressed up now. You look beautiful for your departure, princess."

We stopped off at the nurses' station and Jannie said her good-byes and got some big hugs. Then we finally left St. Anthony's Hospital.

She was well now. The tests on the removed tumor had come back benign. She had a clean bill of health, and I had never felt so relieved in my life. If I had ever forgotten how precious she was to me, and I doubt that I had, I never would again. Jannie, Damon, and little Alex were my treasures.

It took us less than ten minutes to ride home, and Jannie was like a frisky little pup in the car. She had her face out the open window and was gazing wide-eyed at everything and sniffing the smoky city air, which she proclaimed spectacular, absolutely brilliant.

When we got to the house and I parked the car, Jannie climbed out slowly, almost reverently. She stared up at our old homestead as if it were the Cathedral of Notre Dame. She did a three-hundred-and-sixty-degree turn, checked out our neighborhood on Fifth Street, and nodded her approval.

"There's no place like home," she finally whispered. "Just like in the *Wizard of Oz*." She turned to me. "You even got the Batman and Robin kite down out of the tree. Praise the Lord."

I grinned and I could feel something good spreading through my body. I knew what it was. *I wasn't petrified of losing Jannie anymore.* "Actually, Nana climbed out there and got the kite down," I said.

"You, stop." Nana Mama laughed and waved a hand at me.

We followed Jannie inside the house and she immediately picked up Rosie the Cat. She held Rosie close to her face and got licked with Rosie's sandpaper tongue. Then she slowly danced with the family cat for a magical moment or two, just as she had on the night of little Alex's christening.

Jannie softly sang, "Roses are red, violets are blue, I'm so happy I'm home, I love all of you."

It was so fine and good to watch and be a part of — *and yes, Jannie Cross, you're right, there is no place like home. Maybe that's why I work so fiercely to protect it.*

But then again, maybe I'm just rationalizing about the way I am, and probably always will be.

Chapter 74

I WENT TO THE FBI FIELD OFFICE early the next morning. The floor was buzzing with faxes, phones, personal computers, and energy — good and bad. It was already pretty clear that Mitchell Brand wasn't our man, and maybe even that he had been set up.

Betsey Cavalierre had returned from her weekend off. She had a tan, a bright smile, and looked nicely rested. I wondered briefly where she had been, but then I was sucked into the powerful vortex of the investigation again.

The high-tech FBI war room was still in place, but now three of the four walls were covered with possible leads. The FBI point of view was that every avenue must be explored. The director had already gone on record saying that it was the largest manhunt in FBI history. Corporate America was applying enormous pressure. The same thing had happened after the Unabomber had killed a New Jersey businessman in the early nineties.

I spent most of the day in a windowless, seemingly airless conference room watching an endless slide show. along with several agents and other Metro police detectives. Suspects were continuously shown on the big screen, then discussed and placed into three categories: *Discard, Active,* and *Extremely Active.*

At six o'clock that night, Senior Agent Walsh held a meeting that covered the possibility that the crew might strike again soon. Betsey Cavalierre arrived late for the briefing. She sat in the back and observed.

Two FBI behavioral psychologists had worked up a list of potential future targets for the Mastermind. The targets included multinational banks, other top insurance companies, credit card companies, communications conglomerates, and Wall Street firms.

One of the behavioral psychologists, Dr. Joanna Rodman, stated that the robberies demonstrated venom and hatred — the likes of which she'd never seen before. She said the perpetrators relished outwitting authorities and possibly hungered for fame and notoriety.

Dr. Rodman then made her most challenging statement. She believed that the Mastermind would strike again. "I'm willing to bet on it," she said, "and I'm not a betting type of person."

I remained quiet for most of the meeting. I preferred to sit in the back of the class and listen. That was the way I had gone through Georgetown undergraduate and then Johns Hopkins.

Agent Cavalierre would have none of it. "Dr. Cross, what do you think about the possibility of our Mastermind hitting again?" she asked shortly after Dr. Rodman finished speaking. "Care to make *your bet?*"

I rubbed my lower face and I remembered that I'd had the same tic in grad school. I sat up in my seat.

"I'm not a betting person, either. I think the list of potential targets is thorough. I agree with most of what's been said. One person is running this thing. Different crews were recruited for very specific tasks."

I frowned slightly at Betsey, then I went on. "I think the first robbery-murders were supposed to terrify everybody. They did. But in the MetroHartford job, the crew was supposed to operate quickly and efficiently, *without bloodshed.* I didn't see evidence of venom or hatred in the MetroHartford kidnapping. Not from what the hostages told us. That's inconsistent with the earlier bank robberies. The fact that no one was killed makes me believe . . . that it's all over. It's done."

"Thirty million and out?" Betsey Cavalierre asked. "That's it?"

I nodded. "I think the Mastermind's game now is — catch me if you can. And by the way — *you can't.*"

Chapter 75

BETSEY CAVALIERRE came up to me after the briefing ended. "Not to be a total suck-up, but I agree with
you," she said. "I think he might be playing with us. He
may have even set up Mitchell Brand."

"I think it's possible," I said. "Strange and insane as it
seems on the face of it. He has a huge ego, he's compet-
ing, and that's the best thing we have going for us right
now. It's the only small edge that we have."

"We're going to break for the night. Have a drink with
me downstairs, Alex. I want to talk to you. I promise not
to babble about the Mastermind."

I winced. "Betsey, I have to get home tonight. My little
girl came back from the hospital yesterday," I told her.
"Sorry. I can't believe this has happened twice. I'm not
trying to avoid you."

She smiled kindly. "I understand, and it's no big deal. I
just have this sixth sense that you need somebody to talk
to. Go home. I've got plenty to do here. One more thing.

A team of us is heading to Hartford tomorrow. We're going to interview employees and former employees at MetroHartford. You should be part of the group. It's important, Alex. We leave from Bolling field at around eight."

"I'll be there at Bolling. Somehow, we'll get the Mastermind. If he did set up Mitchell Brand, it's his first mistake. It means he's taking chances he doesn't have to take."

I went home and had a fabulous dinner with Nana and the kids, the best in all of Washington that night. Nana had cooked a turkey, which she does once every couple of months. She says that the white meat of a turkey, properly prepared, is too good to have only twice a year, at Christmas and Thanksgiving.

"You see this, Alex?" she asked, and handed me an article she'd clipped from the *Washington Post*. It was a listing compiled by the Children's Rights Council on the best, and worst, places to raise a child. Washington, D.C., was dead last.

"I did see it," I told her. I couldn't resist a little dig. "Now you see why I work late so many nights. I'm trying to help clean up a big mess here in our capital city."

Nana looked me in the eye. "You're losing, big guy," she said.

Irony of ironies, it was the night we always reserved for our weekly boxing lesson. Jannie insisted that I go downstairs with Damon and that she be allowed to watch. Damon had a line ready for the occasion. "You just want to see if I get sent to the hospital, too."

Jannie retorted, "Lame. Besides, Dr. Petito said the boxing lessons, and your 'phantom punch,' had nothing to do with my tumor. Don't kid yourself, Damo, you are no Muhammad Ali."

So we went down to the cellar and we concentrated on footwork — the basics. I even showed the kids how Ali had dazzled Sonny Liston in the first two fights in Miami and Lewiston, Maine, and then done the same to Floyd Patterson after Patterson had taunted him for months before the fight.

"Is this a boxing lesson or about ancient history?" Damon finally asked, his voice a mild complaint.

"Two for the price of one!" Jannie shouted with glee. "Can't beat that. Boxing and history. Works for me." She was back in all her glory.

After the kids went up to bed, I called Christine and got her answering machine again. She wouldn't pick up. I felt as if a knife had been slid between my ribs. I knew I had to move on with my life, but I kept hoping I could get Christine to change her mind. Not if she wouldn't talk to me. Or even let me talk to little Alex. I was missing him badly.

I wound up playing the piano again, and I was reminded that jelly is a food that usually winds up on white bread, children's faces, and piano keys.

I carefully wiped down the piano, then I played Bach and Mozart to soothe my soul. It didn't work.

Chapter 76

THE NEXT MORNING I arrived at Bolling Air Force Base in Anacostia at ten to eight. SAC Cavalierre and three other agents, including James Walsh, got there promptly at eight. The behaviorist from Quantico, Dr. Joanna Rodman, showed up a couple of minutes late. We took off in a Bell helicopter that was shiny black, both official and important looking. We were off hunting the Mastermind. I hoped he wasn't doing the same thing with us.

We arrived at the downtown MetroHartford headquarters at nine-thirty. As I entered the office building, I had the overwhelming feeling that the place had been consciously designed by the insurance company to inspire trust, even awe. The lobby had enormously high ceilings, glinty glass everywhere, polished black-ice floors, and overscaled modern art screaming from the walls. In contrast to the grand public space, the offices inside looked as if they had been designed by either the junior architect of the firm or its resident hack. Warrens of half-walled cubicles filled large, airless rooms on every floor. There was lots of "prairie-dogging" out of the cubes, plenty of fodder for "Dilbert" satire. The FBI had sent agents here before today, but now it was time for the big guns to go to work.

I saw twenty-eight people that day and I quickly found out that few of the MetroHartford's employees had any sense of humor. *What's there to laugh about?* seemed to be the company motto. It also hit me that there were a very few risk-takers among the people I met. Several of them actually said, "You can never be too careful."

My very last interview turned out to be the most intriguing. It was with a woman named Hildie Rader. I was bored and distracted, but her opening line perked me right up.

"I think I *met* one of the kidnappers. He was here in downtown Hartford. I was as close to him as I am to you right now," she said.

Chapter 77

I TRIED NOT to show too much surprise. "Why didn't you tell anybody before?" I asked.

"I called in to the hot line MetroHartford set up. I talked to a couple of ding-a-lings. This is the first anyone *got back to me*."

"You have my full attention, Hildie," I told her.

She was a large woman with a pretty, homey smile. She was forty-two years old and had worked as an executive secretary. She was no longer with MetroHartford, which might have been why no one had interviewed her earlier. She had been fired *twice* by the insurance company. The first time she was let go was during one of the company's periodic and fairly regular belt-tightenings. Two years later Hildie was rehired, but she had been let go three months ago because of what she described as "bad chemistry" with her boss, the CFO of MetroHartford, Louis Fincher. Fincher's wife had been one of the tour-bus hostages.

"Tell me about the man you met in Hartford, the one you believe might have been involved with the hostage-taking," I asked after I'd let her talk.

"Is there any money in this for me?" she asked, eye-balling me suspiciously. "I'm presently unemployed, you know."

"The company is offering a reward for information that leads to a conviction."

She shook her head and laughed. "Hah! That sounds like a long, drawn-out affair. Besides, I should trust the word of Metro?"

I couldn't deny what she'd said. I waited for her to collect her thoughts. I sensed that she was thinking about just how much she wanted to tell me.

"I met him in Tom Quinn's. That's a local watering hole on Asylum Street near the Pavilion and the Old State House. We talked, and I liked him okay. He was a little too charming, though, which set off my warning alarms. The charming ones are usually trouble. Married man? Fruitcake?

"Anyway, we talked for a while, and he seemed to enjoy himself, but nothing came of it, if you know what I mean. He left Quinn's first, actually. Then a couple of nights later, I *met him again* at Quinn's. Only now, everything's changed. See, the bartender is a very good friend of mine. She told me this guy had asked her about me *before* the night I met him. He knew my name. He knew I had worked for Metro. Out of sheer curiosity, I talked to him the second time."

"You weren't afraid of the man?" I asked.

"Not while I was in Tom Quinn's. They all know me, so I'd get help in a nanosecond if I needed it. I wanted to know what the hell this guy was up to. Then it got pretty clear to me. He wanted to talk about MetroHartford more than about me. He was clever about it, but he definitely wanted to talk about the executives. Who was the most demanding? Who called the shots? Even got into their families. He asked specifically about Mr. Fincher. And Mr. Dooner. Then, just like the other time, he left before I did."

I nodded as I finished making a few notes. "You never saw him again, never heard from him?"

Hildie Rader shook her head and her eyes narrowed. "I did hear *about* him, though. I had stayed good friends with Betsy Becton. She's one of the assistants to Mr. Dooner, the chairman. *He* calls the shots at MetroHartford."

I had seen Dooner in action and I agreed with Hildie. He was the boss of bosses at MetroHartford.

"This is interesting," she said to me. "Betsy had met a fella who looked just like my guy from Quinn's. Because he *was* the same guy. He sat down next to her at the coffee bar in the Borders on Main Street. He chatted Betsy up while they sipped expensive caffe mochas, lattes, whatever. He wanted to know about, guess what? *The executives at MetroHartford.* He was one of the kidnappers, wasn't he?"

Chapter 78

DURING THE COURSE OF A LONG DAY, I had learned that nearly seventy thousand people in the Hartford area are employed in the insurance industry. Besides MetroHartford, Aetna, Travelers, MassMutual, Phoenix Home Life, and United Health Care are all headquartered there. On account of this, we had more help than we needed, and more suspects. The Mastermind might have been associated with any of the insurance companies at some time in the past.

After I finished for the day at the insurance company, I got together to share notes with the others at a nearby Marriott. The breakthrough for day one was Hildie Rader's story that one of the crew members had probably been in Hartford a week before the hostages were taken.

"Tomorrow morning we interview both women, Rader and Becton. Get a composite drawing made from their description. As soon as we have that, we'll show it around corporate headquarters. Also, have the composites we made in D.C. sent up here. See if there's a match," Betsey said. She smiled then. "Things are heating up. Maybe they aren't so smart after all."

Around eight-thirty I left the suite to call Jannie and Damon before they went to bed. Nana answered the phone. She knew it was me before I said a word.

"Everything is just fine here, Alex. Home fires are burning nicely without you. You missed a delicious pot roast supper. Soon as I knew you were going to be away, I made your favorite dish."

I rolled my eyes. I couldn't believe it. "Did you really make pot roast?" I asked Nana.

She cackled for a good minute. "Of course not. We had prime ribs of beef, though." Nana cackled even louder. Prime ribs were probably my second-favorite dish — and I was still hungry after the hotel deli food, pastrami and processed cheese on stale rye.

Nana laughed again. "We had turkey sandwiches. But we did finish up with hot, homemade pecan pie. À la mode. Jannie and Damon are right here. We're playing Scrabble, and I'm winning their life savings."

"Nana's winning by a measly twelve points and she *already* had her turn," Jannie said as she took the phone. "Are you all right, Daddy?" she asked, and her voice became motherly.

"Why shouldn't I be all right?" I asked her. I was feeling much better, actually. Nana had made me laugh. "How are you doing?"

Jannie giggled. "I'm good as can be. Damon is being surprisingly nice. He brought my homework from school, and it's all done. Aced! I'm about to take the lead, for good, in our Scrabble game. We all miss you, though. Don't get hurt, Daddy. Don't you dare get hurt."

I was feeling pretty fried, but I trudged back to finish the work session with the FBI agents. *Don't get hurt,* I was thinking as I walked the long hotel corridor. Jannie was beginning to sound like Christine. *Don't get hurt. Don't you dare get hurt.*

Chapter 79

MY MIND WAS SOMEWHERE ELSE when I knocked and Betsey Cavalierre answered the door to her room. It looked like the other agents had gone. She'd changed into a white T-shirt and a pair of jeans, and she wasn't wearing shoes.

"Sorry. I had to call home," I apologized.

"We solved everything while you were gone." She grinned.

"Perfect," I said. "God bless the FBI. You guys are the best. Fidelity, Bravery, Integrity."

"You know the motto on our seal. Actually, everybody was beat. We could try for that drink now, if you'd like. You *can't* have any excuses left. How about the Roof Bar I've read so much about in the elevator? Or we could go see the Connecticut Sports Museum? The Hartford Police Museum?"

"The bar on the roof sounds good to me," I said. "You can show me the city from up there."

The bar actually had a perfect view of Hartford and the surrounding countryside. I could see lighted logos for Aetna and Travelers from where we sat, as well as Route 84 snaking northeast toward the Massachusetts Turnpike. Betsey ordered a glass of cabernet. I had a beer.

"How was everything at home?" she asked as soon as the bartender left with our order.

I laughed. "I have two kids at home now, and they're both terrific, but there is a certain amount of flux and change to our lives."

"I'm one of six girls," she said. "The oldest and most spoiled one. I know all about flux and change in families."

She smiled, and I liked seeing her loosen up. I liked seeing *myself* loosen up.

"You have a favorite?" she asked. "Of course you do, but don't tell me. I know you won't, anyway. I was my father and mother's favorite. Therein lies the recurring problem in my terribly self-involved life story."

I continued to smile. "What's the problem? I don't see any problem. I thought you were perfect."

Betsey nibbled salted nuts out of her hand. She looked me in the eye. "Overachiever syndrome. Nothing I did was ever good enough — *for me.* Everything had to be perfect. No mistakes, no slipups," she said, and laughed at herself. I liked that about her: She had no airs, and her perspective on things actually seemed pretty healthy.

"You still live up to your own high ideals?" I asked.

She finger-combed her dark hair away from her eyes. "I do, and I don't. I'm pretty much where I want to be on the work front. I'm *sooo* good for the Bureau. What's that quote? 'Ambition makes more trusty slaves than need.'

However, I must admit that I'm missing a certain balance in my life. Here's a nice image for a life in balance," she said. "You're juggling these four balls that you've named work, family, friends, spirit. Now, *work* is a rubber ball. If you drop it, it bounces back. The other balls — they're made of glass."

"I've dropped a few of those glass balls in my day. They chip, sometimes they shatter to pieces."

"Exactly."

Our drinks came, and we took the obligatory nervous sips. Pretty funny. We both knew what was going on here, though not where it was going or if it was a good or a really terrible idea. She was warmer and much more nurturing than I had expected. Betsey was a good listener, too.

"I bet you're actually pretty good at balancing work, family, friends. Your spirit seems okay, too," she said.

"I'm not balancing work too well lately. You have good spirit yourself. You're enthusiastic, positive. People like you. But you've heard all that before."

"Not so much that I mind hearing it again." She raised her glass of wine. "Here's to positive spirit, and *spirits*. And here's to prison for life plus life for our friend the Masterprick."

"To prison for life plus life for the Masterprick," I said, and raised my beer.

"So here we are in greater Hartford," she said, staring out at the blurred scrim of city lights. I watched her for a moment, and I was pretty sure that she wanted me to watch her.

"What?" I said.

She started to laugh again and it was infectious. She had a great smile, which featured her dark, sparkling eyes. "What do you mean, *what?*"

"What? Just a simple what," I teased. "You know exactly what I'm talking about."

She was still laughing. "I *have* to ask you this question, Alex. I have no choice in the matter. I have no free will. Here it comes. This could be embarrassing, but I don't care. Okay. Now, do you want to go back to my room? I'd like you to. No strings attached. Trust me. I won't ever cling."

I didn't know what to say to Betsey, but I didn't say no.

Chapter 80

WE WERE BOTH QUIET as we walked out of the hotel bar. I was feeling a little uncomfortable, maybe a lot uncomfortable.

"I kind of like strings," I finally said to her. "Sometimes I even like a little clinging."

"I know you do. Just go with the flow this one time. It'll be good for both of us. This will be nice. It's been building and it has a very fine edge."

A very fine edge.

Once we were inside the hotel elevator, Betsey and I kissed for the first time, and it was gentle and sweet. It was memorable, like first kisses ought to be. She had to stretch way up on her tiptoes to reach my mouth. I knew I wouldn't forget that.

She started to laugh as soon as we pulled apart — her usual burst of humor. "I'm not *that* small. I'm five-three and a lot, almost five-four. Was it any good? Our kiss?"

"I liked kissing you," I told her. "But you are that small."

The taste of her mouth was sweet peppermint, and it lingered with me. I wondered when she had slipped a mint into her mouth. She was sneaky fast. Her skin was soft and smooth to the touch. Her dark hair glistened and bounced lightly on her shoulders. I couldn't deny that I was attracted.

But what to do about it. I had the feeling that this was too much too soon for me. Way too much, way too soon.

The elevator door opened on her floor with a *thud*. I felt a rush of anticipation, and maybe a rush of fear. I had no idea what to make of it, but I knew I liked Betsey Cavalierre. I wanted to hold her close, wanted to know who she was, what she was like to be with, how her mind worked, what she dreamed about, what she might say next.

Betsey said, *"Walsh."*

We quickly stepped back into the elevator car. My heart clutched. *Shit.*

She turned to me and started to laugh. "Gotcha. There's nobody out there. Don't be so nervous! *I am, though.*"

By this time we were both laughing. She was definitely fun to be with. Maybe that was enough for now. I liked being around her, laughing the way we were.

We hugged as soon as we were inside her room. She felt so warm. I let my fingers trail gently down her back, and she sighed softly. I moved my thumb in the tiniest circles all over her back. I gently kneaded her skin and could feel her breathing pick up tempo. My heart was racing, too.

"Betsey," I whispered, "I can't do this. Not yet I can't."

"I know," she whispered back. "Just hold me, though. Holding is nice. Tell me about her, Alex. You can talk to me."

I thought that she was probably right. I could talk to her, and I even wanted to. "It's like I said, I like ties. I'm big on intimacy, but I feel it has to be earned. I was in love with a woman named Christine Johnson. It seemed so right for both of us. There never was a time I didn't want to be with her."

I broke down. I didn't want to, but the sob came out of nowhere. Then I was crying a lot and I couldn't make myself stop. My body was heaving, but I could feel Betsey holding on to me, holding me tight, refusing to let go.

"I'm so sorry." I finally managed a few words.

"Don't be," she said. "You didn't do anything wrong. Not at all. In fact, you did everything right."

I finally pulled back a little and I looked at her face. Her beautiful brown eyes were wet with tears.

"Let's just hug," she said. "I think we both need hugs. Hugs are good."

Betsey and I hugged for a long time and then I went back to my room alone.

Chapter 81

THE MASTERMIND was feeling so goddamned confident, and excited, that he couldn't stand it. *That night, he was there in Hartford.* He had no fear anymore. No one scared him. Not the FBI. Not anyone involved with the case.

How to top oneself? How to reinvent himself? Those were his only concerns. How to get better and better.

He had a plan for tonight — a different kind of plan. This maneuver was so clever, so perverse. He'd never heard of anything like it. It was such a lovely and original "creation."

The most commonplace part was breaking into the small, garden-style apartment on the outskirts of Hartford. He cut out a pane of glass in the door of the loggia, reached in and turned the knob, and *voilà* — he was in.

He listened to the house breathe for a delicious moment. The only sound he could hear was the wind whistling through a stand of trees that overlooked the still, black water of a country pond.

He was a little afraid to be inside the house, but the fear was natural, and intoxicating. The fear made the moment great for him. He slipped on a President Clinton mask — the same kind of mask used in the very first bank robbery.

He quietly made his way toward the master bedroom at the back of the apartment. *This was getting so good.* He almost felt that he belonged here now. Possession was nine tenths of the law. Wasn't that the old saw?

The moment of truth!

He quietly, quietly opened the bedroom door. The room smelled of sandalwood and jasmine. He paused in the doorway until his eyes became accustomed to the low light. He squinted as he stared into the room, studied it, got his bearings. He saw her!

Now! Go! Not a second to lose.

He moved very fast. He seemed to fly across the room and onto the queen-size bed. He fell on the sleeping figure with his full weight.

There was an *ooff*, then a startled cry. He slapped a wad of electrician's tape across her mouth, then handcuffed both slender wrists to a bedpost.

Click-click. So fast, so efficient.

His hostage tried to scream, tried to twist and turn and break free. She had on a yellow silk teddy. He loved the feel of it, so he slipped it off her body. He caressed the silk, ran it over his face. Then back and forth through his teeth.

"It's not going to happen. You can't get away. Stop trying! It's annoying.

"Please try to relax. You're not going to be hurt," he said then. "It's important to me that you *not* be harmed."

He gave her a few seconds to take in what he had said. To understand.

He stooped close until his face was only inches from hers. "I'm going to explain why I'm here, what I plan to do. I will be very, very clear and precise. I trust that you won't tell a soul about this, but if you ever do, I'll come back as easily as I did tonight. I'll get through any security system you can buy, and I will torture you. I will kill you, but first I'll do much worse than that."

The prey nodded. At last — *understanding. Torture* was the magic word. Perhaps it ought to be used more in schools.

"I've been watching and studying you for a while. I think you're just perfect for me. I'm certain, and I'm usually right about these things. I'm right over ninety-nine percent of the time."

The hostage was lost again. He could see it in her eyes. *The lights were on, but nobody was home.*

"Here's the idea, the concept. I'm going to try and give you a baby tonight. Yes, you heard right. I want you to *have* the baby," the Mastermind finally explained. "I've studied your fertility rhythms, your contraceptive program. Don't ask how, but I have. Trust me. I'm very serious about this.

"If you don't have the baby, I will come back for you. *Justine.* If you abort the baby, I will torture you horribly, then kill you. But don't worry, this child will be very special," said the Mastermind. "This child will be a masterpiece. *Make love to me, Justine.*"

Chapter 82

AT NOON THE NEXT DAY, the case seemed to take another terrible, and unexpected, twist. I was in an interview at MetroHartford when Betsey broke in. She asked me to please come out into the hallway. Her face was ashen.

"Oh no, what?" I managed to say.

"Alex, this is so creepy that I'm still shaking. Listen to what just happened. Last night, a twenty-five-year-old woman was raped in her apartment in a suburb outside Hartford. The rapist told her he wanted her to *have his baby*. After he left, she went to a hospital and the police were called in. In their report, it states that the rapist wore a Clinton mask — like the one worn at the first bank robbery, Alex — and also that he called himself a *mastermind*."

"Is the woman still at the hospital? Are the police with her?" I asked. My mind was racing, already filled with possibilities, rejecting the notion of coincidence out of hand. *A mastermind in a Clinton mask, just outside of Hartford?* It was too close.

"She left the hospital and went home, Alex. They just found her dead. He *warned* her not to tell anyone, and not to *abort*. She disobeyed him. She made a mistake. He *poisoned* her, Alex. Goddamn him."

Betsey Cavalierre and I went to the dead woman's apartment, and the scene was beyond horrifying. The woman lay on her kitchen floor, grotesque and twisted. I remembered the bodies of Brianne and Errol Parker. The poor woman had been *punished*. FBI technicians were all over the small garden apartment. There was nothing Betsey or I could do there. The bastard had been right there in Hartford — maybe he still was. He was taunting us.

This was as stressful as any case I'd ever worked. Whoever was behind the robberies and gruesome murders was impossible to trace, to figure out in a meaningful way.

Who the hell was the Mastermind? Had he really been here in Hartford last night and this morning? Why was he taking chances like this?

I worked at the MetroHartford offices until almost seven. I was trying not to show it, but I was close to a burnout. I interviewed several more employees, and then I went to the personnel office and read nuisance mail aimed at MetroHartford. There were stacks of it. Generally, the hate mail came from grieving and angry family members who had been denied claims or felt the process was taking too long — which it usually did. I talked for an hour or so with the head of the building's security, Terry Mayer. She was separate from Steve Bolding, who was an outside consultant. Terry gave me the procedures for mail surveillance, bomb threats, E-mail threats, and even a widely distributed form on how to be alert for possible letter bombs. "We were prepared for a lot of potential disasters," Mayer told me. "Just not for the one that happened."

I was just going through the motions all day. I kept seeing the poisoned woman. The Mastermind had wanted her to have his baby. That probably meant that he didn't have any kids of his own. He wanted an heir, a tiny piece of immortality.

Chapter 83

I RETURNED TO WASHINGTON on the last flight out that night. When I arrived home it was a few minutes past eleven. Bright light illuminated the kitchen windows. The upstairs was dark. The kids were probably asleep.

"I'm home," I announced as I edged open the creaky kitchen door. It needed oil, I noticed. I was falling way behind on my home repairs again.

"You catch all the bad guys?" Nana asked from her cat-bird seat at the table. A paperback book called *The Color of Water* was propped in front of her.

"We're moving in the right direction. The bad guy made a couple of mistakes finally. He's taking a lot of chances. I'm more hopeful than I was. You like the book?" I asked. I wanted to change the subject. I was *home*.

Nana pursed her lips, gave me a half smile. "I'm hopeful. The man can certainly write up a storm. Don't stray off my topic, though. Sit down and talk to me, Alex."

"Can I stand and talk, and maybe put together a little supper for myself?"

Nana frowned, shook her head in disbelief. "They didn't feed you on the airplane?"

"Dinner on the flight was honey-roasted peanuts and a small plastic cup of Coke. It fit with the rest of the day. This chicken and biscuits any good?"

Nana slanted her head to one side. She frowned at me from the sideways angle. "No, it's spoiled. I put it away spoiled. What do you think, Alex? Of course it's good. It's a down-home culinary masterpiece."

I stopped peering into the fridge and stared over at her. "Excuse me. Are we having a fight?"

"Not at all. You'd *know* it if we were. I'm fine myself. You're working too hard again. But you seem to thrive on it. Still the Dragonslayer, right? Live by the sword and all that?"

I took the chicken out of the fridge. I was famished. Probably could have eaten it cold. "Maybe this whacked-out case will be over soon."

"Then there'll be another one and another one after that. I saw a pretty good saying the other day — *There's always room for improvement* — *then you die.* What do you think of that one?"

I nodded and let out a deep sigh. "You tired of being with a homicide detective, too? Can't say that I blame you."

Nana crinkled up her face. "No, not at all. Actually, I enjoy it. But I do understand why it might not be to everyone's liking."

"I do, too, especially on days like today. I don't like what happened between Christine and me. I hate it, actually. Makes me sad. Hurts my heart. But I do understand what she was afraid of. It scares me, too."

Nana's head bobbed slowly. "Even if it can't be Christine, you still need someone. So do Jannie and Damon. How about you get those priorities straight."

"I spend a lot of time with the kids. But I'll work on it," I said as I plopped the cold chicken and fixings in a pan.

"How can you, Alex? You're always working on murder cases. That seems to be your priority these days."

Nana's statement hurt. Was it the truth? "These days, there seem to be a lot of bad murder cases. I'll find someone. Has to be somebody out there will think I'm worth a little trouble."

Nana cackled. "Probably some serial killer. They sure seem attracted to you."

I finally trudged up to bed around one o'clock. I was at the top of the stairs when the phone started to ring. *"Damnit!"* I cursed, and hurried to my room. I picked up before it woke the whole house.

"Yeah?"

"Sorry." I heard a whispering voice. "I'm sorry, Alex."

It was Betsey.

I was glad to hear her voice, anyway. "It's all right. What's up?" I asked.

"Alex, we have a *break* in the case. It's good news. Something just happened. A fifteen-year-old girl in Brooklyn made a claim on the insurance company reward! This is being taken very seriously in New York. The girl says her father was one of the men involved in the MetroHartford job. She knows the others involved, too. Alex, they're New York police detectives. The Mastermind is a cop."

Chapter 84

THE MASTERMIND IS A COP. If it were true, it made sense out of a whole lot of things. It partly explained how he'd known so much about bank security, *and about us.*

At five-fifteen in the morning, I met Betsey Cavalierre and four other FBI agents at Bolling field. A helicopter was waiting for us. We took off into a thick, gray soup that made the ground disappear seconds after we were airborne.

We were pumped up and extremely curious. Betsey sat in the first row with one of her senior agents, Michael Doud. She was wearing a light gray suit with a white blouse, and she looked serious and official again. Agent Doud handed out folders on the suspected New York City detectives.

I read the background material as we flew steadily toward New York. The detectives in question were from Brooklyn. They worked out of the Sixty-first Precinct, which was near Coney Island and Sheepshead Bay. The crib notes said the precinct was a mix of assorted criminals, including the Mafia, the Russian mob, Asians, Hispanics, blacks. The five suspected detectives had worked together for a dozen years and were reportedly close friends.

They were supposed to be "good cops," the file said. There had been warning signals, though. They'd used their weapons more than average, even for narcotics detectives. Three of the five had been disciplined repeatedly. They jokingly called one another "goomba." The leader of the pack was Detective Brian Macdougall.

There were also about a half dozen pages on the fifteen-year-old witness: Detective Brian Macdougall's daughter. She was an honors student at Ursuline High School. She was apparently a loner there and never had many friends. She seemed to be responsible and solid and believable, according to the NYPD detectives who had interviewed her. Her reason for giving up her father was credible, too — he drank and struck her mother often when he was home. *"And he's guilty of the MetroHartford kidnapping. He and his detective pals did it,"* said the girl.

Actually, I felt very good about this. It was the way police work usually went. You put out a lot of nets, you checked them, and every so often something was actually in one of the nets. More often than not, it came from a relative or friend of the perp. Like an angry daughter who wanted retribution against her father.

At seven-thirty, we entered the conference room at One Police Plaza and met up with several members of the NYPD, including the chief of detectives. I was the representative from the Washington police, and I knew Kyle Craig had been instrumental in getting me into the meeting. He wanted me to hear the girl's story firsthand.

Kyle wanted to know *if I believed her.*

Chapter 85

VERONICA MACDOUGALL was already in the large conference room. She wore wrinkled blue jeans and a ratty green sweatshirt. Her curly red hair was unkempt. The darkish, puffy rings under both eyes told me she hadn't slept in a while.

Veronica stared impassively at us as we introduced ourselves around a massive glass-topped mahogany conference table inside what the NYPD called "the Big Building." Chief of Detectives Andrew Gross then introduced the girl. "Veronica is a very brave young woman," he said. "She'll tell her story in her own words."

The girl took a quick, deep breath. Her eyes were small green beads and they were filled with fear. "I wrote out something last night. Organized myself. I'll give my statement, and then there can be questions if you want."

Chief of Detectives Gross broke in gently. He was a heavyset man with a thick gray mustache and long side-burns. His manner was subdued. "That would be fine,

Veronica. However you want to do it. However it happens to go is perfect for us. Take your time."

Veronica shook her head and looked very, very unsteady. "I'm okay. I need to do this," she said. Then she began her story.

"My father is what you people call a man's man. He's very proud of it, too. He's loyal to his friends, and especially to other cops. He's this *'great guy,'* right? Well, there's another side to him. My mother used to be pretty. That was ten years and thirty pounds ago. She needs nice things. I mean, she physically needs things, possessions like clothes and shoes. She *is* her possessions.

"She's not the smartest person in the world, but my father thinks he is right up there and that's why he picks on her unmercifully. A few years back he started to drink a lot. And then he started to get really mean, to hit my mother. He calls her 'the bag,' and 'speed bag.' Isn't that clever of him?"

Veronica paused and looked around the room; she checked our reaction to what she was saying. The conference room was eerily silent. None of us could look away from the teenager and the anger blooming in those green eyes.

"That's why I'm here today. That's how I'm able to do this terrible thing — to 'rat out' my own father. To break the sacred Blue Wall."

She stopped and stared defiantly at us again. I couldn't take my eyes away from her. No one in the room could. This made so much sense: a break coming from a family member.

"My father doesn't realize that I'm actually a lot smarter than he is, and I'm also observant. Maybe I learned that from him. I remember when I was around ten or so, I just knew I was going to be a police detective, too. Pretty ironic, huh? Pretty pathetic, don't you think?

"As I got older I noticed — observed — that my father had lots more money than he ought to have. Sometimes he would take us on a 'guilt trip' — Ireland, maybe the Caribbean. And he always had money for himself. Really good clothes, fancy threads from Barneys and Saks. A new car every other year. A sleek white sailboat parked in Sheepshead Bay.

"Last summer my father was disgustingly drunk one Friday night. I remember he was going out to Aqueduct racetrack with his running-dog detective pals on Saturday. He took a walk to my grandmother's house, which is a few streets away from us. I followed him that night. He was too far gone to even notice.

"My father went to an old gardening shed behind my grandmother's house. Inside the shed, he moved away a work bench and some wooden slats. I couldn't tell exactly what he was doing, so I came back the next day and looked behind the boards. There was money inside — a lot. I don't know where it came from, still don't. But I knew it wasn't his detective's pay. *I counted almost twenty thousand dollars.* I took a few hundred, and he never even noticed.

"I became more observant after that. Recently, over, say, the past month or so, my father and his friends were up to something. His goombas. It was so obvious. They were always together after work. One night I heard him mention something about Washington, D.C., to his pal Jimmy Crews. Then he went away for four days.

"He got home on the fourth afternoon. It was the day

after the MetroHartford kidnapping. He started to 'celebrate' at around three, and he was flying high by seven. That night, he broke my mom's cheekbone. He cut her eye and could have put it out. My father wears this stupid signet ring from St. John's. The Redmen — now the Red Storm, you know. I went to my grandma's shed that night and I found more money. I couldn't believe it. There's so much money there, all cash."

Veronica Macdougall reached under the table and hoisted up a powder blue backpack, the kind kids wear to school. She opened it. She pulled out several stacks of bills and showed us the money. Her face was a mask of shame and pain.

"Here's ten thousand four hundred dollars. It was right there in my grandmother's shed. My father put it there. My father was in on that kidnapping in Washington. He thinks he's so goddamn smart."

Only then, once she was finished telling us what her father had done, did Veronica Macdougall finally break down and cry. "I'm sorry," she kept saying. "I'm so, so sorry." I think she was apologizing for his crimes.

Chapter 86

I BELIEVED HER, and I was still reeling from hearing Veronica Macdougall's chilling confession about her policeman father. An intriguing question was whether the crew of Brooklyn detectives had "masterminded" the earlier bank robberies, too. Had they murdered several people in cold blood before they attempted the Metro-Hartford kidnapping? Was one of the detectives the Mastermind?

I had plenty of time to think about it during an interminable day of politicking and infighting involving the FBI, the mayor, and the New York police commissioner. Meanwhile, the five Brooklyn detectives were put under surveillance, but we weren't given the go-ahead to bring them in. It was frustrating, maddening, like being stuck for a day on the Long Island Expressway in a traffic jam, or on a New York subway. The detectives' attendance records were being checked against the days all of the robberies took place. Credit and spending checks were run on each of them. Other detectives, even snitches, were quietly interviewed. The money found at Brian Macdougall's mother's house had been retrieved and it was definitely part of the ransom.

As of six o'clock, nothing had been decided. None of us could believe the delay. Betsey surfaced briefly and reported that no progress had been made so far. Around seven, I went and checked into a hotel for the night.

I kept getting angrier and angrier. I took a hot shower, and then I leafed through a Zagat's guide looking for a good place to eat downtown. Around nine, I finally ordered from room service. I'd been thinking about Christine and the Boy. I didn't feel like going out. Maybe if Betsey had been available, but she was tied up, raging against the machine at Police Plaza.

I propped myself up in bed and tried to read *Prayers for Rain* by Dennis Lehane. I was on a string of books that I'd enjoyed lately: *The Pilot's Wife, The Pied Piper, Harry Potter and the Sorcerer's Stone,* the Lehane.

I couldn't concentrate. I wanted to take down the five New York detectives. I wanted to be home with the kids, and I wanted little Alex to be part of our family. That was the one thing that had kept me going strong lately.

Finally, I started to think about Betsey Cavalierre. I had been trying not to, but now I remembered our "date" in Hartford. I liked her — it was as simple as that. I wanted to see her again and I hoped she wanted to see me.

The phone in my room rang around eleven o'clock. *It was Betsey.* She sounded tired and frustrated and decidedly nonpeppy for her.

"I'm just finishing up here at Police Plaza. I *hope.* Believe it or not, we're set to take them down tomorrow. You definitely wouldn't believe the bullshit that's gone on today. Lots of talk about the detectives' civil rights. Plus the effect on morale inside the NYPD. Making the arrest 'the right way.' Nobody's willing to say *these are five very bad actors. They're probably killers. Take their sorry asses down.*"

"They're five very bad actors. Take their sorry asses down," I said to her.

I heard her laugh and I could picture her smile. "That's what we're doing, Alex. Bright and early tomorrow morning. We're taking them down. Maybe we'll get the Mastermind, too. I have to be here at least another hour. I'll see you in the morning. *Early.*"

Chapter 87

FOUR O'CLOCK comes very early in the morning. That was the hour we were scheduled to hit the homes of the five detectives. Everything was set. The politicking was done; at least I hoped it was over.

Three-thirty comes even earlier, and that was when we met somewhere in Nassau County out on Long Island. I didn't know much about the area, but it was upscale and pretty, a far cry from Fifth Street and Southeast. Someone on the team said the neighborhood was unusual because a lot of cops and also Mafia people lived there in apparent harmony.

This was a federal case, and Betsey Cavalierre was officially in charge of the arrests. It illustrated the regard in which she was held back in Washington, if not in New York.

"I'm happy to see that everybody is bright eyed and bushy tailed this morning. Night? Whatever time zone we're in." She offered up a joke and got a few smiles from the troops. There were about forty of us, a mix of police and FBI, but the Bureau was definitely in charge of the morning's raids. She divided us into five teams of eight, and I was in her group.

Everybody was ready, and incredibly pumped up. We drove to a split-level house on High Street in Massapequa. No one seemed to be up in the suburban neighborhood. A dog started barking in one of the yards nearby. Dew glistened on every manicured lawn. Life seemed good out here where Detective Brian Macdougall lived with his battered wife and bitterly angry daughter.

Betsey spoke into her Handie-Talkie. She seemed extremely cool under fire. "Radio check." Then, "Team A, through the front door. Team B, kitchen, Team C, sunporch. Team D is backup. . . . *Now. Go!* Take him down!"

The agents and police detectives swarmed toward the house on her signal. Betsey and I got to watch them quickly move in. We were Team D, the backup.

Team A was inside the house fast and clean.

Then so was Team B. We couldn't see the third team from where we were parked. They went in the back.

There was shouting inside. Then we heard a loud *pop.* Percussive, definitely a gunshot.

"Oh, shit." Betsey looked over at me. "Macdougall was waiting for us. How the hell did that happen?"

There were several more gunshots. Someone yelled. A woman began to scream and curse. Was it Veronica Macdougall's mother?

Betsey and I jumped out of the car and moved quickly toward the Macdougall house. We still didn't go inside. I was thinking that four other houses were being hit right now. I hoped there wasn't more trouble like this.

"Talk to me," Betsey said into her Handie-Talkie. "What's happening in there? Mike? What the hell is wrong?"

"Rice is down. I'm outside the master bedroom on the second floor. Macdougall and his wife are inside."

"How is Rice?" she asked, very concerned.

"Chest wound. He's conscious. Wound is sucking bad, though. Get an ambulance here now! Macdougall shot him."

Suddenly a window on the second floor opened. I saw a figure come out of the window and run in a low crouch across the attached garage roof.

Betsey and I sprinted toward the man. I remembered that she'd been a good lacrosse player at Georgetown. She could still move.

"He's *outside!* Macdougall's up on the roof over the garage," she reported to the others.

"I got him," I told her. He was angling toward where the garage roof intersected with a row of feathery-looking fir trees. I couldn't see what was beyond the trees, but I figured it had to be another yard, another house.

"Macdougall!" I yelled at the top of my voice. "Stop! Police! Stop or I'll shoot!"

He didn't look back, didn't stop, and didn't hesitate. Macdougall jumped down into the trees.

Chapter 88

I RAN WITH MY HEAD DOWN, right through a barrier of thick bushes that scraped and cut my arms until there was blood. Brian Macdougall hadn't gotten very far into the yard next door.

I raced for a dozen steps after him, and then I tackled him. I aimed my right shoulder at the back of his knees. I wanted to hurt Macdougall if I possibly could.

He went down hard, but he was as loaded up with adrenaline as I was. He rolled and twisted out of my arms. He popped up fast, and so did I. "You should have stayed down," I told him. "You're not supposed to make mistakes. Getting up was a mistake."

I hit Macdougall with a hard, straight overhand right. It felt very good. His head snapped back about six inches.

I bobbed a little. Macdougall threw a wild hook that missed me completely. I hit him again. His knees buckled, but he didn't go down. He *was* a tough street cop.

"I'm impressed," I told him, taunted him. "You still should have stayed down, though."

"Alex!" I heard Betsey yell as she entered the yard.

Macdougall threw a pretty good punch, but he telegraphed it a little. It glanced off the side of my forehead. I could have taken the punch if it had connected. "That's better," I told him. "Get the weight off your heels, Brian."

"Alex!" Betsey called again. "Take him down, goddamnit! Now!"

I wanted the physical contact with Macdougall, the release, just another minute in the ring. I felt I'd earned it, and he deserved whatever got doled out here. He threw another looping punch, but I sidestepped the hit. He was already tired.

"You're not beating up on your wife or your little girl now," I said. "You're dealing with somebody your own size. I fight back, Macdougall."

"Fuck you," he snarled, but he was gasping for a breath. His face and neck were coated with sweat.

"Are you the man? Are you the Mastermind, Brian? You kill all those people?"

He didn't answer me, so I hit him hard in the stomach. He doubled up, his face tight with pain.

Betsey had come up to the two of us by now. So had a couple of other agents. They just watched; they understood what this was about. They wanted it to happen, too.

"Balls of your feet." I gave Macdougall a fight tip. "You're still fighting back on your heels."

He mumbled something. I couldn't make it out. Didn't much care what he had to say. I hit him in the stomach again. "See? Kill the body," I told him. "I teach my kids the same thing."

I threw another uppercut into his stomach. He wasn't flabby, and the punch felt good, like hitting a heavy bag. Then a sharp uppercut right on the tip of Macdougall's chin. He went down hard on the lawn. He stayed there. He was out.

I stood over him, panting a little, sweating some. "Brian Macdougall. I asked you a question. Are you the Mastermind?"

Chapter 89

THE NEXT TWO DAYS were draining and wildly frustrating. The five detectives were being held at the Metropolitan Correctional Center at Foley Square. It was a secure place where mob informants and crooked policemen were sometimes kept for their own safety.

I interviewed each of the detectives, starting with the youngest, Vincent O'Malley, and ending up with Brian Macdougall, who appeared to be the leader. One after the other, the detectives denied any involvement in the Metro-Hartford kidnapping.

Hours after my initial interview with Brian Macdougall, he asked to see me again.

When the shackled detective was brought into the interrogation room at Foley Square, I had a feeling that something had changed. I could see it in his face.

Macdougall was visibly upset when he spoke: "It's different than I'd thought it would be. In jail. Sitting here on the wrong side of the table. It's more a defensive game, you know. You try and hit the ball back over the net."

"You want anything?" I asked him. "Cold drink?"

"Cigarette?"

I called for cigarettes to be brought into the interrogation room. Someone popped in with a pack of Marlboros, then immediately left. Macdougall lit up and he puffed luxuriously, as if smoking a Marlboro were the greatest pleasure the world had to offer. Maybe it seemed like it now.

I watched his eyes drift in and out of focus. He was obviously bright, thoughtful. The Mastermind? I waited patiently to hear what he wanted from me. He wanted *something*.

"I've seen a lot of detectives do this," he said, then he blew out a cloud of smoke. "You know how to listen. You don't make mistakes."

There was a brief silence. We both had all the time in the world. "What do you want from us?" I finally asked.

"Right question, Detective. I'll get to that soon. Y'know, I was a decent enough cop in the beginning," he said. "It's when those first ideals go that you have to be careful."

"I'll try to remember," I said, smiling faintly, trying not to condescend.

"What keeps you going?" Macdougall asked. He seemed interested in my answer. Maybe I amused him. More likely, he was playing with me, though. That was okay for now.

I looked into his eyes and I saw emptiness, maybe even remorse. "I don't want to disappoint my family, or myself. It's just the way I'm built. Maybe I don't have much of an imagination."

Smoke drifted through his fingers. "You asked me what I wanted? It was the right question. I always act out of self-interest, always have." He sighed out loud. "All right, let me tell you what I'm looking for."

I knew enough to listen, not talk.

"First of all, nobody got hurt from MetroHartford. We've never hurt anybody on any of our jobs."

"What about the Buccieris? James Bartlett? Ms. Collins?" I asked.

Macdougall shook his head. "I didn't do those jobs. You know I didn't do them. *I know you know.*"

He was right; at least I didn't believe they had done the earlier jobs. The style was different for those. Plus, the detectives' attendance logs showed they had worked on several of the days when robberies took place. "Okay. So where do we go from here? You also know that we want to get the person who set up the jobs. That's what we care about now."

"I know that. So here's my offer. It'll be hard for everybody to swallow, but it's nonnegotiable. I want the best deal that *I ever saw as a cop.* That means witness protection inside a country club like Greenhaven. I'm out in ten years maximum time. I've seen that same deal on counts of murder one. I know what can be done and what can't be."

I didn't say anything, but I didn't have to. Macdougall knew I couldn't make the deal by myself. "Let me hear the punch line," I said. "What do we get from you?"

He stared into my eyes. His look was unwavering.

"In return — *I'll give him to you.* I'll tell you how to find the guy who planned the jobs. He's called the Mastermind. I know where he is."

Part Five

ALL FALL DOWN

Chapter 90

THE FBI, THE NYPD, AND THE JUSTICE DE-
partment were holding a series of high-level meetings to try to frame the best possible response to Brian
Macdougall's offer. I was fairly certain that nothing deci-
sive would happen with Macdougall until at least Monday.

At four-thirty I took the shuttle back to Washington.
Betsey Cavalierre and Michael Doud stayed in New York,
just in case something happened.

I had some important business myself. That night, the
kids, Nana, and I went to see *Star Wars: Episode I — The
Phantom Menace.* We had a good time, though we'd
hoped to see more of Samuel L. Jackson in the film. I had
been noticing a subtle change between Jannie and
Damon. Since she'd been sick, Damon was much more
patient with her. Jannie was also pulling some punches
with her brother, torturing him less. They had grown up a

lot in the past few weeks. I figured they were becoming friends, and that would last for the rest of their lives.

Early on Saturday, I decided to have a heart-to-heart with the kids. I had already taken some good counsel from Nana about what needed to be said to them. Her own response was typical Nana: She was sorry as could be about what had happened between Christine and me. As for little Alex, she said she couldn't wait for him to come. "I love babies, Alex. This will *add* ten years to my life." I almost believed her.

"This is not good," Damon proclaimed as he stared across the breakfast table at me. "Is it?"

I grinned at him. "Well, that's only half true. Where do I begin with this?" I said, stumbling a little out of the gate.

"At the beginning," Jannie suggested.

The beginning? Where exactly was the beginning?

I finally just dived into the subject matter. "Christine and I have been very close for a long time. I think you both know that. We still are, but things have changed lately. After the school year, she's going to move away from the Washington area. I don't know exactly where she's going yet. We won't be seeing her as much, though."

Jannie's jaw dropped, and Damon spoke up. "She's different in school, Dad. Everybody says so. She gets mad easy. She always looks sad."

It hurt for me to hear that. I felt it was partly my fault. "She went through a very bad, very scary thing," I said to him. "It's hard for anyone to imagine what it was like for her. She's still recovering from it. It might take a while longer."

Jannie finally spoke, and her voice was surprisingly

small. Her eyes were full of concern and worry. "What about the Big Boy?" she asked.

"Little Alex is going to come live with us. That's the good news I promised."

"Hooray! Hooray!" Jannie shouted, and did one of her impromptu dances. "I love little A. J."

"That's real good," Damon said, and beamed approval. "I'm glad he's coming home."

I was, too, and I wondered how a single moment could be so joyful but also so sad. The Boy was coming to live with us, but Christine was gone. It was official now; I had told Nana Mama and the kids. I hadn't felt so empty and alone for a long time.

Chapter 91

THE MORE DANGEROUS IT WAS, THE BETTER THE THRILL. The Mastermind already knew the truth in that maxim, and this was dangerous indeed. The money was nice, but the money wasn't enough. It was the danger that got his adrenaline flowing and turned him on.

FBI agent James Walsh lived alone in a small rented ranch house out in Alexandria. The house was as plain and unassuming as Agent Walsh himself. It suited his personality perfectly. It was such an "honest" and "forthcoming" abode.

The Mastermind had little trouble getting into the house. Police officers could be incredibly sloppy about security systems in their own homes. Walsh was lax, or maybe he was just arrogant.

He wanted to get in and out quickly, but the Mastermind didn't want to be careless. *The floorboards creaked.* He already knew that — he'd been inside the house before.

The floorboards continued to make distressing noises as he got closer and closer to James Walsh's bedroom.

The more dangerous, the better. The more outrageous, the greater the thrill.

That was how it always worked for him.

He slowly, silently pushed open the bedroom door and he started to enter, when — "Don't move," Walsh said from the semidarkness of the room.

He could just barely see the FBI agent across the bedroom. Walsh had positioned himself behind the bed. He had a shotgun in his hands. Walsh kept the gun under his bed, never slept without it there.

"You can see the gun, mister. It's aimed right at your goddamn chest. I won't miss you, I promise."

"So I see," the Mastermind said, and chuckled softly. "Checkmate, huh? You caught the Mastermind. How clever of you."

Still smiling, he started to walk forward toward Walsh. *The more dangerous, the better.*

"Don't! Stop!" Walsh suddenly yelled at him. "Stop or I'll shoot! STOP!"

"Yes, as you *promised*," the Mastermind said.

He didn't stop, didn't slow down a step, kept coming — inexorably.

Then he heard Agent Walsh pull the trigger. The single action that was supposed to cause his death, stop his world, solve the crime spree. *But nothing happened.*

"Awhh, and you promised, Agent Walsh."

He put his own handgun against the FBI agent's forehead. With his free hand, he brushed across Walsh's crew-cut head.

"I'm the Mastermind; you're not. You've been dying to

catch me, but I've caught you. I *emptied* your shotgun. I'm going to catch all of you. One by one. Agents Walsh, Doud, Cavalierre. Maybe even Detective Alex Cross. You're all going to die."

Chapter 92

I ARRIVED AT JAMES WALSH'S HOME in Virginia around midnight on Sunday. Several of the neighbors were circulating nervously out on the street. I heard an elderly woman mutter and sigh, "Such a nice man. What a shame, what a waste. He was an FBI agent, you know."

I *knew*. I took a deep breath and then I plunged inside the modest house where Walsh had lived and died. The Bureau was there in large numbers and so were the local police. Because an agent had died, the Violent Crime Unit had been called in from Quantico.

I spotted Agent Mike Doud and I hurried over to him. Doud looked ashen and maybe close to losing it.

"I'm sorry," I said to him. He and Walsh had been close friends. Doud lived nearby in the Virginia suburbs.

"Oh, Jesus. Jimmy never said a word to me. I was his best friend, for God's sake."

I nodded. "What do you know so far? What happened?"

Doud pointed toward the bedroom. "Jimmy's in there. I guess he killed himself, Alex. He left a note. Hard to believe."

I crossed the sparsely decorated living room. I knew from talking to him that Walsh had been divorced a couple of years ago. He had a sixteen-year-old son in prep school and another at Holy Cross, where Walsh had gone himself.

James Walsh was waiting for me in the bathroom connected to the bedroom. He was curled up on the off-white tile floor, which was flooded with a lot of his blood. I could see what was left of the back of his head as I entered the room.

Doud came up behind me. He held out the suicide note, which had been placed in a plastic evidence bag. I read it without removing the plastic. The note was to Walsh's two sons.

> *It finally got to be too much for me.*
> *This job; this case; everything else.*
> *Andrew, Peter, I'm truly sorry about this.*
>
> > *Love,*
> > *your dad*

A cell phone sounded and it startled me. It was Doud's phone. He answered but then handed it to me. "It's Betsey," he said.

"I'm on my way to the airport. Oh, Alex, why would he do such a thing?" I heard her voice. She was obviously still in New York. "Oh, poor Jim. Poor Jim. Why would he kill himself? I don't believe it. He's not the type."

Then she sobbed loudly into the phone, and though she was far away, I had never felt closer to her.

I didn't say what I was thinking. I held it inside and it chilled me a little. *Maybe Betsey's gut reaction was right. Maybe James Walsh didn't kill himself.*

Chapter 93

I RETURNED TO NEW YORK CITY early on Monday morning. There was a nine o'clock briefing at FBI headquarters in Manhattan, and I made it just in time. I was holding a lot inside, holding it tight, trying not to look like anything was wrong.

I walked into a formal conference room wearing sunglasses. Betsey must have sensed I was there. She looked up from a mountain of paperwork and she nodded solemnly. I could tell she'd spent a good part of the night thinking about Walsh. So had I.

I took one of the empty seats just as a lawyer from the Justice Department was beginning to address the group. He looked to be in his fifties, rigid and solemn, nearly without affect. He wore a shiny charcoal gray suit that had narrow lapels and looked at least twenty years old.

"An arrangement has been made with Brian Macdougall," he announced to the assembled group.

I looked over at Betsey and she shook her head, rolled her eyes. She already *knew.*

I couldn't believe it. I listened closely to every word out of the Justice lawyer's mouth.

"You are not to speak about anything discussed in this room. We're releasing nothing to the press. Detective Macdougall has agreed to talk to investigators about the overall plan, and the execution of it in the MetroHartford kidnapping. He has valuable information that could lead to the capture of an extremely important UNSUB, the so-called Mastermind."

I was completely shell-shocked, undermined, and I felt totally fucked with. Goddamn Justice had made the deal over the weekend, and I would have bet anything that Macdougall got exactly what he had asked for. It made me physically sick, but that was the way Justice had been working ever since I became a cop.

Brian Macdougall had known exactly what kind of deal he could get from them. Now the only relevant question was, could he give us the Mastermind? How much did he know? Did he know a goddamn thing?

I would find out soon. I got to interview star-witness Detective Macdougall late that morning at the Metropolitan Correctional Center. Detective Harry Weiss was there for the NYPD. Betsey Cavalierre represented the FBI during the session.

Macdougall had two lawyers present. Neither of them wore twenty-year-old suits. They looked slick, very expensive, smart. The detective glanced up as we entered a small booking room where the meeting was to be held. "This stinks, right?" he said. "I happen to agree. But that's the system."

Macdougall the Philosopher sat down between his lawyers, and the session began.

Betsey leaned into me. She whispered, "This ought to be good. Now we get to see what Justice bought."

Chapter 94

THE MEETING started out very badly. Detective Weiss from NYPD Internal Affairs took it upon himself to speak for the rest of us. Weiss found it necessary to start at the beginning and methodically go over Macdougall's previous statement sentence by sentence.

It was excruciating. I badly wanted to interrupt him, but I didn't. Every time Weiss asked another question or launched into a senseless diatribe criticizing Macdougall, I nudged Betsey's foot under the table. To punctuate a couple of embarrassing exchanges she kicked me in the shins.

Macdougall finally had enough of it, too. "You fucking suck!" he blew up at Weiss. "You people are a joke. It's about your *gut*, Weiss, not covering your fat ass. You're wasting my time. Let somebody else ask the questions."

He glared at Weiss, who still seemed not to get it.

"You're *asking all the wrong fucking questions, asshole*," Macdougall finally stood up and shouted at the top of his voice. "You're godawful at your job, you suck, you're wasting everybody's time!"

Macdougall then stomped over to a grimy window that was covered by a heavy metal screen and bars. His lawyers trailed after him. He said something, and they all laughed. *Ho, ho, ho. What a crack-up Brian Macdougall was.*

The rest of us sat at the conference table and watched them. Betsey consoled Weiss, tried to keep up a united front.

"Fuck him," Weiss said with unusual clarity and brevity. "I can ask him anything I want to. We bought that son of a bitch."

Betsey nodded at Weiss. "You're right, Harry. He's arrogant and he's wrong. *Typical detective,*" she said. "Maybe he would respond to Detective Cross. He doesn't seem to like IAD."

Weiss shook his head at first, but then he relented. "Fine, whatever it takes. Whatever works with this asshole. I'm a team player."

"We're all team players," she said, and lightly patted Weiss's arm. She was good. "Thanks for being open to the suggestion."

Macdougall came back to the table and he seemed calmer. He even apologized to Weiss. "I'm sorry. Nerves are a little frayed, you know."

I waited a couple of seconds for his apology to be accepted by Weiss, but the IAD man never said a word. I finally began. "Detective Macdougall, why don't you tell us what you have that's important. You know what you have to tell. You also know what we want to hear."

Macdougall looked at both of his lawyers. He finally smiled.

Chapter 95

"ALL RIGHT, LET'S TRY THAT APPROACH," said Macdougall. "Simple questions and simple answers. I met with the so-called Mastermind three times. Always down in Washington. Each time I saw him, he gave us what he called 'traveling expenses.' That was fifty grand a trip, which made it well worth our while, and also caught our attention, piqued our interest.

"He was *very, very* buttoned-up. Thought everything through. Knew all the angles. Knew what he was talking about. *And* — he told us right off that our cut of the action would be fifteen million dollars. He was very credible when he talked about MetroHartford. He had a concept and a plan that was extremely detailed. We felt it was workable, and it was."

"*How* did he know about you?" I asked. "How did he contact you?"

Macdougall liked the questions, or made it seem as if he did. "There's a lawyer we use sometimes." He looked at the lawyers on either side of him. "Not these two gentlemen. He contacted our *other* lawyer. We don't know exactly how he knew about us, but he knew *what we did, how we worked.* That's useful information, Detective Weiss. Make yourself a note. *Who* would know about us? Somebody in law enforcement? A cop? One of *ours,* Detective Weiss? An agent with the FBI? A cop from D.C.? Maybe somebody in this room? It could be anybody."

Weiss couldn't control himself. His face was red. The collar of his button-down white shirt looked a couple of sizes too small. "But you already know who it is, Macdougall? Isn't that right?"

Macdougall looked at Betsey and me. He shook his head. He couldn't believe Weiss, either. "I'm coming to that, to what I know, and what I *don't* know. Don't underestimate the information that he knew about us. He knew about Detective Cross. And about Agent Cavalierre. He knew *everything.* That's important."

"I agree with you," I said. "Go on, please."

"All right. Before we agreed to the second meeting, we were doing our best to find out who the hell this so-called Mastermind was. We even talked to the FBI about him. We made whatever contacts we could make. We found out nothing. He left no trail.

"So we get to meeting number two and he still doesn't commit. Bobby Shaw tries to follow him after he leaves the hotel. Shaw loses him."

"Which makes you think he might be some kind of cop?" I asked.

Macdougall shrugged. "It definitely crosses our minds. Meeting number three is about whether we were in or out. Half of thirty million dollars — *we already know we're in.* He knows we're in. We try to negotiate a better cut. He laughs, says absolutely not. We agree to his terms. It's his way or we're out.

"He leaves the hotel after the meet. We've got two men following him this time. He's tall, heavy, dark beard — but we think it's probably a disguise. Our two guys almost lose him again.

"But they *don't* lose him. They're very lucky. They see him go into the Hazelwood Veterans Hospital in D.C. He *doesn't* come out again. We don't know what he looks like, but the Mastermind went in there and he stayed. He didn't come out."

Macdougall stopped talking. He let his eyes go slowly down the line from Weiss to Betsey to me.

"He's a mental patient, guys and girl. He's at Hazelwood Veterans Hospital in Washington. He's on the mental health ward. You just have to find him in there."

Chapter 96

FBI AGENTS were immediately dispatched to Hazelwood Veterans Hospital. Files on every current patient, and also the staff, were being pulled and would be evaluated. The Veterans Administration was blocking access to the patients themselves, but that wouldn't last very long.

I spent the rest of a very long day cross-checking copies of files on employees and customers of Metro-Hartford against patient records as they became available from Hazelwood. Thank God for computers. Even if the Mastermind was at the hospital, no one knew exactly what he looked like. His half of the thirty million dollars was still missing. But we were closer to him than we'd ever been. We had recovered nearly all the money from the New York detectives. Only a couple hundred thousand was still missing. All the detectives were trying to play "let's make a deal."

That night around nine-thirty, Betsey and I had dinner in New York at a restaurant called Ecco. She wore a yellow smock, gold earrings and bracelets. It looked good in contrast with her black hair and the tan she still had. I think she knew that she looked good, too. Very, very feminine.

"Is this, like, a date?" she asked once we were seated at a table in the cozy but noisy Manhattan restaurant.

I smiled. "I would say this might qualify as a date, especially if we don't talk about work too much."

"You have my word on it. Not even if the Mastermind walks in here and sits down at our table."

"I'm sorry about Jim Walsh," I told her. We hadn't gotten a chance to talk about it much.

"I know you are, Alex. Me too. He was a really good guy."

"Did it surprise you? That he killed himself?"

She put her hand on top of mine.

"It did — *totally.* Not tonight. Okay?"

For the first time, she opened up and told me a little about herself. She had gone to John Carroll High School in D.C. and been brought up a Catholic. She said that her background was "strict, strict, and more strict. Lots of discipline." Her mother was a homemaker until she died, when Betsey was sixteen. Her father had been a sergeant in the army, then a fireman.

"I used to go out with a girl from John Carroll," I told her. "Cute little uniform."

"Recently?" she asked. Her brown eyes twinkled. She *was* funny. She said the sense of humor came from her old neighborhood in D.C., and also the atmosphere in her parents' house. "If you were a boy in our neighborhood, you had to be funny or you got into lots of fights. My father wanted a boy but got me instead. He was a tough guy but funny, always had a joke. Daddy died of a heart attack on the job. I think that's why I work out every day like such a possessed little maniac."

I told her that my mother and father had both died before I was ten and that my grandmother had raised me. "I work out a lot, too," I said.

"You went to Georgetown, then Johns Hopkins, right?" she asked.

I rolled my eyes, but I was laughing. "You prepared for the meeting. Yes, I have a doctorate in psychology from Hopkins. I'm overqualified for my job."

She laughed. "I went to Georgetown. I was *way* behind you, though."

"Four years. Only four short years, Agent Cavalierre. You were a very good lacrosse player there."

She crinkled up her nose and mouth. "*Oohhh.* Somebody else has been prepping for tonight."

I laughed. "No, no. I actually saw you play once."

"You remember?" she asked with mild astonishment.

"I remember you. You *glided* when you ran. I didn't put it all together at first, but I remember it now."

Betsey asked about my Johns Hopkins training in psych, then my three years in private practice. "But you like being a homicide detective better?" she asked.

"I do. I love the action."

She admitted that she did, too.

We talked a little about people who had been important in our lives. I told her about Maria, my wife, who'd been killed. I showed off pictures of Damon and Jannie from my wallet.

I noticed that her voice got softer. "I've never been

married. Two of my sisters are married, with kids. I love their kids. They call me Auntie Cop."

"Can I ask a personal question?"

She nodded. "Fire away. I can take the heat."

"You ever been close to settling down?" I asked. "Auntie Cop?"

"Is the question personal or professional, Doctor?" I already had the sense that she was incredibly guarded. Her humor was probably her best defense.

"The question is just friendly," I told her.

"I know it is. I can tell, Alex. I've had some good friends in the past — men, a couple of boys. Whenever it got too serious, I always got out of harm's way. *Oops*. There's a slip."

"Just the truth," I smiled, "slipping out ever so slowly."

She leaned in close. She kissed my forehead, then she kissed me gently on the lips. The kisses were sweet and totally irresistible.

"I like being with you," she said. "I like talking to you an awful lot. Are we about ready to leave?"

She and I returned to the hotel together. I walked her to her room. We kissed outside the door and I liked it even more than the first time in Hartford. *Slow and easy wins the race.*

"You're still not ready," she said matter-of-factly.

"You're right. . . . I'm not ready."

"But *you're close*." She smiled, then entered her hotel room and shut the door. "Don't know what you're missing," she called from inside.

I smiled all the way back to my hotel room. I think I did know what I was missing.

Chapter 97

"HERE WE GO!" John Sampson said, and clapped his hands together. "Bad boys, bad boys, where you gonna hide?"

At 6:00 A.M. on Tuesday morning, Sampson and I climbed out of my old Porsche in the staff parking lot of the Hazelwood Veterans Hospital on North Capitol Street in D.C. The large, sprawling hospital was situated a ways south of Walter Reed Army Medical Center, just north of the Soldiers' and Airmen's Home.

Home of the Mastermind? I wondered. *Could that be? According to Brian Macdougall it could — and he had a lot riding on it.*

John and I were dressed in sport shirts, baggy khaki trousers, and high-topped sneakers. We were going to work for a day or two at the hospital. So far, the FBI hadn't been able to identify the Mastermind among the patients or staff members.

The grounds of Hazelwood were surrounded by high

fieldstone walls covered with ivy. The landscaping was sparse: a few deciduous and evergreen shrubs and trees, artificial berms that were evocative of wartime bunkers.

"That's the main hospital," I said, and pointed to a nearby building that was painted pale yellow and rose six stories above us. There were a half dozen smaller, bunker-like buildings on the grounds.

"I've been here before," Sampson said. His eyes narrowed. "Knew a couple of guys from Vietnam who wound up at Hazelwood. They didn't heap high praise on the institution. Place always makes me think of that documentary *Titicut Follies*. You remember that scene where a patient is refusing to eat? So they force a hose down his nose?"

I looked at Sampson and shook my head. "You *really* don't like Hazelwood."

"Don't like the system of dispensing medical care to veterans. Don't like what happens to men and women who get hurt in foreign wars. The people who work here are mostly all right, though. They probably don't even use nose hoses anymore."

"We might need to," I told him, "if we find our guy."

"We find the Mastermind, sugar, we'll definitely use nose hoses."

Chapter 98

WE CLIMBED STEEP STONE STAIRS, then entered the hospital's administration building. We were shown the way to the inner office of Colonel Daniel Schofield, the director of the unit.

Colonel Schofield was there to meet us outside a small private room. Two other men and a petite blond woman were already inside. "Let's go right in," Schofield said. He appeared anxious and upset. What a surprise.

He made stiff, very formal introductions around the room, starting with Sampson and me, then going on to his staff. None of them looked happy to see us.

"This is Ms. Kathleen McGuigan. She's the head nurse on Four and Five, where you and Mr. Sampson will be working. This is Dr. Padraic Cioffi. Dr. Cioffi is the psychiatrist in charge of the mental health units. And Dr. Marcuse, one of the five excellent therapists who work at the hospital."

Dr. Marcuse nodded benignly in our direction. He seemed a pleasant enough man, but nurse McGuigan and Dr. Cioffi sat there stone-faced.

"I've explained the very delicate situation to Ms. McGuigan, Dr. Cioffi, and Dr. Marcuse. To be candid with you, nobody is completely comfortable with this, but we understand that we don't have a choice. *If* this suspected killer is hiding out here, our concern is for everyone's safety. He must be caught, of course. No one disagrees with that."

"He was here," I said, "at least for a while. He might be here now."

"I don't believe he's here," Dr. Cioffi spoke up. "I'm sorry. I just don't see it. I know all of our patients and believe me, none of them is a mastermind. Not even close. The men and women here are deeply, deeply disturbed."

"It could also be a staff member," I told him, then watched his reaction.

"My opinion remains unchanged, Detective."

I needed their cooperation, so I figured it was a good idea to try to make friends, if I could. "Detective Sampson and I will be in and out of here as quickly as is humanly possible," I said. "We do have reason to believe that the killer is, or at least was, a patient at the hospital. I don't know if this makes it better or worse, but I'm a psychologist. I went to Hopkins. I worked as a psych aide at McLean Hospital and also the Institute for Living. I think I'll fit in on the wards."

Sampson spoke up. "Oh, yes, I was once a porter at Union Station. I'll fit in all right, too. Carry that load."

The executive staff didn't laugh and didn't say a word.

Nurse McGuigan and Dr. Cioffi glared at Sampson, who'd had the nerve to make light of the seriousness of the situation, heaven forbid.

I figured I had to take a completely different tack if I was going to get anywhere with them. "Are Anectine or Marplan available at the hospital?" I asked the group.

Dr. Cioffi shrugged. "Of course. But why do you want to know about those drugs?"

"Anectine was used to murder people who worked with the killer. He knows a lot about poisons, and he seems to enjoy watching people die. One of the hold-up gangs has never been found, and it's possible they were killed, too. Detective Sampson and I will need to look at the nursing reports and any case-conference reports for all patients. Then I'll check the daily charts from our most promising leads. We'll work the seven-to-three-thirty shift today."

Colonel Schofield nodded politely. "I expect everyone's full cooperation with these detectives. There could be a killer inside the hospital. It *is* possible, however unlikely."

At seven o'clock, Sampson and I went on duty at Hazelwood. I was a mental health counselor and he was a porter. And the Mastermind? Who was he?

Chapter 99

THAT MORNING, somewhere on the fifth floor of Hazelwood, the Mastermind was incredibly pissed off at his doctor. The useless, worthless quack had taken away his privileges to go off the hospital grounds. The shrink wanted to know why he seemed different lately. What was going on? *What was he holding back, holding inside?*

He stewed in his pitiful little room on the fifth floor. He got angrier and angrier. *Who was he really furious at? Besides the shrink?* He thought about it, then he sat down and wrote a letter.

Mr. Patrick Lee
Owner

Dear Sir:
   I don't fucking understand you. I signed our lease with amendments we agreed upon in good faith. I've held up my end of the deal and you have

*not! You conduct yourself as if you are purposely
defying our lease.*

*Let me remind you, Mr. Lee, that while you
may be the owner of this apartment, once you
take my money, it is my home.*

*This letter will show, for the record, the illegal
actions you have taken against me.*

*You must cease and desist posting eviction
notices on my door. I have paid the rent every
month and on time!*

*You must stop calling me, rambling on in your
loud Cantonese gibberish, and bothering me.*

Stop harassing me!

I ask you one last time.

Stop harassing me!

Immediately.

Or I will harass you!!!

He stopped writing. Then he thought long and hard
about the letter he'd just written. He was losing it, wasn't
he? He was going to blow.

He shut down his PC and went out into the hallway of
the ward. He put on his usual passive and slightly out-of-
it face. The nuts were out in all of their glory. Nuts in ratty
bathrobes, nuts in squeaky wheelchairs, nuts in the nude.

Sometimes, more often than not, he found it impossible to believe that he was here. Of course, that was the
point, wasn't it? No one would guess that he was the Mastermind. No one would ever find him here. He was perfectly safe.

And then he saw Detective Alex Cross.

Chapter 100

SAMPSON AND I both worked the 7:00-to-3:30-P.M. shift that day. When I arrived on Five, I felt I could almost hear an audible stretching of the thin red line between the sane and the mad.

The ward pretty much had the standard institutional look: faded mauve and gray everything, occasional gashes in the walls, nurses carrying trays of little cups, strung-out men in drawstring hospital pants and stained robes. I had seen it all before, except for one thing. The mental health workers carried whistles to sound an alarm if they needed help. That probably meant staff members had been hurt here.

The fourth and fifth floors made up the ward for psychiatric patients. There were thirty-one veterans on Five, the ages ranging from twenty-three to seventy-five. The patients on Five were considered dangerous, either to others or to themselves.

I started my search on Five. Two of the patients on the floor were tall and burly. They somewhat matched the description of the man who'd been followed by detectives Crews and O'Malley. One of them, Cletus Anderson, had a salt-and-pepper beard and had been involved in police work in Denver and Salt Lake City after his discharge from the army.

I found Anderson loitering in the day room on the first morning. It was past ten o'clock, but he was still wearing pajamas and a soiled robe. He was watching ESPN and he didn't strike me as a mastermind criminal.

The decor in the day room consisted of about a dozen brown vinyl chairs, a lopsided card table, and a TV mounted on one wall. The air was heavy with cigarette smoke. Anderson was smoking. I sat down in front of the TV, nodded hello.

He turned to me and blew an imperfect smoke ring. "You're new, right? Play pool?" he asked.

"I'll give it a try."

"Give it a try," he said, and smiled as if I'd made a joke. "Got keys to the pool room?"

He stood up without waiting for an answer to his question. Or maybe he'd forgotten that he'd asked it. I knew from the nursing charts that he had a violent temper but that he was on a truckload of Valium now. Good thing. Anderson was six-foot-six and weighed over two hundred seventy pounds.

The pool room was surprisingly cheery, with two large windows that looked out onto a walled exercise yard. The yard was bordered with red maples and elms, and birds twittered away in the trees.

I was in there alone with Cletus Anderson. Could this

very large man be the Mastermind? I couldn't tell yet. Maybe if he brained me with a pool ball or a cue stick.

Anderson and I played a game of eight ball. He wasn't very good. I let him stay in the game by blowing a couple of chip shots, but he didn't seem to notice. His blue-gray eyes were nearly glazed over.

"Like to wring those fucking bluejays' necks," he muttered angrily after missing a bank shot that wasn't even close to being his best opportunity on the table.

"What did the bluejays do wrong?" I asked him.

"They're out there. I'm in here," he said, and stared at me. "Don't try to shrink-wrap me, okay? Mr. Big Shit Mental Health Worker. Play your shot."

I sank a striped ball in the corner, then I missed another long shot I could have made. Anderson took the cue from me and he stood over his next shot for a long time. Too long, I was thinking. He straightened up suddenly. All six-foot-six of him. He glared at me. His body was getting rigid; he was tensing his large arms.

"Did you just *say* something to me, Mr. Mental Health?" he asked. His hands were large and held the pool cue tightly, wringing its neck. He had a lot of fat on him, but the fat was hard, like on football linemen and some professional wrestlers.

"Nope. Not a peep."

"That s'posed to be funny? Little play on the *peeping* bluejays, which you know I fucking hate?"

I shook my head. "I didn't mean anything by it."

Anderson stepped back from the pool table with the cue stick still clasped tightly in both hands. "I could have sworn I heard you call me a pussy under your breath. Little puss? Wuss? Something derogatory like that?"

I made eye contact with him. "I think our pool game's over now, Mr. Anderson. Please put the stick down."

"You think you can make me put down this cue stick? Probably do, if you think I'm a puss."

I held my mental health–worker whistle to my mouth. "I'm new here and I need the work. I don't want any trouble."

"Well then, you came to the wrong goddamn hellhole, man," he said. "You're the fucking priss. Whistle-blower."

Anderson tossed the pool cue onto the table and he stalked toward the door. He bumped my shoulder on the way.

"Watch your mouth, *nigger*," he said, spitting as he spoke the words.

I didn't give Anderson any more ground. I grabbed him, spun him around, surprised the hell out of him. I let him feel the strength in my arms and shoulders. I stared him down. I wanted to see what happened if he was provoked.

"You watch *your* mouth," I said in the softest whisper. "You be very, very careful around me."

I released my grip on Cletus Anderson and he spun away. I watched the large man leave the pool room — and I kind of hoped he was the Mastermind.

Chapter 101

THE WORST POSSIBILITY I COULD IMAGINE
so far was that the Mastermind might disappear and never
be heard from again. Hunting for the Mastermind had become more like Waiting for the Mastermind, or maybe
even Praying for the Mastermind to do something that
would lead us to him.

Shifts at the veterans hospital began with a thirty-
minute nursing-report-cum-coffee-klatch. During the
meeting each patient was talked about briefly, and privi-
lege changes noted. The report buzzwords were *affect,
compliance, interaction*, and, of course, *PTSD*. At least
half the men on the wards suffered from post-traumatic
stress disorder.

The shift report ended, and my day began. The psychiatric aide's main duty is to interact with patients. I was
doing that, and it reminded me of why I'd gone into psychology in the first place.

Actually, a lot of my past life was rushing back, especially my feelings for and understanding of the terrible power of trauma. So many of these men suffered from it. For them, the world no longer seemed safe or manageable. People around them didn't seem trustworthy or dependable. Self-doubt and guilt were always present. Faith and spirituality were nonexistent. *Why had the Mastermind chosen this place to hide?*

During the eight-hour shift I had a number of specific duties: sharps check at seven (I had to count all the silverware in the kitchen; if anything was missing, which was rare, rooms would be searched); one-on-one specials at eight with a patient named Copeland, who was considered extremely suicidal; fifteen-minute checks starting at nine, checking the whereabouts of all the patients every fifteen minutes and putting a mark by their names on a blackboard in the hallway outside the nurses' station); and baskets (somebody had to empty the garbage).

Each time I went to the blackboard I gave the most likely suspects a slightly bolder chalk mark. At the end of my hour on checks, I found that I had seven candidates on my hot list.

A patient named James Gallagher was on the list simply because he roughly fit the physical description of the Mastermind. He was tall enough, thick chested, and seemed reasonably alert and bright. That alone made him a suspect.

Frederic Szabo had full town privileges, but he was a timid soul and I doubted that he was a killer. Since Vietnam he'd been drifting around the country and had never held a job for more than a few weeks. Occasionally, he spit at hospital staff, but that was the worst offense he seemed capable of.

Stephen Bowen had full town privileges and had once been a promising infantry captain in Vietnam. He suffered from PTSD and had been in and out of veterans hospitals since 1971. He took pride in saying that he'd never held a "real job" since he left the military.

David Hale had been a policeman in Maryland for two years, before he began having paranoid thoughts that every Asian person he saw on the streets had been put there to kill him.

Michael Fescoe had worked for two banks in Washington, but he seemed too spaced-out to balance his own checkbook. Maybe he was faking PTSD, but his therapist at the hospital didn't think so.

Cletus Anderson fit the Mastermind's general physical description. I didn't like him. And he was violent. But Anderson hadn't done a thing to make me suspect he could actually be the Mastermind. Quite the contrary.

Just before shift change, Betsey Cavalierre reached me on the ward. I took the call in the small staff room at the rear of the nurses' station. "Betsey? What's up?"

"Alex, something very strange has happened," she said, and sounded rattled. I asked her what, and her answer gave me a nasty shock.

"Mike Doud is missing. He didn't come in to work this morning. We called his wife, but she said he left at the usual time."

"What is the Bureau doing about it?" I asked.

"We don't think he was in an automobile accident. It's too soon to put out an APB. Except this isn't like Doud. He's a really straight guy, family man, totally dependable. First Walsh," she said. "Now this. What the hell is going on Alex? *It's him, isn't it?*"

Chapter 102

WAS HE HUNTING US? First Agent James Walsh dead, now Doud missing. There was no way to tell if the events were connected, but we had to assume they were. *It's him, isn't it?*

I had set up time to interview Dr. Cioffi at the hospital's administration building, so I kept the appointment. I'd done some background work on Cioffi and a few of the other psychiatrists at Hazelwood. Cioffi was an army veteran himself; he'd done two tours in Vietnam, then he'd worked in seven veterans hospitals before this one. Could he be the Mastermind? He certainly had the background in abnormal psychology. But then again, so did I.

When I was shown into his office, Dr. Cioffi was writing at a pinewood partner's table. His back was to the window. He sat in a cane-and-wood chair covered with a yellow striped fabric that matched the drapes.

I couldn't see him very well, but I knew he could see

me. Oh, the games we play — even we doctors of the mind.

Eventually, he looked up, pretending to be surprised that I was there. "Detective Cross, I'm sorry. I guess the time got away from me."

He shot his cuffs, then rose from his chair and indicated a general sitting area against the far wall. "Dr. Marcuse and I were talking about you the other night. We realized we were pretty tough the day that you and the other detective arrived. I guess we found the idea of the police wandering around the wards a little troubling. Anyway, I've heard rumors that you're an excellent mental health counselor."

I refused to rise to the bait. He was a doctor; I was a *mental health counselor.* I told Cioffi about the list of suspects I had compiled. He took the list from me. Quickly looked over the names.

"I know all of these patients, of course. I'm sure that some are angry enough to be violent. Anderson and Hale have actually committed murders in the past. It's still hard to imagine any of these men organizing a series of daring robberies. And then, of course, why would they still be here if they had all that money?" He laughed. "I certainly wouldn't be." *Is that so, Dr. Cioffi?* I had to wonder.

Next, I spent nearly an hour with Dr. Marcuse, who had a smaller office right next to Cioffi's. I enjoyed his company, and the time flew by. Marcuse was energetic, bright, and trying to be cooperative with the investigation. Or so he made it seem.

"How did you wind up here at Hazelwood?" I eventually asked him.

"Good question, complicated answer. My father was an army pilot. Lost both his legs in the Second World War. I spent time around veterans hospitals from the time I was seven. Hated them with a passion, and with good reason. I guess I wanted to make them better places than what my father knew."

"You succeeding?" I asked.

"I've been here less than eight months. I took over for Dr. Francis, who transferred to another vets hospital in Florida. The money just isn't available for these places. It's a national disgrace, and nobody seems to care. *Sixty Minutes* and *Dateline* should do stories every week on veterans hospitals — until somebody does something about them. Alex, I don't know what to tell you about your killer."

"You don't believe he's here, do you?" I asked.

Marcuse shook his head. "If he is, he really is a mastermind. If he's here, he's got everybody fooled."

Chapter 103

I SEE YOU, DR. CROSS. I see you, but you don't have a clue who I am. I could walk up and touch you.

I'm a lot smarter than you — and also a lot smarter than you think I am. It's a simple fact. It's also verifiable. There have been batteries of intelligence tests. Lots and lots of the finest psychological tests. Have you seen my test scores? Were you impressed?

I was sitting *exactly* one chair away from you in the recreation room the other morning. I studied your face. My eyes rolled over your well-exercised body. I was thinking that maybe I was wrong — and that you weren't really Alex Cross. We were so close I could have jumped up and grabbed you by the throat. Would that have surprised you?

I'll admit, your being here certainly surprised me. I've seen your picture — you're well known — and then there you were. You made all of my paranoid dreams and fantasies come true.

Why are you here, Dr. Cross? Why, exactly? How the hell could you have found me? Are you that good?

That's the question I ask myself over and over, the litany playing inside my head.

Why is Alex Cross here? How good is he?

I'm going to work on a surprise for you now. I'm making a special plan in your honor.

I'm watching you walk away up the hallway, careful not to jangle your keys, and as I'm watching, I'm making a new plan.

You're part of it now.

Be extremely careful, Dr. Cross.

You're much more vulnerable than you think. You have no idea.

You know what? I am going to walk up and touch you. *Gotcha.*

Chapter 104

"THE HOSPITAL seems like a dead end, Betsey. I've looked at everybody — doctors, nurses, patients. I don't know that Sampson or I should go back to Hazelwood after this week. Maybe we got suckered in there by Brian Macdougall. Maybe the Mastermind is playing with us. Do we know anything more about Walsh or Doud?"

She shook her head. I could see the hurt and disappointment in her eyes. "Doud is still missing. There's *nothing*. He's disappeared."

I was sitting in her office and we had our feet propped up on her desk. We were drinking iced tea from bottles. Hanging out, commiserating. Betsey could be a good listener when she wanted, or needed, to be.

"Tell me what you know so far," she said. "Just let me hear it. I want it to roll over my brain."

"We haven't been able to find anything to connect any patient or any staff member at the hospital to MetroHartford or the previous bank robberies. No patient seems capable of the crimes. Even the doctors there aren't terribly impressive. Maybe Marcuse is — but I think he's a good guy. A half dozen of your agents have picked apart everything at Hazelwood. Nothing, Betsey. I'll look over the files again this weekend."

"But you think we've lost him?"

"It's the same old thing — *no suspects*. The Mastermind seems to disappear off the face of the earth when he wants to."

She rubbed her eyes with her fists, then she looked at me again. "The Justice Department is heavily invested in Brian Macdougall's story. They have to keep looking at Hazelwood. Then they'll check every other veterans hospital in the country. That means I'll have to keep looking. But you think Macdougall and his thugs were wrong?"

"Maybe wrong, maybe tricked. Or maybe Macdougall made up the whole story. Macdougall will probably get what he wanted out of this — Camp Fed. As I said, I'll look over the files again. I'm not giving up."

Betsey continued to look out over the cityscape. "So you're planning to work all weekend? That's a shame. You look like you need a break," she said.

I sipped my tea and watched her. "You have something in mind?"

She laughed, and the look on her face was irresistibly coy. She whistled into the neck of her iced-tea bottle. "I think it's time, Alex. We both need some good old-fashioned F-U-N. What do you say I pick you up — around noon on Saturday?"

I shook my head some, but I was laughing.

"Does that mean yes?" she asked.

"It means yes. I think I need a little old-fashioned F-U-N. I'm sure I do."

Chapter 105

I ALMOST COULDN'T WAIT for Saturday afternoon to come. I kept busy with the kids — grocery shopping, a stop at the new petting zoo in Southeast. I kept the Mastermind out of my thoughts. Also Agents Walsh and Doud, Hazelwood Veterans Hospital, murder and mayhem.

Betsey finally picked me up at exactly twelve in her blue Saab. The car was washed, maybe even polished with Turtle Wax, and it looked shiny and new, and the day seemed full of promise.

I knew that Jannie was watching from her bedroom window so I turned, made a funny face, and waved. Jannie waved back, and smiled from ear to ear. She and Rosie the Cat were up there; both of them tuned in to my ongoing soap opera.

I leaned down into the side window of Betsey's Saab. She was wearing a light leather jacket over a white silk blouse. She could really look great when she wanted to, and I guess she wanted to today.

"You're always right on time. Precise. Just like the Mastermind," I kidded her.

"Master*prick*," she corrected. "Wouldn't that be a great ending to this, Alex? I'm him! You catch me because I've made one fatal mistake. It's that I've become infatuated with you."

"You're infatuated?" I asked as I slid into the front seat. "Senior Agent Cavalierre?"

She laughed, and showed a beautiful smile. She was pulling out all the stops. "Giving up my prized weekend, aren't I?"

"So where are we going?" I asked.

"You'll see soon enough. I have a master plan."

"I'm not surprised."

Ten minutes later, she turned the Saab into the circular entrance to the Four Seasons Hotel on Pennsylvania Avenue. Overhanging flags gently rustled in the wind. The courtyard had a lot of brick covered with Boston ivy. Very pretty.

"Is this okay?" She turned and looked at me. Her eyes were a little nervous, a little unsure.

"I think it is," I said. "Convenient, too. Perfect planning."

"Why waste quality time on the road?" Betsey said, and smiled irresistibly. She was pretty outrageous for an FBI agent, especially a smart one with lofty ambitions. I liked her style a lot: She went for what she wanted. I wondered if she usually got it.

She had preregistered, and we were taken directly to a

room on the hotel's top floor. I walked behind her all the way; *I watched her walk.*

"You folks need any help from me?" the youthful but officious hotel bellman asked once we were inside the suite.

I handed him a tip. "Thanks for showing us to the room. If you would just shut the door on your way out. Gently."

He nodded. "The room service here is great, by the way. The best in D.C."

"Thank you. The door," Betsey said, and waved and smiled. "Softly. Bye-bye."

Chapter 106

BETSEY WAS ALREADY SLIPPING off her leather jacket. Then she was in my arms by the time the door clicked shut. We were kissing and moving against each other, and it seemed like a slow, graceful, irresistible dance to me. We were both infatuated, and that's not so bad, I was thinking. Good old-fashioned fun. Isn't that what she had promised?

Betsey felt electric but also very comfortable in my arms. She was a study in contrasts. She was small and light, but also athletic and strong; she was very smart and serious but she was funny, ironic, irreverent. Oh yeah, and she was sexy as hell.

We moved toward the bed and let ourselves fall onto it. I don't know who was leading or who was following. It didn't make any difference. I buried my face in her silk blouse.

I looked into her brown eyes. "You were pretty sure of yourself. Preregistering and all."

"It was time," she said, nothing more.

I took off her soft, creamy white blouse and short black skirt a piece at a time. I gently stroked her silky-smooth face; then her arms, legs, the bottoms of her feet. It must have taken us half an hour to get undressed.

"You have the most wonderful touch," she whispered. "Don't stop. Please don't stop."

"I won't. I like touching, too. Don't *you* stop."

"Oh, God, this is so good! *Alex!*" she screeched, completely out of character.

I kissed her where I'd touched her with my fingers. She was so warm to the touch. She wore a wonderful perfume, which she told me was Alfred Sung's Forever. I kissed her lips, not *forever,* but for a long, long time.

We danced some more, held each other, kissed a lot, stroked each other's bodies. We had all the time in the world. God, I had missed being with someone like this.

"Now. Please?" one of us whispered finally.

It was definitely time.

I entered Betsey slowly, very slowly. I kept going as far as I could inside her. I was on top, but I held my weight on my forearms. We were moving together, and it seemed so effortless and right. She started to hum, no particular song, just sweetness that made me vibrate like a tuning fork.

"I like being with you," I said. "A lot. Even more than I expected."

"Oh, me too. I told you this would be better than chasing after the Mastermind."

"This is *so much* better."

"Now! Please?"

Chapter 107

BETSEY AND I FELL ASLEEP in each other's arms at some point later that afternoon.

I woke up first and saw it was almost six already. It didn't matter what time it was. Not even what day. I called home, checked in on everybody. They were happy I was out — and having F-U-N for a change.

I was. I watched Betsey sleep naked, and I would have been content to do that for a long time. I thought about drawing a warm bath for the two of us. Should I? *Yes, I should. Why not?*

In the bathroom, I spotted a jar of bright blue bubble-bath beads near her things. She was way ahead of me, wasn't she? I wondered if I liked that, and decided that I did.

The tub was filling up slowly when I heard her speak behind me. "Oh, good, I've wanted to have a bubble bath with you."

I looked around at her — she was still naked.

"You thought about this before, huh?"

"Oh, yes. And often. What do you think I'm doing during those endless briefing sessions?"

A few moments later, we were stepping into the tub together. It felt incredibly good: the antidote to the hard work, the tension, the frustration we'd been experiencing over the past month.

"I like being with you so much," Betsey whispered as she stared into my eyes. "I don't want to leave this tub, or you. This is heaven."

"They have excellent room service. The best in D.C.," I reminded her. "They'll probably come right to *tubside*, if we ask nicely."

"Let's find out," Betsey said.

Chapter 108

IT WENT LIKE THAT, dreamily, wonderfully, perfectly, through the rest of Saturday and into Sunday morning. The only problem — the time went too fast.

The more I was around Betsey and the more we talked, the more I liked her; and I had liked her before we went to the Four Seasons. What wasn't there to like? Only once on Saturday did we talk briefly about the Mastermind case. Betsey asked if I thought we were in any danger. She wondered if he might be stalking us. Neither of us had an answer for that one, but we had both brought our guns.

Around ten Sunday morning, we had breakfast served to us at the pool. We sat on chaise lounges cushioned with fluffy blue and white towels. We read the *Washington Post* and the *New York Times*. We got an occasional curious look, but the Four Seasons is a sophisticated hotel chain and the people who stay here, especially at the hotel in Washington, have seen it all — and much, much more.

Besides, I'm sure Betsey and I looked content and happy together.

I should have seen it coming. I don't know why, but suddenly I was thinking about the person behind the robberies, murders, and kidnappings: the Mastermind. I tried to will the thought away. It wouldn't go. The Dragonslayer was back; the job was back.

I looked at Betsey. Her eyes were shut, and she seemed perfectly relaxed. That morning she'd done her nails a bright shade of red. She'd done her lips the same color. She didn't look like an FBI agent anymore. She was sexy and beautiful, and I was loving our time together.

I hated to bother her. She had earned some time off, and she was lying so peacefully on her chaise lounge.

"Betsey?"

Her lips formed a smile. She kept her eyes shut tight. She wriggled her body slightly to get a better position on the chaise lounge.

"Yes. I'd love to go back to the room with you. I'd even give up this toasty feeling on my neck and back for it. We can leave our towels on the chairs. Maybe they'll still be here when we get back."

I smiled, then I lightly massaged her back. "I hate to do this, Betsey. Can we talk about the case? About *him?*"

She opened her eyes. They had become narrowed and focused. Just like that, Betsey was all business. I was amazed at the transformation. If anything, she was worse than I was. "What about *him?*" she asked. "What are you thinking?"

I moved over to the edge of her chair. "We've spent the last two weeks digging around MetroHartford. Then questioning Macdougall. During all that time, we've ignored the banks he hit earlier. Betsey, I want to look through all the old files again. Even the personnel files."

She was a little puzzled. "Okay. I guess. Sure. You've lost me, though. What are you thinking, Alex? What would we be looking for?"

"Four employees were killed at the First Union Bank. There was no rhyme or reason for it. We always assumed he was making an example of them. Why four? It doesn't track for me."

She shut her eyes again. I could see the wheels turning — fast; I could almost hear the gears shift. "He wanted revenge against that particular bank, *and* he wanted his money."

"Sounds like him, doesn't it? He's thorough *and* efficient. Doesn't miss a trick. He'd want it all."

Betsey opened her eyes again. She stared at me. Pursed her shiny red lips. "There's just one thing, though. It's important."

I lightly kissed her lips. "What's that?" I asked.

"I still want to go back to the room with you. *Then* we can go through all the dusty, musty files on the banks."

I laughed. "That sounds like a very wise plan. Especially the first part."

Chapter 109

WE WERE BACK at the FBI field office by three that afternoon. Betsey had called ahead, and the First Union files were waiting in her office. We dug into the files. And dug, and dug. We ordered sandwiches and iced tea from the deli on the corner.

Twice.

"Why are the two of us so driven to do this?" Betsey finally looked over and asked me.

"He probably killed Walsh, and maybe Mike Doud. He's a really sick puppy and he's out there somewhere and that's *scary as hell.*"

She nodded solemnly. "*We're* sick puppies, and look where it got us. Pass me that stack, will you? God, it was so nice and restful and *sunny* at the Four Seasons."

Around eleven o'clock I held up a small black-and-white photo. I was deep into the personnel files from First Union.

"Betsey?" I called out.

"Mmmm?" She was deep into her own stack of files.

"This guy was a security executive at the bank. Betsey, he's a patient on Five at Hazelwood. I know who he is. I've talked to him this week. There's no record at the hospital that he ever worked at First Union. *This is our guy.* He has to be." I passed her the picture.

We quickly agreed that Sampson and I would return to Hazelwood in the morning. In the meantime, she tried to gather all the information she could on a patient named Frederic Szabo. Goddamn nerdy Frederic Szabo!

It was possible that Szabo wasn't connected, but it didn't seem likely. Szabo had been the head of security at First Union Bank. He was a *tall, bearded* patient at Hazelwood. He fit Brian Macdougall's description. His psychiatric profile included recurring paranoid fantasies against many prominent authority figures, including several Fortune 500 companies. He'd just seemed too withdrawn and helpless to be the Mastermind.

The most telling evidence was that the hospital's records *didn't show that he had worked at First Union.* Supposedly, Szabo had been an out-of-work drifter since Vietnam. Of course, we now knew that he'd been lying about those years.

According to his psychiatric profile, Szabo had a paranoid personality disorder. He had a severe distrust of people, especially businesspeople, and believed that they were exploiting and trying to deceive him. He was sure that if he confided in someone, the information would be used against him. During a two-year marriage, from '70 through '71, Szabo had been pathologically hypersensitive and jealous of his wife. When the marriage broke up, he supposedly hit the road. He eventually showed up at

Hazelwood, seeking help three years before the robberies and a year after he'd been let go at First Union. During his frequent stays at Hazelwood he was always cold and aloof. He cut himself off from everyone at the hospital, both patients and staff. He never made a friend, but he basically seemed harmless to others; and *he had grounds and town privileges most of the time.*

After I read the profile again, it struck me that Szabo's job at the bank had been a perfect fit for his disorder. Like a lot of functioning paranoids, Szabo had sought out work in which he could operate in a punitive and moralistic style that would be socially acceptable. As head of security at the bank, he could focus on his need to prevent attacks from anyone at any time. By protecting the perimeters of the banks, he was unconsciously protecting himself.

It was ironic that by setting up a series of successful bank robberies he had proven, at least symbolically, that there was no way to protect himself from attack by others. Maybe that was his point.

His mistrustfulness made treatment at the hospital difficult, if not impossible. He had been in and out of Hazelwood four times in the past eighteen months. Had the veterans hospital been a front for his other activities? Had he chosen Hazelwood as his hideout?

And, most puzzling of all, why was he still there?

Chapter 110

ON MONDAY MORNING I went to work at Hazelwood again. I was outfitted in an overhanging white shirt and corduroy pants that were loose enough to hide the holster strapped onto my leg. An FBI agent named Jack Waterhouse had been added to the staff as an aide. Sampson continued as a porter, but he was working only on Five now.

Frederic Szabo proceeded to do nothing to attract suspicion or reveal himself in any way. For three days straight, he never left the ward. He slept a lot in his room. He occasionally worked on an old Apple laptop.

What the hell was he doing? Did he know we were watching him?

Late on Wednesday, after the work shift, I met up with Betsey in the hospital's administration building. She had on a navy blue suit and blue slingback heels, and she was all business again. She almost seemed like another person at times, preoccupied and distant.

She was clearly as frustrated as I was. "He worked on his master plan for at least four years, right? Presumably, he has fifteen million dollars stashed somewhere. He's killed a lot of people to get it. Now he's sitting on his ass at Hazelwood? Give me a break!"

I told her what I thought about Szabo. "He's extremely paranoid. He's psychopathic. He may even know we're here. Maybe we should pull back from the hospital. Do surveillance from the outside. He has his full grounds and town privileges back from Dr. Cioffi. Szabo can come and go as he likes."

While I talked, Betsey kept pulling at the lapels of her blazer. I was afraid she might start pulling out her hair next.

"But he doesn't *go anywhere!* He's a fifty-year-old slacker! He's a total loser!"

"Betsey, I know. I've been watching Szabo sleep and play games on the Internet for three days."

She snorted out a laugh. "So he's pulled off five perfect crimes — that we know of. And now he's retiring to the farm."

"Yeah. The funny farm," I said.

"Want to hear about *my* day?" she finally asked.

I nodded.

"Well, I visited First Union and I talked with everyone I could find who was there when Szabo was at the bank. He was considered very 'dedicated,' actually. But he was wound tight about efficiency and doing the right thing in *exactly* the right way. Some of the others used it to mock him."

"Mock him in what way?" I asked.

"Szabo had a *nickname,* Alex. Get this — it was the

Mastermind! The name was a *joke*. It was supposed to be a joke on Szabo."

"Well, I guess he's turned the joke around. Now the joke is on us."

Chapter 111

THE STRANGEST THING happened the following morning. As Szabo was passing me in the hall, he rubbed against me. He managed to look flustered and he apologized for supposedly *"losing his balance,"* but I was almost certain he had done it on purpose. Why? What the hell was that all about?

About an hour later, I saw him leaving the ward. I was pretty sure he knew I was watching him go. As soon as he was out, I hurried to the door.

"Where's Szabo going?" I asked the aide who'd just let him out.

"PT. He signed out. Szabo has full grounds and town. He can go wherever he likes."

He had been vegetating on the ward for so long that he'd caught me off guard. "Tell the head nurse that I had to leave," I said.

"Tell her yourself." The aide frowned and tried to blow me off.

I pushed past him. "*Tell her.* It's important."

I let myself off the unit and took the rickety and temperamental elevator down to the lobby floor. PT was physical therapy, and Frederic Szabo hated the gym. I remembered reading it in his nursing notes. Where was he really going?

I hurried outside and saw Szabo skulking across the courtyard between hospital buildings. *Tall and bearded* — like the physical description we'd gotten from Brian Macdougall.

When Szabo walked right past the gym, I wasn't surprised.

He was on the move!

He kept on going and I followed. He seemed kind of nervous and skittish. He finally turned his head in my direction, and I ducked off the path. I didn't think he'd seen me. Had he?

Szabo continued on and walked through the hospital gates. The street outside was filled with traffic. He walked due south. Not a care in the world. Was this the Mastermind?

He hopped into a cab a couple of blocks from the hospital. There were three of them parked in front of a Holiday Inn.

I hurried to one of the other cabs, got in, told the driver to follow.

The driver was Indian. "Where are we going, mister?" he asked.

"I have no idea," I said. I showed him my detective's badge.

The driver shook his head, then he moaned into his hands. "Oh, brother. Just my bad luck. Like the movies — *follow that cab.*"

Chapter 112

SZABO GOT OUT OF HIS CAB on Rhode Island Avenue in Northwest. So did I. He walked for a while — window-shopped. At least that's what it looked like. He seemed more relaxed now. His nervous tics had lessened once he was off the hospital grounds. Probably because he had been faking them.

He finally turned into a squat, dilapidated brownstone building, still on Rhode Island Avenue. The basement floor was a Chinese laundry — A. LEE.

What was he doing in there? Was he skipping out a back door? But then I saw a light flash in a second-floor window. Szabo crossed past it a few times. It was him. *Tall and bearded.*

My brain was starting to overload with possibilities. *No one at Hazelwood knew about Szabo's apartment in D.C.* There wasn't any mention of it in the nursing notes.

Szabo was supposed to be a drifter. Hopeless, harmless, *homeless.* That was the illusion he'd created. I'd finally learned a secret of his. What did it mean?

I waited down on Rhode Island Avenue. I didn't feel in any particular danger. Not yet, anyway.

I waited out on the street for quite a while. He was inside the building for nearly two hours. I didn't see him appear at the windows again. What was he doing in there? Time flies when you're hanging by your fingernails.

Then the light in the apartment blinked out.

I watched the building with mounting apprehension. Szabo didn't come outside. I was concerned. Where was he?

A good five minutes after the light went out upstairs, Szabo appeared on the front doorstep again. His nervous tics seemed to have returned. Maybe they were for real.

He rubbed his eyes repeatedly, and then his lower chin. He twitched and continually pulled his shirt away from his chest. He finger-combed his thick black hair three or four times.

Was this the Mastermind that I was watching? It almost didn't seem possible. But if he wasn't, where did that leave us?

Szabo kept nervously looking around the street, but I was hidden in the dark shadows of another building. I was sure he couldn't see me. What was he afraid of?

He started to walk. I watched him retrace his steps up Rhode Island Avenue. Then he waved down a cab.

I didn't follow Szabo. I wanted to — but I had an even stronger urge. A hunch I needed to play. I hurried across the street and entered the brownstone where he'd spent most of the afternoon.

I *had* to find out what Szabo had been doing in there. I finally had to admit — he was driving *me* crazy. He was giving me nervous tics.

Chapter 113

I USED A SMALL, very useful lock pick and got into Szabo's apartment in less time than it takes to say "illegal entry." No one was ever going to know I'd been in there.

I was planning to take a quick look around the apartment, then get right out again. I doubted he'd left evidence linking him to the MetroHartford kidnapping, or any of the bank jobs. I needed to see his place, though. I had to know more about Szabo than the doctors and nurses at Hazelwood had written in their reports. I needed to understand the Mastermind.

He had a collection of sharpened hunting knives, and he also collected old guns: Civil War rifles, German Lugers, American Colts. There were souvenirs from Vietnam: a ceremonial sword and a battalion flag of the K10 NVA Battalion, North Vietnamese. Mostly, he had books and magazines in the apartment. *The Evil That Men Do. Crime and Punishment. The Shooting Gazette. Scientific American.*

So far, no big surprises. Other than that he *had* the apartment in the first place.

"Szabo, are you *him?*" I finally asked out loud. "Are you the Mastermind? What the hell is your game, man?"

I quickly searched the living room, a small bedroom, then a claustrophobic den that obviously served as an office.

Szabo, is this where you plotted everything out?

An unfinished handwritten letter was lying on the desk in his den. It seemed he'd been working on it recently. I began to read.

> *Mr. Arthur Lee*
> *A. Lee Laundry*
>
>   *This is a warning, and if I were you, I'd take it very seriously.*
>   *Three weeks ago, I dropped off some dry cleaning to you. Before I send out my cleaning, I <u>always</u> enclose a list of <u>all articles</u> in the dry cleaning bag, <u>and</u> a brief description of each article.*
>   <u>*I keep a copy for myself!*</u>
>   *The list is <u>orderly</u> and <u>efficient</u>.*

The letter went on to say that some clothes of Szabo's were missing. He'd spoken to someone at the laundry and been promised the clothing would be sent right over. It wasn't.

>   *I march right down to your cleaners. I meet with YOU. I am enraged that YOU too can stand*

*there and tell me you don't have my clothes. Then
for the final insult. You tell me my doorman
probably stole them.*

*I don't have a fucking doorman! I live in the
same building you do!*

Consider yourself <u>warned</u>.

Frederic Szabo

What the hell was this? I wondered as I finished reading the odd, crazy, and seemingly inconsequential letter.

I shook my head back and forth. Was the A. Lee Laundry his next target? Was he planning something against
Lee? The *Mastermind?*

I opened the drawers in a small credenza and found
more letters, written to other companies: Citibank, Chase,
First Union Bank, Exxon, Kodak, Bell Atlantic, scores of
others.

I sat down and skimmed through the letters. All of it
was hate mail. Crazy stuff. This was Frederic Szabo as
he'd been described in his hospital workups. Paranoid,
angry at the world, a curmudgeonly fifty-one-year-old
who had been fired from every job he'd had.

I was getting more confused rather than clearer about
Szabo. I ran my fingers along the top of a tall filing cabinet. There were papers up there. I pulled them down and
took a look.

*There were blueprints of the banks that had been
robbed!*

And a layout of the Renaissance Mayflower Hotel!

"Christ, it is him," I muttered out loud. What were the
blueprints doing here, though?

I don't remember exactly what happened next. Maybe it was shifting light or motion in the room that I caught out of the corner of my eye.

I turned away from Szabo's work desk. My eyes went wide with surprise, then total shock. My heart skipped.

A man was coming at me with a hunting knife clasped in his hand. He was wearing a President Clinton mask. He was screaming my name!

Chapter 114

"CROSS!"

I reached out both hands to try and stop the arm chopping down toward me. It held a hunting knife much like the ones on display in the other room. My hands wrapped around the powerful arm. If this was Szabo, he was stronger and a lot more agile than he'd looked at the hospital.

"What are you doing?" he screamed. "How dare you? How dare you touch my personal property?" He sounded completely crazy. "These letters are *private!*"

I pivoted off my right leg and yanked the hand holding the knife. The blade stuck several inches into the wooden desk. The masked man grunted and cursed.

Now what? I couldn't chance bending down to get my gun from my ankle holster. The masked man easily wriggled the knife free. He swung it in a small, lethal arc. He missed the thrust by a few inches. The blade whistled past my temple.

"You're going to die, Cross," he screamed.

I spotted a cut-glass baseball on his desk. It was the only thing resembling a weapon that I saw anywhere. I grabbed it. Sidearmed it at him.

I heard a crunching sound as the paperweight struck a glancing blow off the side of his skull. He roared loudly, angrily, like an injured animal. Then he wobbled backward. He didn't go down.

I bent quickly and pulled at my Glock. It hitched once, then came free in my hand.

He flailed at me again with the large knife.

"Stop!" I yelled. "I *will* shoot you."

He kept coming. He roared out words that were unintelligible. He took another swipe with the knife. This time, he cut me on the right wrist. It burned, hurt like hell.

I fired the Glock. The bullet hit him in the upper chest. *It didn't stop him!* He spun sideways, righted himself, and he was on me, screaming, "Fuck you, Cross. You're *nothing!*"

He was too close for me to swing, and I didn't want to shoot again and kill him if I didn't have to. I drove my head hard into his chest. I aimed for the general area where he'd been wounded.

He screamed, a horrifying, high-pitched moan. Then he dropped the knife.

I wrapped both arms as tight as I could around him. My legs churned hard. I kept driving him across the room until we hit a wall. The whole building shuddered.

Somebody in the next apartment banged on a wall and complained about the noise.

"Call the police!" I yelled. *"Call nine one one."*

I had him pinned to the floor, and he was moaning

loudly that I'd hurt him. He continued to struggle and fight. I hit him squarely on the jaw, and he finally stopped. Then I pulled off the rubber mask.

It was Szabo.

"You're the Mastermind," I gasped. "It *is* you."

"I didn't do anything," he snarled back. He started to struggle again. He cursed loudly. "You broke in to my house. You fool! You're all goddamn fools. Listen to me, asshole. Listen! *You got the wrong man!*"

Chapter 115

IT WAS A MADHOUSE, and that certainly seemed appropriate for the dramatic capture. A team of FBI technicians arrived at Frederic Szabo's apartment in less than an hour. I recognized two of them, Greg Wojcik and Jack Heeney, from past jobs. They were the FBI's best, and they began to expertly take the place apart.

I stayed on and watched the painstaking search. The techies were looking for false walls, loose floorboards, anywhere Szabo might have concealed evidence, or possibly hidden fifteen million dollars.

Betsey Cavalierre got to the apartment just after the technical crew. I was glad to see her. Once Szabo's bullet wound was treated and bandaged, Betsey and I tried to question him. He wouldn't talk to us. Not a word. He seemed crazier than ever; manic one moment, then quiet and unresponsive the next. He did what he was known for at Hazelwood — he spit at me, several times. Szabo spit until his mouth was dry, then wrapped his arms around himself and was silent.

He shut his eyes tight. He wouldn't look at either of us, wouldn't respond in any way. Finally, he was taken away in a straitjacket.

"Where's the money?" Betsey asked as we watched Szabo leave the building.

"He's the only one who knows, and he sure as hell isn't talking. I have never, ever felt more out of it on a case."

The next day was a rainy, miserable, godawful Friday. Betsey and I went to the Metropolitan Detention Center, where Frederic Szabo was being held.

The press was gathered in large numbers everywhere outside the building. Neither of us said a word as we passed through them. We hid under and behind a big black umbrella and the streaking rain as we hurried inside.

"Pitiful goddamn vultures," Betsey whispered to me. "*Three* things are certain in this life: death, taxes, and that the press will get it wrong. They will, you know."

"Once somebody writes it wrong, it *stays* wrong," I said.

We met with Szabo in a small, anonymous-looking room attached to the cell block. He was no longer confined in a straitjacket, but he looked out of it. His court-appointed lawyer was present. Her name was Lynda Cole, and she didn't seem to like Szabo much more than we did.

I was surprised that Szabo hadn't gone after a bigger-name attorney, but just about everything he did surprised me. *He didn't think like other people.* That was his strength, wasn't it? It was what he loved about himself, and maybe it was what had brought him down.

Once again, Szabo wouldn't look at us for several minutes. Betsey and I tried a steady battery of questions, but he was completely, stubbornly unresponsive. His dosage of Haldol had been increased, and I wondered if that had anything to do with his listlessness. Somehow I doubted it. I felt he might be playacting again.

"This is hopeless," Betsey finally said after we'd been there for over an hour. She was right. It was futile to spend any more time with Szabo that day.

She and I got up to leave, and so did Lynda Cole, who was small like Betsey and very attractive. She hadn't said more than a dozen words during the hour. There wasn't any need for her to talk if her client didn't. Szabo suddenly looked up from a spot on the table. He'd been staring at it for at least twenty minutes.

He looked straight at me and he finally spoke. "You got the wrong man."

Then Frederic Szabo grinned like the craziest person I had ever met in my life. And I've met some very crazy people.

Chapter 116

BETSEY CAVALIERRE and I returned to Hazelwood and the mountains of grunt work that still had to be done there. Sampson met us. By ten-thirty that night, we'd gone through everything we could find at the hospital. We had managed to identify nineteen staff members who'd spent time with Szabo. The shortlist included six therapists who'd seen him.

Betsey and I tacked their pictures up on one wall. Then I walked back and forth staring at them, hoping for a blinding insight. Where the hell was the money? How had Szabo actually controlled the robbery-murders?

I sat down again. Betsey was sipping her sixth or seventh Diet Coke. I'd matched her coffee for Coke. Intermittently, we had revisited the mystery of James Walsh's supposed suicide and the sudden disappearance of Michael Doud. Szabo had refused to answer any questions about the two agents. Why would he murder the two of them? What was his real plan? Goddamn him!

"Could Szabo really be behind all this, Alex? Is he that clever? That goddamn evil? That nuts?"

I pushed myself up from the desk I was working at. "I don't know anymore. It's late again. I'm fried, Betsey. I'm out of here. Tomorrow's another day."

The overhead lights were blinding and hurtful. Betsey's eyes were red rimmed and vacant as they stared up at me. I wanted to hug her some but half a dozen agents were still working in the office. I ached to hold her in my arms, to talk to her about anything but the case.

"Good night," I finally said. "Get some sleep."

"Night, Alex." *I miss you,* she mouthed.

"Be careful," I said. "Be careful going home."

"I always am. *You* be careful."

I got home somehow and climbed upstairs to bed. I'd been working too hard for too long. Maybe I *did* need to quit the Job. I hit the pillow hard. At about twenty past two I woke up. I'd been having a conversation with Frederic Szabo in my sleep. Then I'd talked to someone else from the investigation. *Oh, brother.*

It was a bad, bad time to be awake. I usually don't remember my dreams — which probably means I'm repressing them — but I woke with a clear and very disturbing image of the last couple of minutes.

The bank robber Tony Brophy had been describing his meeting with the Mastermind; how he'd been sitting behind bright lights and could only see a silhouette of the man. The silhouette he described didn't match the shape of Frederic Szabo's head. Not even close. He had talked about a big hooked nose and large ears. He'd mentioned the ears a couple of times. *Big ears, like a car with both doors open.* Szabo actually had small ears and a regular nose.

But there was someone else who came to mind! Jesus! I jumped out of bed. I stared out my window until my mind was more focused and clear. Then I called Betsey.

She picked up after the second ring. Her voice was a soft, muffled moan.

"It's Alex. Sorry to call you, to wake you. I think I know who the Mastermind is."

"Is this a bad dream?" she muttered.

"Oh, definitely," I told her. "This is our worst nightmare."

Chapter 117

THERE WERE TWO MASTERMINDS. It sounded crazy to me at first, but then I was almost sure it had to be the answer to so many things about the investigation that didn't make sense.

Szabo was one Mastermind, but he'd been given the name as a joke because he was too efficient, too perfect. There was someone else. A second Mastermind. This person wasn't a joke to his peers — he had no *peers;* he didn't write hate mail from his room at a veterans hospital.

It took me a few minutes to convince Betsey that I might be right. Then we called Kyle Craig. We went two-on-one until Kyle was convinced enough to let us move forward — in a whole new and mind-boggling direction.

At eleven that morning, Betsey and I boarded a plane at Bolling field. Up until a few weeks earlier I'd never been to Bolling, but lately I seemed to be flying out of there more often than out of National, or Ronald Reagan, as it's now called.

Just past one o'clock we landed at Palm Beach International Airport in south Florida. It was ninety-five degrees outside, humid as hell. I didn't care about the heat. I was excited, pumped up about possibly solving the puzzle. We were met by FBI agents, but Betsey was in charge, even in Florida. The local agents deferred to her.

We got on I-95 North once we left the small, very well run airport. We proceeded about ten miles, then headed east toward the ocean and Singer Island. The sun looked like a lemon drop melting in bright blue skies.

I'd had time on the flight to think about my theory of two Masterminds. The more I thought it through, the surer I became that we were on the right track, finally. A vivid image kept flashing through my mind.

It was a photograph of a therapist named Dr. Bernard Francis. The photo had been stapled to Francis's personnel file at Hazelwood. Two other photos had been hanging on the walls of Dr. Cioffi's office. I'd seen them there when I interviewed him. Bernard Francis was tall and balding, with a broad forehead and a hooked nose. He also had large ears, floppy ones. *Like a car with both doors open.*

Francis had been Frederic Szabo's therapist for nine weeks in '96, and then for five months last year. At the end of the year he had transferred to Florida, supposedly to work at the veterans hospital in north West Palm. Once I'd established a link to Francis, several other connections followed. According to the nursing notes, Dr. Francis had accompanied Szabo off the grounds on at least three occasions last year. The trips weren't unusual in themselves, but under the circumstances they were very interesting to me.

During the plane ride to Florida, I also reread the actual notes Dr. Francis had made about Szabo in '96 and then last year.

One of the very insightful early notes posed the question: *Did pt. actually spend the past twentysome years wandering the country performing odd jobs? Somehow, this doesn't ring true. Suspect pt. has a very active fantasy life and may be withholding from us. What really precipitated pt.'s. stay at Hazelwood this year?*

Betsey and I knew the answer to that question, and we suspected Francis had found out, too. In February of '96, Frederic Szabo had been fired from his job as head of security at First Union. There had been a series of unsolved robberies at First Unions in Virginia and Maryland. Szabo had blamed himself for the lapse in security, and then so had the bank. They finally fired him.

Soon after that he had a nervous breakdown and checked himself into Hazelwood, which was where the fun and mind games began.

Chapter 118

WE SET UP a round-the-clock surveillance post outside Dr. Francis's condominium on Singer Island. The place was a sprawling four-bedroom penthouse with a roof deck; it was right on the water. It seemed beyond the means of the average therapist at a veterans hospital. Of course, Dr. Francis didn't consider himself an average therapist.

Francis was spending the evening entertaining a blond woman who looked to be about half his age. To give him his due, he was a slender man of forty-five and appeared to be in good shape. She was a stunning beauty, though; she wore a black string bikini with high-heeled black pumps. She was constantly rearranging her cleavage and pushing her long blond hair out of her eyes.

"Very fetching," Betsey said, and frowned. "Looks like she's caught herself a real killer date."

Betsey, two other agents, and I camped out in a Dodge van in a parking lot behind the condos. The lot was nearly full, and the van blended in. It had a periscope that allowed us to watch Francis and his guest as they barbecued steaks on his deck. The FBI had already identified the blond woman as a dancer at an "upscale topless steak house" in West Palm. She had previous arrests for soliciting and prostitution in Fort Lauderdale. Her name was Bianca Massie and she was twenty-three years old.

We watched the good doctor as he frequently hugged and fondled the blond woman while cooking dinner. Then the two of them disappeared inside for about ten minutes. They came out again, and during the meal they played footsie and stroked one another. They finished a second bottle of Stag's Leap cabernet, then disappeared inside again.

"What can we see in there?" Betsey asked one of the agents. "I need a picture."

"Our man on the other roof can see inside the condo through several of the southern-exposure windows," one of the agents reported.

"It's an easy-sleazy bachelor pad. Expensive furniture, lots of etchings. Bose sound system, free weights. The doc has a black Lab he probably uses to pick up more ladies on the beach."

"I don't think he picked her up," I said. "More likely, he leased her for the night."

"He and the young lady are *intimately* involved at the moment. The black Lab seems to have taught the doc a few things. He knows some doggy tricks. Our lookout says that his ears and nose are much larger than a certain other part of his anatomy."

That got a laugh from the group. It also eased the tension. We were a little fearful for the girl, but we were close enough to get inside in a hurry.

The lookout continued to report on what he saw. "*Oops,* the doc would appear to be a premature ejaculator. The young lady doesn't seem to mind. *Awhh,* she kissed him on top of his head, poor baby."

"You get what you pay for," Betsey said.

Finally, the blond woman left and the steamy movie was over for the night. Dr. Francis stayed out on the deck, sipping a snifter of brandy, watching the moon ride high over the Atlantic.

"Ahh, the good life," Betsey said. "Moon over Miami and all that neat stuff."

"He only had to kill about a dozen people to get his place in the sun," I said.

Francis's cell phone rang around midnight. We listened to the call from the surveillance van. The call definitely got our attention. Betsey and I exchanged glances.

The caller sounded nervous. "Bernie, they're all over this place again. They're looking at staff now. They —"

Francis cut in. "It's late. I'll call you in the morning. *I'll call you.* Don't call me here. I've told you that. Please, don't do it again."

Dr. Francis hung up angrily. He drained the rest of his brandy.

Betsey elbowed me. She was smiling for the first time since we'd been watching Francis. "Alex, you recognize the voice on the other end?" she asked.

I sure did. "The lovely and talented Kathleen McGuigan. Nurse McGuigan is part of this. It's all starting to come together, isn't it?"

Chapter 119

IT WAS REALLY EASY to loathe Dr. Bernard Francis. He was human scum, the worst of the worst, a killer who liked to make his victims suffer. It made the late-night-surveillance job easier, almost bearable. So did the idea that Francis was the Mastermind, and that we were close to nailing him to the walls of his pink stucco, Mediterranean-style condo.

Kathleen McGuigan didn't try to call Francis back that night. And he didn't call her. Around one o'clock, he went inside to bed and turned on his alarm system.

"Sweet dreams, you bastard," Betsey said as the house lights went off.

"We know where he lives. We know he did it — if not exactly how. But we can't bring him down?" one of the agents complained once Francis had turned in for the night.

"Patience, patience," I said. "We just got here. We'll get Dr. Francis. We just want to watch him a little longer.

We need to be absolutely sure this time. And, we want the money he stole."

Betsey and I finally left the surveillance van around two in the morning. We took one of the Bureau's sedans. She drove off Singer Island. Everyone else was staying at a Holiday Inn in West Palm. We headed north on I-95.

"Is this okay?" she asked once we were on the interstate. She looked more vulnerable than I was used to seeing her. "There's a Hyatt Regency a few exits north."

"I like being with you, Betsey. Right from the first time we met," I told her.

"Yeah. I can tell, Alex. But not enough, huh?"

I looked over at her. I liked Betsey even more when she was a little unsure of herself. "You want candor and honesty at two-fifteen in the morning?" I joked.

"Absolutely, relentlessly."

"I know this is a little crazy, but —"

She finally smiled. "I can handle crazy."

"I don't know exactly what's going on in my life right now. I'm floating with the tide a little bit. This isn't like me. Maybe that's a good thing."

"You're also still trying to get over Christine," she said. "I think you're doing it the right way. You're being brave."

"Or very foolish," I said, and smiled.

"Probably a little of both. But proactive. You're untroubled and simple on the surface — in a good way. But you're complex — in a good way. You're probably thinking 'I could say the same about you.'"

"Not really. Actually, I was thinking that I'm lucky to have met you."

"This doesn't have to go anywhere special, Alex. It's already special to me," she said. Her eyes were so beautiful, incandescent. "Anyway, will you come home with me tonight? Home away from home. My humble room at the Hyatt?"

"I'd love to, more than anything."

When we parked outside the hotel entrance, Betsey leaned in close and kissed me. I pulled her against my chest and held her tight. We stayed like that for a couple of minutes.

"I'm going to miss you so much," she whispered.

Chapter 120

THE REST OF THE NIGHT flew by, and I think both of us hated to see it go. I kept thinking about what Betsey had said — *that she was going to miss me.* She and I were back inside the FBI surveillance van by nine the following morning. The van already smelled bad. Dry ice sat in twin buckets in the corner, throwing off a vapor and making the cramped space almost livable.

"What's happening, gentlemen?" Betsey asked the agents crowded into the van. "Did I miss any fun? Is the Masterprick up yet?"

We were told that Francis was up, and that he hadn't called Kathleen McGuigan yet. I had an idea and made a suggestion. Betsey like it a lot. We called Kyle Craig and got him at home. Kyle liked the idea, too.

Agents in Arlington, Virginia, arrested Nurse McGuigan at a little past ten that morning. She was questioned, and denied knowing anything about a relationship between Dr. Bernard Francis and Frederic Szabo. She also denied any involvement in the scheme. She said that the allegations against her were ridiculous. She hadn't called Francis the night before, and we were welcome to check her phone records.

Agents, meanwhile, were searching McGuigan's house and yard. Around noon, they found one of the diamonds from the MetroHartford job. McGuigan panicked and she changed her story. She told the FBI what she knew about Dr. Francis, Frederic Szabo, and the robberies and kidnappings.

"*Yes, yes, yes, yes,*" Betsey Cavalierre said, and jumped around the back of the surveillance van when she heard the news. She bumped her head on the van roof. "That *hurts.* I don't care. We've got him! Dr. Francis is going down."

At a little past two that afternoon, she and I walked across the manicured front lawn and up the brick stairway into Francis's building. My heart was thudding in my chest. This was it. It had to be. We took the elevator up to the fifth floor — the penthouse, the Mastermind's lair.

"We've earned the right to do this," I told her.

"I can't wait to see his face," Betsey said as she rang the bell. "Cold-blooded piece of shit. *Ding-dong,* guess who's at the front door? This is for Walsh and Doud."

"And the little Buccieri boy — all the others he killed."

Dr. Francis answered the door. He was tan, dressed in Florida Gators sweatpants, a Miami Dolphins T-shirt, no socks or shoes. He didn't look like a cold-blooded and heartless monster. So often they don't.

Betsey told him who we were. She then explained to Dr. Francis that we were part of the team investigating the

MetroHartford kidnapping and several bank robberies back East.

Francis seemed momentarily confused. "I don't think I understand. Why are you here? I haven't been in Washington, well, in nearly a year. I don't see how I can help you with any bank robberies up north. Are you sure you have the right address?"

I spoke up. "May we come in, Dr. Francis? This is the right address. Trust me on that. We want to talk to you about a former patient of yours named Frederic Szabo."

Francis managed to look even more confused. He was playing his part well, and I guess I wasn't surprised.

"Frederic Szabo? You're kidding me, right?"

"We kid you not," Betsey said emphatically.

Francis became petulant. His face and neck flushed. "I'll be *in my office* at the hospital in West Palm on Monday. The hospital is on Blue Heron. We can talk about my former patients there. Frederic Szabo? Jesus! That was almost a year ago. What has he done? Is this about his crank letters to the Fortune Five Hundred? You people are incredible. Please leave my home now."

Dr. Francis tried to slam the door in my face. I stopped it with the heel of my hand. My heart continued to beat hard. This was so good — we had him.

"This can't wait until Monday, Dr. Francis," I told him. "It can't wait at all."

He sighed but continued to look incredibly pissed off. "Oh, all right. I was just making myself coffee. Come in if you must."

"We must," I told the Mastermind.

Chapter 121

"WHY THE HELL ARE YOU HERE?" Francis asked again as we followed him through an all-glass loggia that looked down onto the rolling surf of the Atlantic several floors below. The view was spectacular, worth at least a couple of murders. The afternoon sun created countless stars and diamonds that danced on the water's surface. Life was so very good for Dr. Bernard Francis.

"Frederic Szabo figured it all out for you, didn't he?" I said, just to break the ice. "He had an elaborate fantasy for revenge against the banks. He had all the know-how, the obsession, the contacts. Isn't that how it happened?"

"What the hell are you talking about?" Francis looked at Betsey and me as if we were as deranged as some of his mental patients.

I ignored the look and the condescension in his voice. "You heard about his plans in your therapy sessions with Szabo. You were impressed by the detail, the precision. He'd thought through everything. You also learned he hadn't been a drifter all those years since the war. You found out he'd worked for First Union Bank. Surprise, surprise. He'd been a security executive. He *really did* know about banks and how to rob them. He was crazy, but not in the way you had thought."

Francis flicked on a coffeemaker on the kitchen counter. "I won't even dignify this horseshit with a response. I'd offer you both coffee, but I'm angry. I'm really pissed off. Please finish with your nonsense, then you can both leave."

"I don't want coffee," I said. "I want you, Francis. You killed all those people, without any remorse. You murdered Walsh and Doud. You're the madman, the Mastermind. Not Frederic Szabo."

"It's you who is crazy. You're *both* crazy," Dr. Francis said. "I'm a respected physician, a decorated army officer."

Then he smiled — almost as if he couldn't help it — and the look on Francis's face said it all: *I can do anything I want to do. You're nothing to me. I do what I want to.* I'd seen that horrible look before. I knew it well. Gary Soneji, Casanova, Mr. Smith, the Weasel. Francis was a psychopath, too. He was as crazy as any of the killers I'd caught. Maybe he'd spent too long being underappreciated working in veterans hospitals. Undoubtedly, it went a lot deeper than that.

"One of the bank-crew members you interviewed remembered you. He described you as tall, broad forehead, hooked nose, large ears. That's not Frederic Szabo."

Francis turned away from his coffee making and let out a harsh, unpleasant laugh. "Oh, that's very compelling evidence, Detective. I'd like to hear you present it to the district attorney in Washington. I'll bet the D.A. would get a good belly laugh out of it, too."

I smiled back at him. "We already have talked to the D.A. She didn't laugh. By the way, Kathleen McGuigan has talked to us, too. Since you didn't return her call, we went to see her. You're under arrest for robbery, kidnapping, and murder. Dr. Francis, I see that you aren't laughing anymore."

I sensed that his mind was racing way ahead of the conversation. "You notice that I'm not rushing to call my lawyer, either."

"You should," I told him. "There's something else you should know. Szabo finally talked this morning. Frederic Szabo kept a diary of your sessions, Doctor. He kept notes. He wrote about your interest in his plans. You know how efficient Frederic can be. How thorough. He said you asked more questions in his therapy sessions about the robberies than you asked about him. He showed you his blueprints for everything."

"We want the money, the fifteen million dollars," Betsey told Francis. "If we recover the money then everything will go easier for you. That's the best offer you're going to get."

Francis's disdain was blossoming. "Let's suppose for a moment that I was this Mastermind you speak of. Don't you think I'd have a stunning escape plan figured? You couldn't just barge in here and capture me. The Mastermind wouldn't allow himself to be caught by two peons like you."

It was finally my turn to smile. "I don't know about that, Francis. We peons might surprise you. I think you're on your own now. Did Szabo *give you an escape plan, too?* He probably didn't."

Chapter 122

"ACTUALLY, HE DID," Francis said, and his voice was at least an octave lower than it had been. "There was always a slim, slim possibility that you'd catch me. That I'd be faced with life in jail. That's totally unacceptable, you understand. It isn't going to happen. You *do* understand that?"

"No, actually, it is going to happen," Betsey said with a firmness to match Francis's statement. Meanwhile, my hand was already reaching for my gun.

Suddenly, Francis broke for the glass door that led out onto the rooftop deck. I knew there was nowhere for him to go out there. *What was he doing?*

"Francis, no!" I shouted.

Betsey and I pulled our guns simultaneously, but we didn't fire. There was no reason to kill him. We rushed out through the door and followed Francis in a sprint across the weathered wooden deck.

When he reached the far wall of the roof deck, Francis

did something I wouldn't have ever imagined, not in a hundred lifetimes of police work.

He dived off the deck — which was five floors above the street. Bernard Francis went down headfirst. He'd break his neck for sure. There was no way he'd live.

"I don't believe it!" Betsey screeched as we got to the edge of the deck and looked down.

I didn't believe what I saw, either. Francis had made a dive five stories down to a shimmery blue swimming pool. He surfaced and began to stroke rapidly toward the pool's far wall.

I had no choice and I didn't hesitate. I jumped off the high roof deck after Dr. Francis.

Betsey was no more than half a step behind me.

We both yelled as we cannonballed all the way down to the pool.

I hit the surface of the water with my backside first, and I was punished severely. My body went *splat*. My insides felt as if they'd been hastily rearranged.

I shot to the bottom, *hit* it pretty hard, but then I was paddling to the surface, swimming as fast as I could toward the far wall. I was trying to clear my head, to focus my eyes, to think clearly about stopping the Mastermind's escape.

I climbed out of the pool and saw Francis running onto the property of the bordering condominiums. He was throwing off water like a duck.

Betsey and I started after him. Our shoes were squeaking and sloughing water. Nothing mattered except that we had to catch him.

Francis was picking up speed, and I did the same. I guessed he must have had a car parked in one of the neighboring lots — or maybe even a boat in a nearby marina.

I was gaining very little ground for all my efforts. Francis was running barefoot, but it didn't seem to slow him down.

He peered over his shoulder and saw us. Then he straightened his head and saw something that changed everything.

Up ahead of Francis in the parking lot were three FBI agents. They had their guns drawn, aimed at him. They were yelling for him to stop.

Francis came to a dead stop in the crowded lot. He looked back at us, then faced the three agents. He reached into his pants pocket.

"Francis, don't do it!" I yelled as I ran toward him.

But he didn't pull a gun. He had a clear bottle in his hand. He poured the contents into his mouth.

Dr. Francis suddenly clawed at his throat. His eyes bulged to double their normal size. He fell to his knees, which cracked hard against the pavement.

"He poisoned himself," Betsey said in a hoarse voice. *"My God, Alex."*

Francis rose from the ground with a burst of strength. We watched in horror as he thrashed wildly around the parking lot, flailing both arms, doing a strange, straight-backed dance. He was frothing from the mouth. Finally, he smashed his face into a silver Mercedes SUV. Blood spattered onto the hood.

He screamed, tried to tell us something, but it came out a tortured gargle. He had a severe nosebleed. He twitched and spasmed, and there was nothing any of us could do to help him.

More agents were flooding into the parking area. So were condo residents and visitors. There was nothing any of us could do for Francis. He'd killed people, poisoned some. He had murdered two FBI agents. Now we were watching him die, and it was horrifying. It was taking a long time.

He fell and thudded heavily to the ground again. His head cracked hard against the pavement. The spasms and twitching slowed noticeably. A terrible gargling sound escaped from his throat.

I got down on my hands and knees beside him. "Where is Agent Doud? Where's Michael Doud?" I pleaded. "For God's sake, tell us."

Francis stared up at me, and he said the last words I wanted to hear. *"You've got the wrong man."*

Then he died.

Epilogue

THE RIGHT MAN

Chapter 123

THREE WEEKS HAD PASSED, and my life was finally returning to something approaching normal. Not a day went by that I didn't think about getting out of police work, though. I didn't know if it had been the intensity of the Mastermind case, or an accumulation of cases, but I was experiencing all the basic symptoms of job burnout.

Most of the fifteen million dollars from Francis's share hadn't been found, and that was driving everybody at the FBI a little crazy. Locating it was consuming all of Betsey's time. She was working weekends again, and I hadn't seen much of her. She had said it all in Florida, I suppose. *I'm going to miss you so much.*

Tonight was Nana Mama's fault; at least I blamed her for it. Here we were — Sampson and I — trapped inside the ancient and venerable First Baptist Church on Fourth Street near my house.

All around Sampson and me, men and women were *sobbing*. The minister and his wife were busy telling everybody that the outpouring of emotion was for the best — just to let it all out, the anger, the fear, the poison inside. Which just about everybody in the church was doing. Everybody but Sampson and me seemed to be crying their eyes out.

"Nana Mama owes us big time for this little number," Sampson leaned in and said in a whisper.

I smiled at what he'd said, his lack of understanding of this woman he'd known since he was ten years old. "Not in her mind. Not to her way of thinking. We still owe Nana for all the times she saved our little butts when we were growing up."

"Well, she does have a point there, sugar. But this wipes out a lot of old debts."

"You're preaching to the choir," I told him.

"No, the choir's busy *wailing*," he said, and chuckled. "This is definitely a three-hankie evening."

John and I were squeezed in tight between two women who were weeping and shouting prayers and amens and heartfelt petitions. The occasion was something called "Sister, I'm Sorry," a special church service that was gaining popularity in D.C. Men came to churches and other venues to pay tribute to the women for all the physical and emotional abuse they had taken, and for the abuse they might have given women in their lifetimes.

"It's so good of you to come," the woman next to me suddenly proclaimed in a voice loud enough for me to hear over the shouting and screaming around us. She hugged my shoulder. "You're a good man, Alex. One of the few."

"Yeah, that's my problem," I muttered under my breath. But then, loud enough for her to hear, I said, "Sister, I'm sorry. You're a good woman, too. You're a sweet-heart."

The woman grabbed me harder. She was a sweetheart, actually. Her name was Terri Rashad. She was in her early thirties, attractive, proud, and usually joyful. I had seen her around the neighborhood.

"Sister, I'm sorry," I heard Sampson say to the woman standing beside him in the church pew.

"Well, you damn well ought to be sorry," I heard Lace McCray say. "But thank you. You're not as bad as I thought you were."

Sampson eventually nudged me and whispered in his deep voice, "It's kind of emotional when you get into it. Maybe Nana was right to have us come."

"She knows that. Nana is always right," I said. "She's like an octogenarian Oprah."

"How're you doing, sugar?" John finally asked as the singing and screeching and sobbing crescendoed.

I thought about it for a few seconds. "Oh, I miss Christine. But we're happy to have the Boy with us. Nana says it will *add* years to her life. He lights up our whole house, morning to night. He thinks we're all his *staff*."

Christine had left for Seattle at the end of June. At least she'd finally told me where she was going. I'd gone over to Mitchellville to say good-bye to her. Her new SUV was packed up. Everything was ready. Christine gave me a hug and then she started to cry, to heave against my body. "Maybe someday," she whispered. *Maybe someday.*

But now she was out in the state of Washington, and I was here in the Baptist church in my neighborhood. I figured Nana Mama was trying to get me a date. It was a funny idea, actually, and I finally started to laugh.

"You sorry for the sisters, Alex?" Sampson asked. He was getting gabby. I looked at Sampson, then around the church.

"Sure I am. Lots of good people here, trying to do the best they can. They just want to be loved a little bit now and then."

"Nothing wrong with that," Sampson said, and clasped me hard around the shoulder.

"No. Nothing at all. Just trying to do the best we can."

Chapter 124

A COUPLE OF NIGHTS LATER, I was home playing the piano on the sunporch at around eleven-thirty. The rest of the house was silent, nice and peaceful, the way I like it sometimes. I had just gone up, checked on the Boy, and found him sleeping like a precious little angel in his crib. I was playing Gershwin, one of my favorites, "Rhapsody in Blue."

I was thinking about my family, about our old house on Fifth Street and how much I loved it here in spite of everything that was wrong with the neighborhood. I was starting to get my head on straight again. Maybe all that screeching and crying in the Baptist church had helped. Or maybe it was the Gershwin.

The phone rang, and I hurried to the kitchen to get it before it woke everyone up, especially little Alex, or A. J., as Jannie and Damon had started to call him.

It was Kyle Craig.

Kyle almost never called the house and never this late.

This was how everything had started on the Mastermind case — with Kyle.

"Kyle," I said, "why are you calling me here? What's wrong? I can't start on another case."

"It's bad, Alex. I don't even know how to tell you this," he said in the softest, quietest voice. "Oh, shit, Alex . . . Betsey Cavalierre is dead. I'm at her place now. You should come here. Just come."

I hung up the phone a minute or so later. I must have — because it was back on its hook. My legs and arms had turned to jelly. I was biting the inside of my cheek and I tasted blood. I was reeling. Kyle hadn't told me everything, just that I should come to Betsey's house. Someone had broken in there and killed her. Who had killed her? Jesus! Why?

I was throwing on some clothes to go and meet Kyle when the phone rang a second time. I snatched it up. It had to be somebody else with the bad news. Probably Sampson, or maybe Rakeem Powell.

I heard a voice on the line. It froze everything inside of me.

"I just wanted to congratulate you. You did wonderful work. You caught and punished all my little minions, as I thought you might. Actually, they were put there for that very purpose."

"Who is this?" I asked. But I thought I knew who it was.

"You know who it is, Dr. Detective Cross. You're a smart-enough fellow. You knew that catching the good Dr. Francis was a little too convenient. Also my detective friends in New York — Mr. Brian Macdougall and his crew. And of course there's still the matter of all that missing money. I'm the one you call Mastermind. That's a name I can live with. It fits. I am *that good.*

"Good night for now. I'll see you soon. Oh. And have a nice time over at Betsey Cavalierre's. *I certainly did.*"

Chapter 125

I CALLED SAMPSON first and asked him to come out and be with Nana and the kids. Then I raced out to Woodbridge, Virginia, and Betsey's house. I drove the HOV lane all the way at speeds up to a hundred.

I had never been there before, but I didn't have any trouble finding her house. There were cars double-parked everywhere on the street. Several were Crown Victorias and Grand Marquises. I figured most of them were FBI. EMS was there, too. I could hear the burping screams of more sirens racing to the murder scene.

I took a deep breath before I walked inside. Suddenly I felt dizzy. Kyle was still there, directing the Bureau's Violent Crime Unit as it began to collect evidence. I shook my head: I doubted they would find much here. They hadn't at crime scenes where the Mastermind had been involved before this.

A few FBI agents were crying. I had cried during the car ride here, but right now I needed to be as clear and focused as possible. This was the only chance I would get to see Betsey's house close to the way the killer had seen it, the way he had left it for us.

It looked as if there had been a break-in. A window in the kitchen had been tampered with. FBI techs were videotaping it now. I couldn't help noticing Betsey's things, her style, her home. On the refrigerator was the *Newsweek* cover of the American Women's World Cup soccer champion Brandi Chastain and the headline "Girls Rule!"

The house looked to be close to a hundred years old and was filled with country clutter. Andrew Wyeth paintings, photos of loons in autumn on a gorgeous lake. On a hallway table I noticed a reminder for Betsey's next mandatory shooting qualifier at the FBI range.

Finally, I did the really hard thing, the impossible thing. I walked down a long hallway that led back from the living room. The master bedroom was at the end of the hall. It was easy to tell that she had been murdered there. The FBI's activity centered around the rear bedroom. The murder scene. It had happened right here.

I still hadn't spoken to Kyle, hadn't bothered him, hadn't pulled him away from the VCU team and their search of the place. Maybe we would get lucky this time. And maybe not.

Then I saw Betsey and I lost it. My left hand flew to my face as if it had a mind and will of its own. My legs buckled badly. My entire body shook.

I could hear *his* goddamn voice ringing inside my head: *Oh. And have a nice time over at Betsey Cavalierre's. I certainly did.*

He had stripped off her nightclothes. I didn't see them

anywhere in the bedroom. Her body was covered with blood. He'd used a knife this time — he'd punished her. There was blood everywhere I looked, but especially between her legs. Her beautiful brown eyes were staring right up at me, but she saw nothing, and never would again.

The medical examiner turned around and saw me standing there. I knew the man, Merrill Snyder. We had successfully worked together before — but nothing like this.

"She might have been raped," he whispered. "At any rate, he used the knife on her. Maybe he was cutting away evidence. Who the hell knows, Alex. This is sick. You have any ideas?"

"Yes," I said in a low voice. "I want to kill him for this, and I will."

Chapter 126

THE KILLER WAS RIGHT THERE inside Betsey Cavalierre's house. He was feeling sadness and hatred — *theirs* — and he thrived on it. This was the supreme thrill for him, a great, great moment in his life.

To be here with the police and FBI.

To rub elbows, chat, and listen to them curse him and shed tears for their fallen compatriot, to smell their fear. They were in a rage — against him.

And yet they were powerless to do anything.

He was *counting coup*. He was in control.

He even revisited Betsey Cavalierre, who had believed she would one day rise to the top of the Federal Bureau.

What incredible hubris on her part.

Did she truly believe she was one of the best, the top brains in the FBI? Of course she did. They all thought they were so goddamn smart these days.

Well, she didn't look so smart right now, naked and

coated with her own blood, violated in every way he could imagine.

He saw Alex Cross coming out of the bedroom. Cross looked humbled, finally. Humbled, but also self-righteous and angry.

He made certain he had his game face on, and then he walked right up to Alex Cross.

This was the moment.

"I'm so sorry about Betsey," said Kyle Craig, *the Mastermind*. "I'm so sorry, Alex."

More
James Patterson!

Please turn this page
for a
bonus excerpt
from

VIOLETS ARE BLUE

a new
Little, Brown book
available
in November 2001.

Prologue

WITHOUT ANY WARNING

Chapter One

Nothing ever starts where we think it does. So of course this doesn't begin with the vicious and cowardly murder of an FBI agent and good friend named Betsey Cavalierre. I only thought that it did. My mistake, and a really big and painful one.

I arrived at Betsey's house in Woodbridge, Virginia, in the middle of the night. I'd never been there before, but I didn't have any trouble finding it. The FBI and EMS were already there. There were flashing red-and-yellow lights everywhere, seeming to paint the lawn and front porch with bright, dangerous streaks.

I took a deep breath and walked inside. My sense of balance was off. I was reeling. I acknowledged a tall, blond FBI agent I knew named Sandy Hammonds. I could see that Sandy had been crying. She was a friend of Betsey's.

On a hallway table I saw Betsey's service revolver. Beside it was a printed reminder for her next shooting qualifier at the FBI range. The irony stung.

I forced myself to walk down a long hallway that led from the living room to the back of the house. It looked to be close to a hundred years old, and was filled with the kind of country clutter that she'd loved when she was alive. The master bedroom was situated at the end of the hall.

I knew instantly that the murder had happened in there. The FBI techs and the local police were swarming around the open door like angry wasps near a threatened hive. The house was strangely, eerily quiet. This was as bad as it gets, worse than anything else. Ever.

Another one of my partners was dead.

The second one brutally murdered in two years.

And Betsey had been much more than just a partner.

How could this have happened? What did it mean?

I saw Betsey's small body sprawled on the hardwood floor, and I went cold. My hand flew to my face, a reflex I had no control over.

The killer had stripped off her nightclothes. I didn't see them anywhere in the bedroom. The lower body was coated with blood. He'd used a knife. He'd punished Betsey with it. I desperately wanted to cover her, but I knew I couldn't.

Betsey's brown eyes were staring up at me, but they saw nothing. I remembered kissing those eyes, and that sweet face. I remembered Betsey's laugh, high-pitched and musical. I stood there for a long time, mourning Betsey, missing her terribly. I wanted to turn away, but I didn't. I just couldn't leave her like this.

As I stood there in the bedroom, trying to figure out something coherent about Betsey's murder, the cell phone in my jacket pocket went off. I jumped. I grabbed it, but then hesitated. I didn't want to answer.

"Alex Cross," I finally spoke into the receiver.

I heard a machine-filtered voice, and it cut right through me. I shuddered against my will.

"I *know* who this is, and I even know where you are. At poor, dear, *butchered* Betsey's. Do you feel a little bit like a puppet on a string, Detective? You should," said the Mastermind, "because that's what you are. You're my favorite puppet, in fact."

"Why did you kill her?" I asked the monster on the other end of the phone line. "You didn't have to do this."

He laughed a mechanical laugh, and the hairs on the back of my neck stood up. "You ought to be able to figure that out, no? You're the famous Detective Alex Cross. You have all those big, important cases notched on your belt. You caught Gary Soneji, Casanova. You solved Jack and Jill. Christ, you're impressive."

I spoke in a low voice. "Why don't you come after me right now? How about tonight? As you say, you know where I am."

The Mastermind laughed again, quietly, almost under his breath. "How about I kill your grandmother and your three kids tonight? I know where *they* are, too. You left your partner with them, didn't you? You think he can stop me? John Sampson doesn't have a chance against me."

I hung up and sprinted out of the house in Woodbridge. I called Sampson in Washington, and he picked up on the second ring.

"Everything okay there?" I gasped.

"Everything's fine, Alex. No problems here. You don't sound too good, though. What's up? What happened?"

"He said he's coming for you and Nana and the kids," I told John. "The Mastermind."

"Not going to happen, sugar. Nobody will get past me. I hope to hell he tries."

"Be careful, John. I'm on my way back to Washington *right now*. Please be careful. He's crazy. He didn't just kill Betsey, he defiled her."

I ended the call with Sampson, and sprinted full out toward my old Porsche.

The cell phone rang again before I got to the car.

"Cross," I answered, still running as I spoke, trying to steady the receiver against my chin and ear.

It was him again. He was laughing maniacally. "You can relax, Dr. Cross. I can hear your labored breathing. I'm not going to hurt them tonight. I was just fucking with you. Having some fun at your expense.

"You're running, aren't you? Keep running, Dr. Cross. But you won't be fast enough. You can't get away from me. It's you I want. You're next, Dr. Cross."

Part One

THE CALIFORNIA MURDERS

Chapter Two

United States Army Lieutenant Martha Wiatt and her boyfriend, Sergeant Davis O'Hara, moved at a fast pace as the evening fog began to roll in like a sulfurous cloud across Golden Gate Park in San Francisco. The couple looked sleek, even beautiful, in the waning light of day.

Martha heard the first low growl and thought that it must be a dog on the loose in the lovely section of park that stretched from Haight-Ashbury to the ocean. It came from far enough behind them that she wasn't worried. "The Big Dawg!" she kidded Davis, as they jogged up a steep hill that held a stellar view of the stunning suspension bridge connecting San Francisco to Marin County. "Big Dawg" was a pet expression they used for everything oversize — from jetliners, to sexual apparatus, to very large canines.

Soon the thick fog would blanket the bridge and bay completely, but for now it was a gorgeous sight, incomparable, one of their favorite things in San Francisco. "I love this run, that beautiful bridge, the sunset — the whole ball of wax," Martha said in a steady, relaxed cadence. "But enough bad poetry. It's time for me to kick your well-formed, athletic-looking butt, O'Hara."

"That sounds like cheap-shot, female chauvinism to me," he grunted, but he was grinning, showing off some of the whitest teeth she had ever seen, or run her tongue across.

Martha kicked up her pace a notch. She'd been a cross-country star at Pepperdine University, and she was still in great shape. "And that sounds like the beginnings of a gracious loser's speech," she said.

"We'll see about that, won't we. Loser buys at The Abbey."

"I can already taste a Dos Equis. Mmm-mmm good."

Suddenly the two runners' playful exchange was interrupted by a much louder growl. It was closer, too.

It didn't seem possible that a dog had covered so much ground so fast. Maybe there were a couple of "Big Dawgs" loose in the area.

"There aren't any cats in this park?" Davis asked. "I mean, like a *mountain* lion variety of cats?"

"No. Of course not. Get real, pal. We're in San Francisco, not the middle of Montana." Martha shook her head. Moisture jumped off her close-cropped reddish brown hair. Then she thought she heard footsteps. *A runner and a large dog?*

"Let's get out of these woods, okay?" Davis asked.

"I hear you. I don't necessarily disagree. Last one to the parking lot is dog chow."

"Not funny, Lieutenant Martha. Bad joke. This is getting a little spooky."

"I don't know about big cats around these parts, but I think I just spotted a little pussy."

Another loud *growl* — and it was really close. Right on the heels of the two of them. Gaining ground fast.

"C'mon! Let's go. Let's move it," said Martha Wiatt. She was a little afraid now, running as fast as she could, and that was very fast.

Another eerie growl pierced the gathering fog.

Chapter Three

Lieutenant Martha Wiatt had definitely picked up her pace. She put some distance between herself and Davis. It wasn't that hard. She did triathlons *for fun.* He worked behind a desk, though God knows, he certainly looked good for an accountant.

"C'mon, c'mon. Keep up with me, Davis. Don't fall back," she called over her shoulder.

Her boyfriend for the past year didn't answer. Well that settled any future debate about who was in better shape, who was the real athlete. Of course, Martha had known that all along.

The sounds of the next growl and also heavy footsteps crushing leaves were really close again. They were catching up to her.

But *what* was catching up to her?

"Martha! There's something behind me. Oh God! Run! *Run, Martha!*" Davis shouted. "Get the hell out of here!"

Adrenaline charged through her. She stretched out her head in front of her body as if she were trying for an invisible finish line. Her arms and legs moved in synch, like efficient pistons. She leaned her weight forward, the way all good runners do.

She heard more screams behind her. She looked back — but she couldn't see Davis anymore. The screams were so terrifying that she almost stopped running. But Davis had been attacked by something vicious. Martha rationalized that she had to get help. The police. Somebody.

Her boyfriend's screams were ringing in her ears, and she was running in total panic, not aware of where she was going. She stumbled over a pointy rock and cartwheeled down a steep hill. Martha crashed into the base of a small tree, but at least it stopped her fall.

In a daze, she managed to pull herself up. Jesus, she was pretty sure she'd broken her right arm. Cradling it with the left, she ran forward in a clumsy stumble. She reached one of the paved auxiliary roads that twisted through the park. Davis's screams had stopped. What had happened to him? She had to get help.

She saw a pair of headlights approaching, and Martha ran out into the middle of the road. She straddled the double center lines and felt like a total madwoman. *For God's sake, this was San Francisco.*

"Please stop, please stop. Hey! Hey! Hey!" she waved her good arm, and shouted at the top of her voice. "Stop! I need help!"

The white van sped straight for her, but then, thank God, it skidded to a stop. Two men jumped out and ran to her. They would help. The van said *Red Cross* on its hood.

"Help me. Please," Martha said. "My boyfriend is hurt."

Everything went from bad to worse. One of them hit her with a closed fist. Before Martha realized what was happening, she went down hard. Her chin struck the pavement, bouncing like a wet ball. She was knocked almost unconscious by the powerful blow.

She looked up, tried to focus her eyes, and wished she hadn't. Blazing red eyes stared down at her. A mouth was open wide. *Two* mouths. She had never seen such teeth in her life. They were like sharpened knives. The incisors were huge.

She felt the teeth bite into her cheeks, then her neck. How could that be? The teeth tore into her, and Martha screamed until her throat was raw. She rolled and twisted and kicked out at her attackers, but it did no good. They were incredibly strong. Both of them were growling.

"Ecstasy," one of them whispered against Martha's ear. "Isn't it beautiful? You're so lucky. You were chosen out of all the beautiful people in San Francisco. You and Davis."

Chapter Four

It was a perfect, blue-skied morning in Washington — well, almost perfect. The Mastermind was on my cell phone. "Hello, Alex. Did you miss me? I missed you, partner."

The bastard had been making obscene, threatening phone calls to me every morning for over a week. Sometimes he just cursed at me for several minutes; this morning, he sounded positively civil.

"What's your day look like? Any big plans?" he asked.

Actually, yes — I was planning to catch him. I was inside an FBI van that was already on the move. We were tracing his call and should have the exact location very soon. A court order had been put through the FBI, and the phone company was involved in "trapping" the call. I was in the rear of the speeding van with three Bureau agents and my partner, John Sampson. We had left my house on Fifth Street as soon as the call came in; we were heading onto I-395 North. My job was to keep him on the line until the trace was completed.

"Tell me about Betsey Cavalierre. Why did you pick her instead of me?" I asked him.

"Oh, she's much, much prettier," the Mastermind said. "More *fuckable.*"

One of the techie agents was talking in the background. I tried to listen to both conversations. The agent said, "He's living up to his name. We've got a wire tap and *should* be able to trace this call immediately. It isn't happening for some reason."

"Why the hell not?" Sampson asked, and moved closer to the agents.

"Don't know exactly. We're picking up different locations, but they keep changing. Maybe he's on a cell phone in a car. Cell phones are harder to trace."

I could see that we were getting off the D Street exit. Then we headed into the Third Street tunnel. Where was he?

"Everything all right, Alex? You seem a little distracted," the Mastermind said.

"No, I'm right here with you, partner. Enjoying our little breakfast club."

"I don't know why this is so goddamn hard," the FBI techie complained.

Because he's the Mastermind, I wanted to yell at him.

I saw the Washington Convention Center on the right.

The van was really clipping along, doing sixty or seventy on the city streets.

We passed the Renaissance Hotel. Where the hell was the Mastermind calling from?

"I think we have a fix on him. We're real close," one of the young agents said in an excited voice.

The FBI van stopped suddenly; it was chaos inside. Sampson and I pulled out our guns. We had him. I couldn't believe we had him.

Then everyone inside the van groaned and cursed. I looked outside and saw why. I shook my head in disgust.

"Jesus Christ, do you believe this shit!" Sampson yelled, and pounded the wall of the van. We were at 935 Pennsylvania Avenue, the J. Edgar Hoover Building, which is FBI headquarters.

"What's happening now?" I asked the agent in charge. "Where the hell is he?"

"Shit, the signal is *roaming* again. It's moving outside Washington. Okay, now it's back in the city. Christ, the signal just skipped out of the country."

"Good-bye, Alex. For now anyway. As I told you before, you're next," the Mastermind said, and then he hung up on me.